*H. G. Wells: Early Writings in
Science and Science Fiction*

→ *H. G. Wells:*

Early Writings in
Science and Science Fiction

Edited,

with critical commentary and notes,

by

ROBERT M. PHILMUS

and

DAVID Y. HUGHES

UNIVERSITY OF CALIFORNIA PRESS

Berkeley • Los Angeles • London

University of California Press
Berkeley and Los Angeles, California
University of California Press, Ltd.
London, England
Copyright © 1975 by H. G. Wells
ALL RIGHTS RESERVED
Introductions, copyright © 1975
by The Regents of the University of California
ISBN: 0-520-02679-9
Library of Congress Catalog Card Number: 73-91673
Printed in the United States of America

TO OUR PARENTS

Sine quibus non

Contents

Contents

Preface

This idea of a kind of "ground swell" in the ether, coming up
from the uttermost bounds of space, recording itself as it passes
our little eddy of planets in the swaying of our compasses, and
in solar storms, and so going on into the illimitable beyond, appears
to us to be so powerful and beautiful as to well-nigh justify that
hackneyed phrase, "the poetry of science."

> "An Excursion to the Sun"[1]

The primary purpose of this anthology is to make
available in one volume a selection of H. G. Wells's hitherto
unreprinted writings of the 1880s and 1890s relating to
science and the sciences. That these have not had the
attention they merit is no doubt in part because the
original printed versions are to be found scattered among
a variety of publications. Of the 28 pieces included here,
12 first appeared in the *Saturday Review*, 3 in the *Pall
Mall Gazette*, 3 in the *Fortnightly Review*, 2 in the *Science
Schools Journal*, 2 in the *Gentleman's Magazine*, and 1
each in *Chambers's Journal*, *Knowledge*, the *National
Observer*, *Nature*, the *New Review*, and *Science and Art*.[2]
Together these essays, reviews, and fiction permit the
reader to follow the outline of Wells's intellectual development. Crucial to that development is his early discovery

[1] Wells's review of Sir Robert Ball's *The Story of the Sun*, "An Excursion
to the Sun," *PMG* 58 (Jan. 6, 1894): 4.

[2] The selections are not statistically representative: included here are all the
essays relating to science from, e.g., the *Gentleman's Magazine* and *Chambers's*
known to be by Wells, whereas his publications in the *PMG* are proportionately
much greater than might be inferred from the number we have selected.
(Incidentally, for purposes of tabulation, the episodes from the *National Observer Time Machine* are counted together as one item, as are those from the
New Review.)

of something like a principle of "complementarity."[3] Incipient in one of his first literary efforts, "A Talk with Gryllotalpa" (1887), is a distinction between two basic "standpoints" towards phenomena, and especially towards things human. There is what he later calls "the absolute standpoint" of perceiving things "at a distance," so to speak, in terms approaching astronomical magnitudes: from this perspective of "infinite space" man seems "infinitesimal." But there is also a standpoint wherefrom man looms large because everything in the universe is viewed in relation to "the [human] eye that sees." Either standpoint, cosmic or human, has its pitfalls. The danger of the cosmic view is a disregard for what Wells terms "the unique," the individuality of all phenomena. The human perspective, on the other hand, too readily lends itself to the fallacy of a complacent anthropocentrism. Recognizing that each perspective can by itself lead to distortion, Wells relies on both, though the principal focal point of his writings gradually shifts from cosmic to human. In his essays and fiction prior to *The Time Machine*, and to a large extent in *The Time Machine* itself, the cosmic evolutionary process dominates his field of vision; but thereafter Wells telescopically, as it were, begins to zero in on man—without, however, losing sight of the larger universe in which man finds himself situated. Corresponding to this change in focus is an altered vision of the prospects for the human species. The view of nature's laws disposing of what man proposes gives way to the idea of "artificial" evolution, man's consciously taking charge of his future by shaping his sociocultural environment, over which he can exert control.[4]

The foregoing represents the gist of the argument of the general introduction (chapter 1) and its continuation in the remarks that precede the other five sections of the

[3] See chapter 1 and note 18.

[4] For a discussion of Wells's concept of "artificial" evolution and the influence of "Weismannism" on its development, we refer the reader especially to chapters 1 and 6.

anthology (chapters 2-6). These remarks are meant to be suggestive and to guide the reader to perceive the coherence of Wells's thought; they do not pretend to be exhaustive, and as their footnotes sometimes indicate, they might be expanded in more than one direction. As for the grouping of the texts selected, the intention was to bring them "into closer and more exact relations"[5] than might be observable if they had been presented all together, simply in chronological order. It is hoped that classifying these texts under the rubrics they suggest will clarify Wells's vision of "the poetry of science."

[5] *EA*, p. 11.

Acknowledgments

We wish to thank Darko Suvin of McGill and David Ketterer of Sir George Williams University for looking over parts of this book at various stages of its incompletion; R. D. Mullen of Indiana State University, Patrick Parrinder of Cambridge, and J. P. Vernier of the Université de Rouen for offering helpful hints on the Selective Bibliography that was the starting point for this anthology; Harris Wilson of the University of Illinois Wells Archive and members of the library staffs of the British Museum and the Bodleian and Radcliffe Science Libraries for their kind and indispensable assistance; and the administrators of the College of Engineering Fund of the University of Michigan for a grant for travel.

The works of H. G. Wells contained herein are reprinted with the permission of A. P. Watt and Son, Limited, literary agents for the Wells estate, and their New York affiliate, Collins-Knowlton-Wing, Incorporated.

R. M. P.
D. Y. H.

Abbreviations

ACW   Amy Catherine Wells's list of cue-titles in the Wells Archive at the University of Illinois, Urbana.

AtlEd   The Atlantic Edition of H. G. Wells's Works, 28 volumes (London: T. Fisher Unwin, 1924-1927).

CPM   *Certain Personal Matters* (London: Lawrence and Bullen, 1898 [1897]).

EA   *Experiment in Autobiography* (Toronto: Macmillan of Canada, 1934).

GR   Gordon N. Ray, "H. G. Wells's Contributions to the *Saturday Review*," *The Library* 16 (5th series, 1961): 29-36.

GW   Geoffrey H. Wells, *H. G. Wells: A Bibliography, Dictionary and Subject-Index* (London: George Routledge, 1926).

PMG   *Pall Mall Gazette*

SR   *Saturday Review*

I. *Introduction: Outlines*

A variety of biological and historical suggestions and generalizations, which, when lying confusedly in the human mind, were
cloudy and opaque, have been brought into closer and more exact
relations ... a plainer vision of human possibilities and the
conditions of their attainment, appears. I have made the broad
lines and conditions of the human outlook distinct and unmistakable for myself and for others ....
I have a brain good for outlines.

Experiment in Autobiography[1]

H. G. Wells wrote what he later described as "various
sketches, dialogues and essays" (also drama criticism and
book reviews) both before and during the period when he
was working on his best science fiction. The quantity of
this "journalistic" output is considerable. Over two
hundred items published between 1887 and 1898,[2] most
of them pseudonymous or unsigned, can be attributed to
him,[3] and there are undoubtedly more which may yet be
discovered. Of this early journalism, Wells reprinted only
a tiny fraction.[4] In his own judgment, "Much of that stuff

[1] *EA*, pp. 11, 15.

[2] These dates encompass almost all of Wells's science journalism (see the
bibliographical Appendix). With very few exceptions, the journalistic pieces Wells
published after 1898 have little to do with science per se.

[3] See D. Y. Hughes and R. M. Philmus, "The Early Science Journalism of
H. G. Wells: A Chronological Survey," *Science-Fiction Studies* 1 (1973): 98-114.
We have included an expanded version of that bibliography, in alphabetical
rather than chronological order, as an appendix to this anthology. In the case
of unsigned or pseudonymous essays and reviews, we have relied here as there
on *GW*, *ACW*, and *GR* (as, and unless otherwise, indicated).

[4] In *CPM* (1897): "The Extinction of Man," "Incidental Thoughts on a Bald
Head," "The Man of the Year Million" (reprinted there as "Of a Book Unwrit-
ten"), "Through a Microscope," and "From an Observatory"; in *A Modern
Utopia* (1905): "The Scepticism of the Instrument"; and in *AtlEd* (1924-27):

1

was good enough to print but not worth reprinting."[5]

Perhaps because almost none of "that stuff" is readily accessible, virtually no one up to now seems to have questioned Wells's verdict.[6] "That stuff," however, includes, *inter alia*, most of his essays and reviews on scientific subjects, along with a few early "essayistic" short stories and fictional dialogues. All of these are potentially of value—albeit in varying degrees—for understanding *The Time Machine, The Island of Doctor Moreau, The First Men in the Moon*, and Wells's other achievements in science fiction and for determining the progress of his thinking that led him to *A Modern Utopia* and his later social tracts. But besides their heuristic worth, not all the early writings are otherwise ephemeral. Many of them— among which belong (hopefully) most, if not all, of those reprinted here—have some intrinsic worth as literature. In that offhand, colloquial style of which he is a master, Wells speculates on the nature and destiny of man.

His thinking on this subject has its basis in science. It is not simply certain scientific ideas that impressed themselves decisively on his mind while he was studying at South Kensington, but also—and more tellingly—the scientific method, the perspective, and many of the philosophic assumptions of the sciences.

Above all, Wells assimilated the critical spirit of scientific inquiry. In his early essays and reviews concerned with the teaching and popularizing of science, he consistently denigrates any pedagogy which seeks to inculcate mere fact without attending to the process of discovery

---

"Scepticism . . ." and "Through a Microscope." In addition, two essays included here were reprinted in other periodicals: "Zoological Retrogression" in *Living Age* 19 (Nov. 7, 1891): 363-367, and *Scientific American* 65 (Oct. 10, 1891): 228 (excerpts only, and heavily cut, under the title "Degeneration and Evolution"); and "Human Evolution, an Artificial Process," excerpted and summarized under the title "Human Evolution: Natural or Artificial? An Argument Against Natural Selection," *Review of Reviews* 14 (Nov. 1896): 605-606.

[5] *EA*, p. 309.

[6] The one exception is Bernard Bergonzi, who reprints *The Chronic Argonauts* (from *Science Schools Journal* [1888]) as an appendix to *The Early H. G. Wells: A Study of the Scientific Romances* (Toronto: University of Toronto Press, 1961).

and validation. "Not knowledge, but a critical and inquiring mental habit, is the aim of science teaching"[7]—this
is his constant theme. The most essential feature of science
is its experimental method: not that a thing is so, but
why it is so; not the belief, but the grounds of belief.
Though the word *experiment* figures in the title of only
one of his many books (significantly, however, that one
attempts to give the history of his mental development),
the young Wells was continually experimenting with ideas.
Virtually all his essays and reviews dealing with science
set out to prove, or rather test, hypotheses by referring
to the evidence for them and examining their consequences. And the same "method" informs much of his
fiction, particularly his science fiction.[8]

If what he calls the "fundamental principles of [literary]
construction" come from the structure of experiment, his
temporal and spatial perspective on the human condition
derives its "order of magnitude" (so to speak) from the
scope of scientific inquiry, especially the scope of the
science he was most knowledgeable about, biology.

For Wells, as for his contemporaries, the center of
biological thinking had become the theory of evolution.
That theory entailed, among other consequences, a radical
reorientation of conceptions of space and time. The newly
posited entanglement of species in the destiny of one
another reopened the question of man's relation to (the
rest of) nature and to the universe at large in part because
it rendered the idea of isolation (itself a spatial concept)
anachronistic, if not obsolete.[9] From the standpoint of

[7] "The Sins of the Secondary Schoolmaster," *PMG* 59 (Dec. 15, 1894): 2. Wells
reiterates this point in many of the essays he published at about the same time
(see Appendix, nos. 35, 65, 78, 80, 82, and 87).

[8] Recognizing Poe and A. C. Doyle as his precursors in this regard, Wells
writes in "Popularising Science," *Nature* 50 (July 26, 1894): 301:

> The taste for good inductive reading is very widely diffused; there is a keen
> pleasure in seeing a previously unexpected generalisation skilfully devel-
> oped.... The fundamental principles of construction that underlie such
> stories as Poe's "Murders in the Rue Morgue," or Conan Doyle's "Sherlock
> Holmes" series, are precisely those that should guide a scientific writer.

[9] Of course, exploration of the "Dark Continent," especially in the 1880s, also

evolutionary theory, no place, not even an island, is exempt from the process of natural selection, which provides a basis of comparison—that is, connection—between any two geographical locations, no matter how far apart they might be.[10]

If the conceptual bridging of distances in space was a concomitant of Darwin's theory, the telescoping of time was a necessity. Evolution enlarged human consciousness of time: most obviously, because for the theory to be true this planet must be older than anyone before Darwin had supposed it to be;[11] but also, in another way, because confirmation of the theory partly depends on viewing geological and biological time as a whole. Thus the Darwinian hypothesis did not simply encourage a panoramic view of the total natural history of the earth (and on a smaller, analogous scale, of the developmental history of a species), it required such a view as evidence of the truth of evolution. And once human consciousness opens itself to the possibility of conceiving the entire past of the evolutionary process, why not attempt to project the course of that process a similar, or greater, "distance" into the future? For the young Wells, with the lectures of Thomas Huxley fresh in his mind, this extension of the temporal perspectives of evolutionary theory seemed not merely possible; it seemed logical.

The cosmic perspective that his study of science suggested to him was presumably expounded in one of Wells's earliest essays, "The Universe Rigid." That essay was never published[12] and the manuscript is apparently no

contributed to destroying that sense of "isolation." Significantly, however, the imperialistic enterprise in Africa was often rationalized in the terms of Social Darwinism.

[10] See, for example, the comparison between the earth and Mars in *War of the Worlds* (1898): "We men ... must be to [the Martians] at least as alien and lowly as are the monkeys and lemurs to us. The intellectual side of man already admits that life is an incessant struggle for existence, and it would seem that this too is the belief of the minds upon Mars." *AtlEd*, 3: 215.

[11] See Stephen Toulmin and June Goodfield, *The Discovery of Time* (London: Hutchinson, 1965), especially pp. 222-24.

[12] Frank Harris, then editor of the *Fortnightly Review*, printed "The Redisco-

longer extant; but according to the summary Wells gives of it in the *Experiment*, his hypothesis sounds very much like one Laplace employs to argue for determinism:[13]

'The Universe Rigid' . . . gave me a frame for my first scientific fantasia, *The Time Machine*, and there was moreover a rather elaborate joke going on . . . about a certain 'Universal Diagram' I proposed to make, from which all phenomena would be derived by a process of deduction. (One began with a uniformly distributed ether in the infinite space of those days and then displaced a particle. If there was a Universe rigid, and hitherto uniform, the character of the consequent world would depend entirely, I argued along strictly materialist lines, upon the velocity of this initial displacement. The disturbance would spread outward with ever increasing complication.)[14]

Wells details a similar hypothesis in the version of *The Time Machine* published in the *New Review*. There he specifies the consequence: seen in this way, "the universe is a perfectly rigid unalterable apparatus, entirely predestinate," "in which things [are] always the same."[15] However, he repeatedly qualifies that notion by saying that the universe appears "rigid" only "from the absolute standpoint."

---

very of the Unique"; but reading "The Universe Rigid" (for the first time) in galley proofs, he rejected that as "incomprehensible." See *EA,* pp. 172, 293-96, and Geoffrey West, *H. G. Wells: A Sketch for a Portrait* (London: Gerald Howe, 1930), pp. 91-92.

[13] Compare Pierre Simon Laplace (1749-1827), as quoted in translation by Roger Hahn in *Laplace as a Newtonian Scientist* (Los Angeles: William Andrews Clark Memorial Library, 1967), p. 17:

The present state of the system of nature is evidently a resultant of what it was in the preceding instant, and if we conceive of an Intelligence who, for a given moment, embraces all the relations of beings in the Universe, It will be able to determine for any instant of the past or future their respective positions, motions, and generally their affections [i.e., properties].

[14] *EA*, p. 172.
[15] For the text of the *New Review Time Machine*, see chapter 3.

The qualification is crucial. Without it, the argument for a Universe Rigid seems incompatible with the position Wells defends in another of his earliest essays, "The Rediscovery of the Unique," where his contention that *"All being is unique,* or, nothing is strictly like anything else"[16] implies not only the "individuality" of everything but also the unillusiveness of the possibilities for self-determination. This concept of uniqueness does not contradict that of a Universe Rigid: for Wells these two ideas do not exclude one another because each sees the universe from a different point of view, each represents a different focus of perception. "From the absolute standpoint," "outside" space and time, it appears as if natural laws entirely govern and inexorably determine the course of the cosmos; but from the human standpoint, the future, whatever it may look like, will be shaped at least in part through human initiative and human effort. More particularly, the laws of evolution do not rule out the possibility of self-transformation, Lamarckian or otherwise.[17]

In stressing the compatibility of views which seem in conflict as a result of different "standpoints" of perception, Wells anticipates the concept of "complementarity."[18] As early as "Zoological Retrogression" (1891), he uses the term "opposite idea" not as a synonym for "antithesis"

[16] See also chapter 2.

[17] See below.

[18] In atomic physics, "complementarity" is a more inclusive and generalized application of Heisenberg's Uncertainty Principle. As named and defined by Niels Bohr—briefly in "The Quantum Postulate and the Recent Development of Atomic Theory" (1927) and at length in "The Quantum of Action and the Description of Nature" (1929)—"complementarity" means that different approaches ("standpoints" in Wells's terminology) are necessary to reveal all aspects of phenomena and that the results of these experimental approaches are "complementary" rather than mutually exclusive. See Bohr, *Atomic Theory and the Description of Nature* (Cambridge: Cambridge University Press, 1934):

> The fundamental postulate of the indivisibility of the quantum of action . . . forces us to adopt a new mode of description designated as *complementary* in the sense that any given application of [some] classical concepts [of physics] precludes ["because of the coupling between phenomena and their observation"] the simultaneous use of other classical concepts which in a different connection are equally necessary for the elucidation of the phenomena. ("Introductory Survey," p. 10; emphasis in original)

or "negation," but in the sense of "essential complement."[19] Later, in "The Scepticism of the Instrument"
(1904), he criticizes "formal logic" for (among other things)
being unable to deal with complementarities. He objects
to the logicians' habit of treating diverse ideas "by projecting them upon the same plane," thereby creating antino-
mies where no real conflict is present. As an example, he
singles out the putative opposition between "predestination and free-will."[20] His argument, in effect, is that the
contradiction between these two views is specious since
one derives from a cosmic, the other from a human standpoint.

The tension between the cosmic and human standpoints
in Wells is greatest in *The Time Machine*.[21] Thereafter,
although continuing to recognize their complementarity,
Wells gradually comes to place increasing emphasis on
the efficacy of human effort.[22] His stance, however, is not
to be confused with what he identified as anthropocentrism, the notion that nature is teleologically oriented
towards *homo sapiens*. Though a number of his contemporaries (most articulately Samuel Butler[23]) balked at the
devastating effects of a theory of chance natural selection
on the concept of natural teleology, Wells did not. For
him, the idea that nature *per se* has a *telos*, a purpose
or intent in conformity with human ideals, was part and
parcel of an anthropocentric view of nature that Darwin
provided decisive evidence against. Wells's attack on

[19] For the text of "Zoological Retrogression," see chapter 5.

[20] "The Scepticism of the Instrument," *AtlEd*, 9: 348-51.

[21] See the introduction to chapter 3.

[22] Perhaps the personal motive behind this emphasis was Wells's feeling that
with *The Time Machine* he was "fairly launched at last," having escaped the
constrictions of his social environment through individual effort (see *EA*, chapter
8). Christopher Caudwell (the pseudonym of St. John Sprigg) makes this point,
somewhat perversely, in chapter 4 ("H. G. Wells: A Study in Utopianism") of
Studies in a Dying Culture (London: John Lane, 1938), pp. 73-95. See also Robert
P. Weeks, "Disentanglement as a Theme in H. G. Wells's Fiction," *Papers of
the Michigan Academy of Science, Arts, and Letters* 39 (1954): 439-44.

[23] See R. M. Philmus, *Into the Unknown: The Evolution of Science Fiction
from Francis Godwin to H. G. Wells* (Berkeley: University of California Press,
1970), pp. 110-14.

anthropocentricity is virtually the starting point in the development of his thinking that led him from *The Time Machine* to *A Modern Utopia* and beyond.

Wells regarded evolution less as a "theory" than as the central fact of biology, geology, and solar physics. Its corollary, diametrically at odds with anthropocentrism, was that *homo sapiens* is an accident and an episode of natural history. At least until about 1896, Wells was preoccupied with that notion; essay after essay assaults the anthropocentric fallacy. Life might have been built up of compounds other than carbon ("Another Basis for Life") and might have reached or surpassed our mental level ("Intelligence on Mars"). Animals and plants possess nervous organizations higher than is commonly recognized,[24] whereas the human brain is an instrument of dubious precision and accuracy ("Scepticism of the Instrument"). Man, moreover, remains subject both to instinctual drives inherited from apelike ancestors and to the accidents and necessities imposed by nature ("Human Evolution, An Artificial Process"), so that both from within himself and from without he faces powerful adversaries to his humanity. Natural law, universal and absolute, does not respect man's "present ideals" or his anthropocentric sense of his own self-importance ("Zoological Retrogression"; "Bio-Optimism").

At bottom, Wells was at this time considering the eventuality of man's extinction, and this he linked to a lack of "plasticity" (a term whose meaning changed for him but which at first meant simply evolutionary adaptability as opposed to "rigidity"). Thus,writing in 1891 on "degeneration as a plastic process in nature," he doubts that man has the plasticity of his "forebear," the Silurian mud-fish, which, inert in the shallows, transformed its swim bladder into a lung ("Zoological Retrogression"). As late as the end of 1894 he still judges extinction the likely

---

[24] This is Wells's implication in "The Life of Plants," *SR* 82 (Aug. 8, 1896): 131-32; and "The Mind in Animals," *SR* 78 (Dec. 22, 1894): 683-684.

price nature will exact for man's rigidity compared to prolific, short-lived species that rapidly breed countless numbers of progeny subject to the continuous action of natural selection ("The Rate of Change in Species"). And he has two essays in 1893-1894 on the special threat to *homo sapiens* arising from the fact that dominant species invariably fall to some humble creature that nature is quietly preparing in the "abyss" ("The Extinction of Man"; "On Extinction"; see also the conclusion of "Zoological Retrogression").

Plasticity is evolutionary adaptability, and the force adapted to is natural selection. This being the period of *The Time Machine*, Wells focuses on beginnings and endings—final causes—but not in a teleological sense. He simply foreshortens the action of natural selection according to the panoramic temporal perspective suggested by the study of Darwinian theory.[25] Man's "forebear" thus becomes a mud-fish and his "competitor" a field mouse; and perhaps men will someday evolve into colonial polyplike organisms, "human trees with individuals as their branches" ("Ancient Experiments in Co-Operation"). All is possible, given the chance operations of natural selection.

Because he felt it was incompatible with the continuous change "towards things that are forever new" ("The 'Cyclic' Delusion") consequent on natural selection, Wells resisted August Weismann's theory of germ-plasm when it first came to his attention late in 1894. In company with Darwin and Herbert Spencer, Wells believed that natural selection works mostly on chance variations but also on traits acquired by an individual creature during the course of its life and inherited by subsequent generations (Lamarck's theory of heredity).[26] He therefore at first

[25] In "The Scepticism of the Instrument," Wells recalls how the comparative anatomy stressed by Huxley encouraged rapid extrapolation backward in time and how this approach was complemented by a course in embryology where radical ontogenetic evolution was swiftly "recapitulated" (*AtlEd*, 9: 336-37).

[26] Generally Wells is as vague as Darwin about his reliance on Lamarck's theory that inheritable traits are acquired through the use or disuse of faculties,

opposed the anti-Lamarckian thrust of the germ-plasm theory, especially because it seemed to him that Weismann's notion of the continuity, hence immortality, of "germ cells" was merely an updated version of mystical theories of the "pre-formation" of all individuals at the beginning of time and thus precluded any change whatever ("The Biological Problem of To-Day"). In other words, the doctrine struck Wells as being teleological and seemed to eliminate the role of natural selection. However, notwithstanding his initial objections, he had apparently accepted "Weismannism" by early March of 1895,[27] and in August of that year was lamenting that "the doubts thrown upon the inheritance of acquired characteristics have deprived us of our trust in education as a means of redemption for decadent families" ("Bio-Optimism"). That is, no force for transformation can remain except the molding action of natural selection operating on chance variations. Wells's belief in that force had reached its high water mark.

The drift of biological science was setting against the "pedigree morphology" of Wells's days at the Royal Col-

organs, etc. At only one or two points in his discussion of Vertebrata in the *Text-Book of Biology* does Wells allude to Lamarck (and never by name)—when he writes, for example, of the tiger's "noiseless approach learnt from nature in countless millions of lessons of success and failure" (*Text-Book of Biology*, 2d ed. [London: W. B. Clive, 1894], pt. 1, p. 129. However, Wells's early belief in Lamarckianism does reveal itself in his misgivings about Weismann; and a Lamarckian theory is implied in the Time Traveller's explanation of how the human species degenerated and diverged into the Eloi and the Morlocks.

[27] In an essay entitled "Incidental Thoughts on a Bald Head," printed in the *PMG* for March 1, 1895, Wells remarks: "Professor Weissmann [*sic*] has at least convinced scientific people of this: that the characters acquired by a parent are rarely, if ever, transmitted to its offspring" (*CPM*: 158). This realization on Wells's part was apparently somewhat belated, for Alfred Wallace, writing in the *Fortnightly* some years earlier, had declared: "Owing to the researches of Galton and Weismann . . . the balance of opinion amongst physiologists now seems to be against the heredity of any qualities acquired by the individual after birth" ("Human Selection," *Fortnightly Review*, n.s. 48 [1890]: 325-26). Along with Weismann, Darwin's cousin Francis Galton stressed the action of chance variations and rejected that of acquired characteristics in the evolution of species. Darwin himself resisted their demonstrations and held to his theory of pangenesis. For an illuminating discussion of the matter, see Peter J. Vorzimmer, *Charles Darwin: The Years of Controversy* (Philadelphia: Temple University Press, 1970), pp. 254-61.

lege of Science and moving towards the founding of a science of genetics. On Wells the effect was to redirect his attention, at about the beginning of 1895, sharply away from vistas of the last man (or last buffalo or last dinosaur) to what might be called "sibling morphology"—that is, measurement of physically varying traits in living populations, preferably in a single litter or seedbed,[28] or measurement designed to determine whether any traits are linked so that they stand or fall as a bundle ("Bye-Products in Evolution"; "Concerning Skeletons"). His essays on "sibling morphology" reveal that whether the course of evolution appears uncontrollable or not very much depends upon the time-scale applied. Wells now chose to view evolution in the short run, hence as a process whose direction might be determinable.

The next question, of course, is that of human control of the process. Could natural selection be supplanted as the agency dictating which among the plastic possibilities of life would be realized? Genetic manipulation was not conceivable, for the simple reason that a science of genetics was still decades away. In attempting his affirmative answer, what Wells did is surprising. He in effect dropped biological evolution from his calculations. The type (species) he now regarded as being, for practical purposes, stable and invariable: there could be no change through the inheritance of acquired characteristics (Lamarck having been discredited to Wells's mind); and given the span between one human generation and the next, natural selection presented too long-range and indeterminate a prospect as far as any immediate amelioration of the human condition was concerned. The question therefore became: to what extent is the mortal individual plastic in his lifetime; to what extent, after birth, is he, or can he be, shaped? In "The Limits of Individual Plasticity" Wells replied that there seem to be no definite limits to

---

[28] See "Discoveries in Variation," *SR* 79 (Mar. 9, 1895): 312; and "Fallacies of Heredity," *SR* 78 (Dec. 8, 1894): 617-18.

what might be accomplished upon living flesh by surgery, chemical treatment, and hypnosis. This he meant literally; and despite his satirical reservations about the idea as it appears in *The Island of Doctor Moreau*, he nevertheless defended its scientific credibility against charges levelled against it in some reviews of that book.[29]

He now turned finally, before the end of 1896, to what he termed "artificial evolution" ("Human Evolution, An Artificial Process"), meaning education and behavioral engineering. Man, he said, in his capacity of "culminating ape," remains the victim of natural selection; but he may be redeemed from his bondage through education, which confirms him in his capacity of "artificial man," "the highly plastic creature of tradition, suggestion, and reasoned thought." Here he speaks as he would for years to come, and by the beginning of 1897 he already imagines the vanguard of the New Republicans, Samurai, and Open Conspirators: "one may dream," he writes, "of an informal, unselfish, unauthorised body of workers, a real and conscious apparatus of education and moral suggestion . . . shaping the minds and acts and destinies of men" ("Morals and Civilisation").

[29] See "Correspondence: 'The Island of Dr. Moreau'," *SR* 82 (Nov. 7, 1896): 497.

II. *Enormous Repudiations*

He began stark ... as though he came into the world of letters
without ever a predecessor. In style, in method and in all that
is distinctively *not* found in his books, he is sharply defined, the
expression in literary art of certain enormous repudiations.
"Stephen Crane from an English Standpoint"[1]

What Wells in 1900 acutely remarked of Stephen Crane
could as truly be applied to himself, for his own repudiations, partly documented in the *Experiment in Autobiography*, were also enormous. Consistently, if not quite
systematically, Wells began his career as a writer by
defining himself against what he identified as the prevailing opinions of his time. His earliest surviving literary
efforts show how soon an antithetical way of thinking
became his habitual method of approach; his last books
give evidence that he retained a polemical cast of mind
throughout his life.

Among Wells's first publications were pseudonymous
contributions to the *Science Schools Journal*, which he
founded late in 1886 with the help of his friend and fellow
student William Burton.[2] The best of those early pieces
are two "essayistic" short (short) stories, "A Talk with
Gryllotalpa" and "A Vision of the Past" (1887).[3] "Gryllotalpa," published over the name "Septimus Browne," is
brief indeed. But in it Wells outlines the antithesis that
preoccupies much of his writing through the 1890s. With

[1] H. G. Wells, "Stephen Crane from an English Standpoint," *North American
Review* 171 (Aug. 1900): 241-42.
[2] See *EA*, pp. 194-95; and *GW*, pp. 58-60.
[3] For "A Vision of the Past," see chapter 5.

great economy he brings into confrontation the anthropocentric view of the world and the cosmic perspective which
perceives man as "less than an iota in the infinite universe"
(the perspective of Tennyson's "sad astrology," according
to whose "boundless plan" the stars are "Cold fires, yet
with power to burn and brand/ His nothingness into
man.")[4] Significantly, though anthropocentrism arbitrarily gets "the last word," the notion of the "infinitesimal
littleness of man" receives far the largest share of the
exposition.

"Gryllotalpa" reveals—albeit obliquely—Wells's critical
attitude not simply towards any particular belief but also,
and more tellingly, towards its grounds and consequences,
which are usually inextricable and often indistinguishable
from one another. For example, the anthropocentrism of
Gryllotalpa's interlocutor requires that the sun be viewed
as "not so big as the eye that sees it." This kind of
anthropocentrism, that is, both depends upon and results
in a total distortion of any scientific perspective regarding
natural phenomena.

Scientists themselves sometimes perpetrate distortion,
which has its origin in certain deeply enculturated habits
of thought permeating the nature of language itself. "The

---

[4] *Maud* (1855), XVIII, ll. 634, 637-38. A similar cosmic perspective figures
in the works of Thomas Hardy, most explicitly and sustainedly in *Two on a
Tower* (1882), in the preface (1895) to which he announces that his intention
was "to set the emotional history of two infinitesimal lives against the stupendous
background of the stellar universe, and to impart to readers the sentiment that
of these contrasting magnitudes the smaller might be the greater to them as
men." From *The Works of Thomas Hardy in Prose and Verse* (The Wessex
Edition, 20 vols. [London: Macmillan, 1912-13], 12:viii). In the novel proper,
an authorial voice remarks:

At night, when human discords and harmonies are hushed, in a general
sense, for the greater part of twelve hours, there is nothing to moderate
the blow with which the inifinitely great, the stellar universe, strikes down
upon the infinitely little, the mind of the beholder. ... Having got closer
to immensity than their fellow creatures, they [Swithin and Viviette] saw
at once its beauty and its frightfulness. They more and more felt the contrast
between their own tiny magnitudes and those among which they had
recklessly plunged, till they were oppressed with the presence of a vastness
they could not cope with even as an idea, and which hung about them
like a nightmare. (12:68-69)

Fallacy of the Common Noun"—also of the concepts of number and statistics—lies in the built-in assumption that "beings" with the same name are identical. But, Wells argues in "The Rediscovery of the Unique" (1891), "we only arrive at the idea of similar beings by an unconscious or deliberate disregard of an infinity of small differences" which science now enables us to measure with a fair degree of precision. "The work of Darwin and Wallace," emphasizing the importance in evolution of minute variations in species, "was the clear assertion of the uniqueness of living things." The violation of this uniqueness, the imposition of a "rigid reasonableness" of "clockwork" uniformity, epitomizes the anthropocentric tendency to reduce phenomena to logical categories without bothering to investigate the limits and limitations of the human mind, from whose predispositions those categories arise.

The repudiation of anthropocentricity which becomes explicit in Wells's essays and short stories of the 1890s is symptomatic of his pervasive antagonism to any idea the basis of which its adherents conspicuously fail to recognize. Ignorance of the grounds of belief is characteristic of "rigidity" (a word which has considerable latitude of meaning for him but which in its present context comprehends complacency, credulity, and dogmatic arrogance); and rigidity is something Wells continuously defines himself against, irrespective of the "truth" of the belief in question. This is especially evident in "The Flat Earth Again" (1894), which appeared anonymously in the *Pall Mall Gazette*[5] shortly after the *National Observer* began serializing the first published version of *The Time Machine*.[6] The *PMG* dialogue, subtitled "A Study in Popular Argument," examines the grounds for believing the earth round. In it a "perverse person" refutes the demonstrations usually advanced in support of that prop-

[5] "From September [1893] onwards he was a regular contributor" to the *PMG* (West, *op. cit.*, p. 99).

[6] Compare "The Flat Earth Again" with the first episode of the *National Observer Time Machine* (chapter 3), printed two weeks earlier.

osition. Having disposed of these—which "are no more proofs than they are poetry"—he himself produces evidence from astronomy in favor of a round earth—evidence, however, "quite unknown to the generality of people." At that point a lady among his audience triumphantly exclaims that she had known all along the earth was round: as in "Gryllotalpa," but this time with unmistakable irony, Wells gives complacency "the last word."

Continuing his virtually uninterrupted diatribe against rigidity of thought is "The Limits of Individual Plasticity" (1895), one of the many essays and review-articles Wells submitted to the *Saturday Review*.[7] This essay, the substance of which he incorporates as chapter 14 of *The Island of Doctor Moreau* (1896), attacks the notion "that a living thing is at the utmost nothing more than the complete realization of its birth possibilities." Superficially, Wells's argument here may seem to contradict the cosmic determinism implicit in Gryllotalpa's conception of man's infinitesimal littleness vis-à-vis the universe at large. But in fact the discrepancy is specious. Like "The Rediscovery of the Unique," "Individual Plasticity" takes a standpoint complementary to that of Gryllotalpa. The *SR* essay is not concerned with what man is, seen from the spatial and temporal viewpoint of astronomy, so much as with the complementary perspective that focuses on man close up, as it were, to examine the limits of what he can make of himself. Against the position of a rigid determinism which would severely restrict man's possibilities for control over his nature and destiny, Wells proposes instead the idea of "plasticity"—"that a living thing might be ... so moulded and modified that at best it would retain scarcely anything of its inherent form and disposition." Unlike naive anthropocentric beliefs which are oblivious to scientific data, the notion of "plasticity"—which would become, in a highly modified version, the basis of Wells's idea for

[7] According to Gordon Ray's bibliography, Wells published frequently in *SR* for a number of years, starting in November 1894.

"artificial evolution"—can be urged on scientific grounds. Indeed, "Individual Plasticity" seriously offers examples of accomplishments in surgery, hypnotism, and the like as proof that biological plasticity is scientifically plausible. Only later, in *Moreau*, does Wells satirically balance the "plastic" possibilities of the organism against the limitations inherent by nature in it. At the same time, *Moreau* also takes into account the ethical and theological implications of "taking living creatures and moulding them into the most amazing forms."

The scope of Wells's repudiations of course includes religious and theological commonplaces. He called *Moreau* a "theological grotesque,"[8] by which he meant (at least in part) that Darwin's theory enormously aggravates the problem of theodicy: a god who would allow the cosmic pain and suffering evolution necessarily entails would have to be like Doctor Moreau. As for the God of traditional religion, Wells, disagreeing with Grant Allen's thesis that the worship of God could only have come about through worshipping the dead, dryly comments: "there are at least a dozen different ways . . . by which a man may arrive at worshipping a stone." Yet "On Comparative Theology" (1898) also recognizes a will to believe: the age of science does not mean the end of what Wells calls superstition. The "symbolist type of mind" in men of all ages, he says, inclines towards "Fetishism," towards a belief in secret cosmic correlations obtaining among diverse phenomena; and from "Fetishism" of this sort science itself is not entirely immune. Apart from the Baconian fetishism of cause and effect common to most scientists, Wells notices the need of a few scientists for an "intensely superstitious science," a "systematised Fetishism" which propounds a "transcendent parallelism or systematisation of phenomena." Witness the comparative anatomist's (e.g., Sir Richard Owen's) penchant for finding structural correspondences among all living things, correspondences well

[8] *AtlEd*, 2:ix.

beyond the pale of cause and effect. After all, Wells suggests, there is no real difference between the positing of anatomical analogies among, say, the nephric organs of animal species and the older notion of "microcosm," that the individual bears analogy to the universe as a whole.

While rejecting "each and every transcendentalism" actually offered him, Wells nevertheless admits the lure of the concept of some mystical, all-encompassing synthesis. As always, he feels the pull of opposite ideas, of diverse ways of looking at things. In this instance, he concedes an "imperative to believe . . . that the whole of being has an interaction and correlation beyond the system of causes that the scientific method reveals."

The selections immediately following illustrate the range and complexity of Wells's repudiations. As such they represent a fair sampling of the other hitherto unreprinted writings of his included herein and from here on grouped, for the most part, on the basis of their thematic similarities.

A TALK WITH GRYLLOTALPA

I once saw a picture for that part of the book, "Pilgrim's Progress," wherein we learn about Christian going through that dark valley where he met Apolly[o]n; and the way in which the painter had drawn this picture fell in and fitted so nicely with sundry things I had been thinking a great deal about, that I could not forbear writing something thereon. The worthy man who had done this drawing had so studied and laboured in doing the sky that it was the most terrible sky, I think, I have ever seen in a picture, for, in some parts were inky clouds, and in some the lightning glared, and in parts stars were falling, and one part was so cunningly painted with vermilion and yellow that it seemed as if hell must be yawning below it. And the lower part of the picture, moreover, was made exceedingly cold-looking and desolate. And, after much looking, I found that this painter had not forgotten either Christian or the devil, but had put in two of the littlest figures conceivable near the middle of the picture to represent them.

Now, as I was thinking about this picture, who should come in to see me but my friend, Gryllotalpa,[1] who straightway fell into quite a frensy of admiration at this device of it.

Now, Gryllotalpa is one very deep in the new learning, and he fell to at once talking about, what he called, the "infinitesimal littleness of men," and said many fine things about the cerulean depths of infinite space and the starry heavens, and the onward progress of the race as revealed to us by evolution, some of which matters I fancied he had talked about before to me. Then I said to Gryllotalpa, "Gryllotalpa, it is like taking walnuts with cold meat to hear you discourse on that picture, which heretofore had

"Talk With Gryllotalpa"
Science Schools Journal, no. 3 (Feb. 1887), pp. 87-88. [*GW*; signed "Septimus Browne"]

[1] That is, "mole cricket," so named for its appearance and habits.

little taste for me. Do you really feel akin to the Christian in that vastness?"

Says Gryllotalpa, "I think, my dear old friend, that that picture, which, to you, unlearned in the vast mysteries of physical science, is so insipid, is a far grander picture of a state of man than any I have seen for some time. The old devices of a big man and a devil a little bigger are quite wrong in every way. Man is less than an iota in the infinite universe. He is a Link in an Infinite Chain of Causation and a Factor in a Limitless Sum." Then, said I, interrupting him, "To whom is he thus?" Says Gryllotalpa, in tone of remonstrating surprise, "To me."

"It seems," said I, "that you must have a very extensive mind; for, as for me, I can conceive only of man as altogether the biggest thing in my world." "Ah," cried he, "I see you know nothing of descriptive astronomy or speculative chemistry, nor have you studied the doctrine of the degradation of energy nor looked into ætiology, which is the dropping of plumb-lines into the past just to see how very bottomless it is; neither have you heard what is known in human physiology on the psychological side."

"True it is, Gryllotalpa," said I, "that I have not even dabbled in any of those things, but thou that hast drunk deep of the draught of knowledge will, perhaps, tell me one thing I am curious to know? By what do you, men of the new learning, measure things, that you say, as you do, that a planetary system is a greater thing than a man?" He answered "That 'twas by 'sun's distances,' and miles, and feet, and inches," and seemed somewhat scornful with me. "Then," said I, "despise me not, O Gryllotalpa, but it seems to me that there is somewhat of a general perspective effect which you men of the new learning in your course of taking to pieces and examining all the parts of the universe, now and then lose sight of. A sun may be a big thing millions of miles away, but, surely, here it is not so big as the eye that sees it. Your duty to aid in the developing of humanity is a vast thing, doubtless, but nearer, and every day before you, is your duty to serve your neighbour."

I will not tell what Gryllotalpa said, because I ever love to have the last word. And, in truth, I hardly fancy I *could* tell, for it was strange sayings, concerning "truth in the absolute" and the like (to me) incomprehensible things.

THE REDISCOVERY OF THE UNIQUE

The original title of this paper was "The Fallacy of the Common Noun." This was subsequently altered to the present superscription, which the author considers to be equally expressive and far preferable on account of its quiet grandeur. Either will convey the suggestion of our intent to most of our readers, but there are possibly a few, here and there, to whom both are unmeaning. To these we may perhaps, by way of introductory advertisement, or prospectus, address a few remarks on the scope, value, and necessity of our matter.

The Rediscovery of the Unique is the rediscovery of a quite obvious and altogether neglected common fact. It is of wide—almost universal—interest, and of quite universal application. To altogether practical people it is of value as showing the criminal injustice of cab regulations and an inspection of weights and measures; to those who love the subtle subjective rather than objective crudities, and who find it impossible to repeat facts, it is an inestimably precious justification; while to scientists it is important as destroying the atomic theory. It startles the philosopher dwelling in pure reason by giving logic such a twist as tall towers sometimes get from lively yet conservative earthquakes. It should, it will, decimate every thoughtful man's views as a pestilence thins a city. Among other things, after half a century of destructive criticism, it reinstates miracles and prophecy on their old footings. It shows that those scientific writers who have talked so glibly of the reign of inflexible law have been under a serious misconception. It restores special providences and unverified assertions to the stock of credible things, and liberty to the human imagination. To clergymen, forced to controversy in urban parishes; to classical scholars who

"Rediscovery of the Unique"
Fortnightly Review, n.s. 50 (1891): 106-111. [Signed]

as schoolmasters find *Spencer's Education* a curse and a threat,[1] to the softer and illogical sex everywhere, this rediscovery comes as a special boon and blessing. Properly financed it might be established as a cult; and those refuges for the feeble refined from vulgar and militant scepticism, the congregations of Theosophical Buddhism and mystic Catholicism, have a third rival. A new saying might be, and as a matter of fact is, being started in the marketplace: "Let us be unique"—in shoals; for the ambition of our young men and maidens to be at any sacrifice "lively and eccentric," is the unconscious moral aspect of this great rediscovery.

The bare thing itself, like the theory of gravitation, may be expressed in a sentence, though like that theory it is the outcome of many centuries of thought. In a sentence it is, *All being is unique*, or, nothing is strictly like anything else. It implies, therefore, that we only arrive at the idea of similar beings by an unconscious or deliberate disregard of an infinity of small differences. No two animals, for instance, are alike, as any bird or dog-fancier or shepherd can tell. Any two bricks, or coins, or marbles, will be found on examination to differ in size, shape, surface, hue—in endless details as you make your investigation more searching and minute. "As like as two peas in one pod," is a proverb which, like most proverbs, embalms a misconception: one can easily see for oneself when peas are in season. And so in the smallest clod of earth and in the meanest things of life there is, if we care to see it, the unprecedented and unique. As we are taught in the vision of Saint Peter, and more dimly by Wordsworth, there is really nothing around us common and negligible. Thus, with a brief paragraph and a minute's thought, the scales

---

[1] See Herbert Spencer, "What Knowledge is of Most Worth," in *Education: Intellectual, Moral, and Physical* (New York: D. Appleton, 1860), pp. 1-87. Spencer favors the rigors of science rather than the vagaries of classical studies as a training for health, self-preservation, livelihood, parenthood, artistic production and appreciation, and the advancement of ethics and religion.

drop from the reader's eyes and he makes the rediscovery of the unique.

Its logical consequences are so enormous that we would beg his patience for a moment to make sure of our position before proceeding to them. We may imagine some objections to what we have said. The case of two bullets following each other from a mould might perhaps be raised by an unscientific person, but actually the same mould never turns out two bullets alike: it has gained or lost heat and expanded or contracted; there is just a little more wear since the last bullet was cast; the lead itself is rising or falling in temperature and its impurities vary. Again, the little crystals of a precipitate seem identically alike till we test them with micrometer, microscope, polarizer, and micro-chemical tests; then we find quite acceptable individualisms of size, imperfection, strain, and so on. The stars of heaven and the sands of the sea are not evidently unique beings only on account of distance and size respectively. Everywhere repetition disappears and the unique is revealed as sense and analysis grow keener. And since adjectives are abstracted from nouns, it follows that uniqueness goes beyond things and reaches properties. The red of one rose petal seems the same as the red of another, because the man who sees them is blinded through optical insufficiency and mental habit. Put them side by side, is the shade the same? If you think so, take counsel with some artist who can really paint flowers. All learning nowadays tends to become practical, and we may yet see schools of metaphysicians in the fields, engaged severally in plucking daisy petals apart.

Hence the *common noun* is really the verbal link of a more or less arbitrarily determined group of uniques. When we take the term distributively the boundaries grow suddenly vague. It is the constant refrain in the teaching of one of the most eminent of living geologists[2] that every-

---

[2] Here the name John Wesley Judd appears in Wells's hand in a copy of "The Rediscovery" in the Wells Archive. Professor Judd, who taught Wells

thing passes into everything else by "insensible gradations." He holds up to his students a picture of the universe
not unlike a water-colour sketch that has fallen into a
water-butt and "run." The noun "chair," for instance, is
definite enough to the reader—till he thinks; then behold
a borderland of dubiety! Rocking chairs, lounge chairs,
settees; what is this nondescript—chair or ottoman? and
this—chair or stool? Here, again, have we a garden chair
or seat, or a *cheval-de-frise*? and where do you draw the
line between chair and firewood? But the ordinary person,
when he speaks of a number of chairs, never feels the
imminence of this difficulty. He imagines one particular
unique sitting apparatus with which he is familiar, and,
taking a kind of vicious multiple mental squint at it, sees
what is utterly impossible in the real world—so many
others identical with it.

For, on the theory of our rediscovery, *number* is a
purely subjective and illusory reduplication of uniques.

It is extremely interesting to trace the genesis of this
human delusion of number. It has grown with the growth
of the mind, and is, we are quite prepared to concede,
a necessary feature of thought. We may here remark,
parenthetically, that we make no proposal to supersede
ordinary thinking by a new method. We are, in harmony
with modern biology, simply stating a plain fact about
it. Human reason, in the light of what is being advanced,
appears as a convenient organic process based on a fundamental happy misconception, and it may—though the
presumption is against such a view—take us away from,
rather than towards, the absolute truth of things. The
raison d'etre of a man's mind is to avoid danger and get
food—so the naturalists tell us. His reasoning powers are
about as much a truth-seeking tool as the snout of a pig,
and he may as well try to get to the bottom of things
by them as a mole might by burrowing. This, however,

---

geology at the Royal College of Science (*EA*, p. 183), is named in a similar
context in "The Scepticism of the Instrument" (*AtlEd*, 9: 340).

is outside the scope of the present paper, and altogether premature.

The first substantives of primitive man were almost certainly not ordinary common nouns. They were single terms expressive of certain special relationships between him as the centre of the universe and that universe. There was "Father," who fed him; "Home," where he sheltered; and "Man," the adversary he hated and plotted against. Similarly, in the recapitulatory phases of a child's development, it uses "Pa," "Ma," "Pussy," strictly as proper nouns. Such simple terms become common as experience widens and analogies appear. Man soon exhausted his primitive stock of grunts, weird mouthings, and snorts; his phonetic, in fact his general, memory was weak, and his capacity of differentiation therefore slight; he was in consequence obliged to slur over uniqueness, and lump similar-looking things together under what was, for practical purposes, the same sound. Then followed the easy step of muddling repeated substantives into dual and plural forms. And then, out of a jumble of broken-down substantives and demonstratives grew up the numbers—grew and blossomed like a grove of mental upas trees.

They stupify people. When we teach a child to count, we poison its mind almost irrevocably. When a man speaks of a thousand of bricks, he never dreams that he means a unique collection of uniques that his mind cannot grasp individually. When he speaks of a thousand years, the suspicion never crosses his mind that he is referring to a unique series of unique gyrations on the part of the earth we inhabit; and yet, if he is an educated man, he knows perfectly well that the shape of the earth's orbit and the earth's velocity are things constantly changing! He is inoculated with the arithmetical virus; he lets a watch and a calendar blind him to the fact that every moment of his life is a miracle and a mystery.

All that is said of common nouns and number here has an obvious application to terms in logic. It is scarcely necessary to say more to strictly logical people, to convince them of the absurdity of being strictly logical. They fancy the words they work with are reliable tools, instruments of steel, while they are rather like a saw or axe of ice when the thermometer fluctuates about zero centigrade.

The most indisputable corollary of the rediscovery is the destruction of the atomic theory. There is absolutely no ground in human experience for a presumption of similar atoms, the mental entanglement that created one being now unravelled, and similarly the certainty of all the so-called laws of physics and chemistry is now assailable.

Here a most excusable objection may be anticipated and met. "I grant," the scientist will say—in fact, does say— "that any presumption in favour of identically similar atoms disappears upon analysis; I grant that our original suspicion of such atoms arose from a mental imperfection; yet I still keep my theories intact with—experimental verification." Thus the whirligig of time brings round its revenges; here is science taking up the cast-off armour of religion and resting its claims on prophecy! The scientist predicts a planet, an element, or a formula, and the thing either comes almost as he said, or—he makes a discovery. Now the unique fact of averages explains the whole matter.

It is a well-known fact that at any theatre during the run of a fairly successful piece, on every recurring Monday, Tuesday, or other day in the week, almost exactly the same number of people will come nightly and distribute themselves in almost exactly the same way through the house. So many will go to the pit, so many to the dress circle, so many to the boxes, so much "paper" stuffing will be required to give a cheerful plumpness to the whole. The manager can give all these numbers beforehand within a very small fraction of the total. Yet not one of these spectators is exactly the same as another; each one has his individual cares and sorrows, desires and motives, and comes and goes in accordance with the necessities of his unique life. Now and then there is a break in the even succession of attendances; a madman, perhaps, comes to the theatre, fires off a pistol and clears out the gallery; but take a sufficiently large theatre, a sufficiently large number of times, and it becomes impossible* to define the result of average attendance from the sum of the actions of a number of imagined indistinguishably similar persons. So with atoms—it is possible to think of them as unique things each with its idiosyncrasies, and yet regard the so-called verification of the atomic theory with tranquillity. But when the mad atom comes along, the believer in the unique remains tranquil, while the ears of the chemist get hot, his manner becomes nervous and touchy, and he mumbles certain unreasonable things about "experimental error." Or possibly, as occurred lately with an antic atom on a sensitive plate, he fancies jealous or curious spooks are upsetting his experiments.

We may here call attention to the unreasonable width of "margin of experimental error" allowed to scientists. They assert, for instance, in illustration of this atomic theory of theirs, that in water, hydrogen and oxygen invariably exist in the definite and integral ratio of one to eight. Any truthful chemist, if the reader can get one and "heckle" him, will confess that the most elaborate and accurate analyses of water have given fractional and variant results; the ratio of the compounds gets wrong, theoretically speaking, sometimes to the left of the decimal place. The chemist gets results most satisfactory to himself by taking large quantities and neglecting fractions. The discrepancies so often noted by beginners in practical physics and chemistry between experimental and theoretical results are frequently extremely startling and instructive in this connection. At the beginning a student is naive—honest; but presently he gets into the way of manipulating his apparatus—a laboratory euphemism.

Leaving the scattered atoms of the ordinary chemist,

*Apparently a slip for "possible."

we may next allude briefly to the bearings of the rediscovery on morality. Here we are on ground where we modestly fear almost to tread. There is the dire possibility of awakening the wrath and encountering the rushing denunciations of certain literary men who have taken public morality under their protection. We may, however, point out that beings are unique, circumstances are unique, and that therefore we cannot think of regulating our conduct by wholesale dicta. A strict regard for truth compels us to add that principles are wholesale dicta: they are substitutes of more than doubtful value for an individual study of cases. A philanthropist in a hurry might clap a thousand poor souls into ready-made suits all of a size, but if he really wanted the people properly clothed he would send them one by one to a tailor.

There is no reason why a man who has hitherto held and felt honestly proud of high principles should be ashamed of sharing a common error, provided he is prepared for a frank abandonment; but though a principle, like a fetich, may be still convenient as a missile weapon, or entertaining as a curiosity, its supposed value and honourableness in human life vanishes with our rediscovery.

Finally we may turn away from proofs and consequences and note briefly how this great rediscovery grew to a head. The period of darkest ignorance, when men turned their backs on nature and believed in mystic numbers, has long passed away; even the skulls of the schoolmen have rotted to dust by this time, and their books are in tatters. The work of Darwin and Wallace[3] was the clear assertion of the uniqueness of living things; and physicists and chemists are now trying the next step forward in a hesitating way—they must take it sooner or later. We are on the eve of man's final emancipation from rigid reasonableness, from the last trace of the trim clockwork thought of the

---

[3] Wells alludes to the importance Darwinian theory places on minute variations among individuals of the same species as the origin of new species.

seventeenth and eighteenth centuries. The common chemist is a Rip Van Winkle from these buried times. His grave awaits his earliest convenience, yawning.

The neat little picture of a universe of souls made up of passions and principles in bodies made of atoms, all put together so neatly and wound up at the creation, fades in the series of dissolving views that we call the march of human thought. We no longer believe, whatever creed we may affect, in a Deity whose design is so foolish and little that even a theological bishop can trace it and detect a kindred soul. Some of the most pious can hardly keep from scoffing at Milton's world—balanced just in the middle of those crystalline spheres that hung by a golden chain from the battlements of heaven.[4] We no longer speculate
"What varied being peoples ev'ry star,"[5]
because we have no reason at all to expect life beyond this planet. We are a century in front of that Nuremberg cosmos, and in the place of it there looms a dim suggestion of the fathomlessness of the unique mystery of life. The figure of a roaring loom with unique threads flying and interweaving beyond all human following, working out a pattern beyond all human interpretation, we owe to Goethe,[6] the intellectual father of the nineteenth century. Number—Order, seems now the least law in the universe; in the days of our great-grandfathers it was heaven's first law.

So spins the squirrel's cage of human philosophy.

Science is a match that man has just got alight. He thought he was in a room—in moments of devotion, a temple—and that his light would be reflected from and display walls inscribed with wonderful secrets and pillars carved with philosophical systems wrought into harmony. It is a curious sensation, now that the preliminary splutter is over and the flame burns up clear, to see his hands

---

[4] See *Paradise Lost*, Bk. II, ll. 1047-1053.

[5] Alexander Pope, *An Essay on Man* (1733-34), Epistle I, l. 27.

[6] See the Earth Spirit's speech in Goethe's *Faust*, Part I, "Night," ll. 501-509.

lit and just a glimpse of himself and the patch he stands on visible, and around him, in place of all that human comfort and beauty he anticipated—darkness still.

THE FLAT EARTH AGAIN

A Study in Popular Argument

"I am a Zetetic,"[1] said the perverse person, "and the world is flat."

"What nonsense you talk!" said the young lady.

"Prove that the world is round," said the perverse person, smiling blandly at the company.

"Every one knows it is round," said the young lady, and refused to degrade her intellect by any further notice of the question.

"The earth is ascertained to be round," began the schoolmaster, feeling nervously with all his fingers out at the nose piece of his eyeglasses; "the earth is ascertained to be round from—from the following considerations: First, circumnavigation. If we start from a point on the earth's surface, we can sail round the globe and return at last to the place whence we started."

"Similarly," said the perverse man, "London must be of a globular shape, because I can start on the Inner Circle from Charing Cross Station, and, travelling eastward from it, presently return, via Victoria, to Charing Cross again."

The schoolmaster looked annoyed. "Circumnavigation," he said, "is only the first consideration. There is next the fact that the water surfaces of the earth are curved. If, for instance, I stand on the shore and watch a ship receding, I can see it go over the curve, first the hull being hidden, then the lower parts of the sails, and finally the topmasts. This shows that the surface of the ocean is curved and—"

"But that," interrupted the perverse man, "does not show anything about the shape of the solid earth. Surely

"Flat Earth Again"
PMG 58 (April 2, 1894):3. [*ACW*]
    [1] That is, a sceptic.

water may have a curved surface when standing on a perfectly flat base. You know a drop of water on a greasy plate, for instance, always has this outline. (He drew on a piece of paper the outline we have marked A, and handed it round).

A

Moreover, if the earth were brick-shaped, or the shape of a thin book, the water upon it would still not spread itself as a level sheet of water. It would be attracted toward the centre of gravity of the earth, wherever that might be, and its surface would tend to assume a spherical curve around that centre. If I draw this figure of a brick-shaped earth with its centre of gravity at CG, the curved line above will show how the water would lie.

B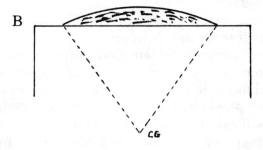

Any one not absolutely ignorant of physics will admit that, and yet the round earth people have tried again and again to drag in this absolutely irrelevant matter of the curve of the water surface. You will remember Proctor managed to confuse the issue with some absurd bet about the Bedford Level a few years ago."[2]

[2] Richard A. Proctor mentions this "bet" in a footnote to his *Old and New Astronomy* (London: Longmans, 1892), p. 76. The bet was to prove "the rotundity of the earth" to someone deluded "by a charlatan [into believing] that the earth's surface is plane," the basis of the proof being measurements "on a range of water six miles long" between two bridges spanning the Bedford Level Canal. The proof, though cogent, was rejected, for anyone "unable to understand the astronomical evidence of the earth's rotundity must be beyond the influence of evidence."

The schoolmaster looked thoughtful. "What you say sounds plausible. But there is still a third proof of the earth's rotundity. The shadow of the earth upon the moon, as we see it in eclipses, is always round, and only a spherical body can invariably throw a round shadow."

"How do you know it is the shadow of the earth?" said the perverse person.

"Well, we know the moon is a satellite of the earth . . . H'm. I am afraid that is rather like assuming that the earth is a round planet in space." He became meditative.

"You see," said the perverse person, with the air of one who closes a discussion; "your first two proofs were not proofs at all, and your third begged the question. Have you any more?"

"There is a point raised by Mr. Alfred Russel Wallace on this controversy. If the earth is flat, we could see the Alps in England."[3]

"Well, suppose it is a little curved—like a saucer upside-down; that is some way from proving it round."

"You see," pursued the temporary Zetetic, "how feeble all these common arguments for the rotundity of the earth are, how difficult it is to prove this little assertion. Yet thoughtless people will interrupt you with pishing and poohing, will say they *know* the earth is round, and get viciously angry with the flat earth proposition. But dogmatism apart, I do not believe one educated man in twenty could produce a sufficient reason—other than his credulity —for his belief in the roundness of the earth. The point is that you teach things at school as proofs the world is round that are no more proofs than they are poetry. The

Proctor, whose pompous rhetoric Wells satirizes, delicately omits mentioning that the man who in 1870 accepted the bet and devised the proof was Alfred Wallace, who for 20 years thereafter silently suffered the lawsuits and other persecutions of the flat-earth advocates. Wallace divulges the facts in his autobiography, *My Life: A Record of Events and Opinions*, 2 vols. (New York: Dodd, Mead, 1905), 2: 381-393. We have found no evidence that Wells was aware of Wallace's involvement.

[3] We have not been able to trace the source of Wells's citation of Wallace here (but see note 2).

only satisfactory consideration so far as I have been able to ascertain is quite unknown to the generality of people. It is not even found in the text-books of Physical Geography. It is the apparent rotation of the stars round a south as well as a north pole. I know of none other that would be comprehensible by even an ordinary well-educated person."

"So you do admit the world is round after all?" said the schoolmaster, brightening into a glow of triumph.

"You have not proved it," said the perverse person.

"I said it was round," said the young lady, "all along."

THE LIMITS OF INDIVIDUAL PLASTICITY

The generalizations of heredity may be pushed to extremes, to an almost fanatical fatalism. There are excellent people who have elevated systematic breeding into a creed, and adorned it with a propaganda. The hereditary tendency plays, in modern romance, the part of the malignant fairy, and its victims drive through life blighted from the very beginning. It often seems to be tacitly assumed that a living thing is at the utmost nothing more than the complete realization of its birth possibilities, and so heredity becomes confused with theological predestination. But, after all, the birth tendencies are only one set of factors in the making of the living creature. We overlook only too often the fact that a living being may also be regarded as raw material, as something plastic, something that may be shaped and altered, that this, possibly, may be added and that eliminated, and the organism as a whole developed far beyond its apparent possibilities. We overlook this collateral factor, and so too much of our modern morality becomes mere subservience to natural selection, and we find it not only the discreetest but the wisest course to drive before the wind.

Now the suggestion this little article would advance is this:that there is in science, and perhaps even more so in history, some sanction for the belief that a living thing might be taken in hand and so moulded and modified that at best it would retain scarcely anything of its inherent form and disposition; that the thread of life might be preserved unimpaired while shape and mental superstructure were so extensively recast as even to justify our regarding the result as a new variety of being. This proposition is purposely stated here in its barest and most startling form. It is not asserted that the changes effected

"Limits of Individual Plasticity"
SR 79 (Jan. 19, 1895): 89-90. [*GW, GR*]

would change in any way the offspring of such a creature, but only that the creature itself as an individual is capable of such recasting.

It may be that the facts to be adduced in support of this possibility will strike the reader as being altogether too trivial and familiar for their superstructure. But they are adduced only to establish certain principles, and these principles, which are perfectly established by these small things, have never been shown conclusively to be necessarily limited to these small things. For reasons that it would not be hard to discover, they have in practice been so restricted in the past, but that is the sum of their assured restriction. Now first, how far may the inherent bodily form of an animal be operated upon? There are several obvious ways: amputation, tongue-cutting, the surgical removal of a squint, and the excision of organs will occur to the mind at once. In many cases excisions result in extensive secondary changes, pigmentary disturbances, increase in the secretion of fatty tissue, and a multitude of correlative changes. Then there is a kind of surgical operation of which the making of a false nose, in cases where that feature has been destroyed, is the most familiar example. A flap of skin is cut from the forehead, turned down on the nose, and heals in the new position. This is a new kind of grafting of part of an animal upon itself in a new position. Grafting of freshly obtained material from another animal is also possible, has been done in the case of teeth, for example. Still more significant are the graftings of skin and bone—cases where the surgeon, despairing of natural healing, places in the middle of the wound pieces of skin snipped from another individual, fragments of bone from a fresh-killed animal; and the medical student will at once recall Hunter's cock-spur flourishing on the bull's neck.[1] So much for the form.

[1] John Hunter (1728-1793), the great pioneer vivisectionist and surgeon, performed many curious animal transplants. See the article on Hunter by F. H. B. (Francis Henry Butler) in the eleventh edition of the *Encyclopaedia Britannica (1910)*.

The physiology, the chemical rhythm of the creature, may also be made to undergo an enduring modification, of which vaccination and other methods of inoculation with living or dead matter are examples. A similar operation is the transfusion of blood, although in this case the results are more dubious. These are all familiar cases. Less familiar and probably far more extensive were the operations of those abominable medieval practitioners who made dwarfs and show monsters, and some vestiges of whose art still remain in the preliminary manipulation of the young mountebank or contortionist. Victor Hugo gives us an account of them, dark and stormy, after his wont, in "L'homme qui rit."[2] But enough has been said to remind the reader that it is a possible thing to transplant tissue from one part of an animal to another, or from one animal to another, to alter its chemical reactions and methods of growth, to modify the articulation of its limbs, and indeed to change it in its most intimate structure. And yet this has never been sought as an end and systematically by investigators. Some of such things have been hit upon in the last resort of surgery; most of the kindred evidence that will recur to the reader's mind has been demonstrated as it were by accident—by tyrants, by criminals, by the breeders of horses and dogs, by all kinds of untrained men working for their own immediate ends. It is impossible to believe that the last word, or anything near it, of individual modification has been reached. If we concede the justifications of vivisection, we may imagine as possible in the future, operators, armed with antiseptic surgery and a growing perfection in the knowledge of the laws of growth, taking living creatures and moulding

[2] Victor Hugo's novel *L'homme qui rit* (1869) contains, among other things, a passage concerning supposed Chinese practices of "molding" men in quaintly shaped vases, where the growing child is confined until it fills up "the embossments of the vase with its compressed flesh and twisted bones," thus producing a dwarf "of any desired shape." Moreau cites this passage from *The Man Who Laughs*, trans. William Young (New York: Appleton, 1885), p. 17, in *AtlEd*, 2: 89-90. Compare the practices of the Selenites in *The First Men*, *AtlEd*, 6: 240-241.

them into the most amazing forms; it may be, even reviving the monsters of mythology, realizing the fantasies of the taxidermist, his mermaids and what-not, in flesh and blood.

The thing does not stop at a mere physical metamorphosis. In our growing science of hypnotism we find the promise of a possibility of replacing old inherent instincts by new suggestions, grafting upon or replacing the inherited fixed ideas. Very much indeed of what we call moral education is such an artificial modification and perversion of instinct; pugnacity is trained into courageous self-sacrifice, and suppressed sexuality into pseudo-religious emotion.

We have said enough to develop this curious proposition. It may be the set limits of structure and psychical capacity are narrower than is here supposed. But as the case stands this artistic treatment of living things, this moulding of the commonplace individual into the beautiful or the grotesque, certainly seems so far credible as to merit a place in our minds among the things that may some day be.

ON COMPARATIVE THEOLOGY

Humour, I take it, is the perception, the persistent remembrance of the fluctuating illogical quality of men and things, of men more than of things. And it is one of the humours of life that man the egregious, defines himself as a reasonable soul. Continuously and completely rational beings may perhaps exist, but no man is continually and completely rational. First he is limited since he has no ultimate data; and secondly, he forgets. One must be very powerfully observant or very powerfully introspective to realise how much of the conscious daily life of man, quite apart from instinct, is the creation of external suggestion and chance, and ill-read experience, distorted memory, and forgetfulness. And even when this is realised, the industrious anthropologist may quite easily forget it again in pursuit of some attractive theory of mental processes. Mr. Grant Allen, for instance, forgets it, directly the stress of theory-building begins. He would have us believe that all gods are the apotheosis of dead ancestors, that whenever we worship, or whatever we worship, we worship directly or indirectly a dead tribal "boss." He would have us believe that all sacred stones were sepulchral stones, and sacred trees, sepulchral trees, and generally he drives to death one admirable and indisputable explanation of why men worship. For to any one who has given any close attention to his own mental processes or the mental processes of other people, it is certain there are at least a dozen different ways, primary separate ways, by which a man may arrive at worshipping a stone, and to any one not blind and strenuous in pursuit of something "fresh and original" in anthropological theory, it is perfectly obvious that individuals out of the billions of ape men and men the ages have

"Comparative Theology"
A review of Grant Allen's *The Evolution of the Idea of God* and an anonymous book, *The Canon; an Exposition of the Pagan Mystery Perpetuated in the Cabala as the Rule of All the Arts: SR* 85 (Feb. 12, 1898): 211-213. [Signed]

seen, must have traversed every one of these possible ways. No doubt stones have been stuck upon graves to keep down the dead, but no doubt they have been stuck up in other places for endless reasons or for no reason at all—"for fun" as boys say when they do a thing out of excess of energy. And an isolated stone, naturally or artificially standing out, admits of endless interpretations and has carried them all. It was personified and worshipped for its own sake, it was regarded as great medicine, it was amusing, it was fearful, it was queer, it was disliked, oddities of form suggested grotesque phallic interpretations, it was associated with or identified with something else; the point of view affected the interpretation, it may have had its sombre and its genial aspects. The same man in different moods may have regarded it in very various ways. He forgot, new suggestions came. Only with the coming of organized tradition and complex powers of language, only when savagery was over and the barbaric stage reached, when men talked freely and the Word grew potent, only then would the treatment of the remarkable stone grow at all uniform. A man then would remember what he told another man, would remember what he had been told. In one community one point of view could get the upper hand, in another, another. In each community there would be a struggle for existence of the possible interpretation of the stone of the district. The erection of sepulchral stones, their identification with worshipful corpses, the promotion to godhead no doubt occurred. Mr. Grant Allen's collection of unauthenticated evidence in the matter proves nothing but that. It barely proves that. It does not prove that all other possible interpretations did not also occur.

Then again, Mr. Grant Allen propounds a beautiful theory of "stages" in the worship of the dead, "Corpse worship," "Ghost worship," "Shade worship," which answer to the "three stages of preservation or mummification, burial and cremation." There never were such stages.

The primitive man, the early paleolithic man probably did many different things with a human dead body. He left it about and beasts devoured it. He was carnivorous and buried it and dug it up and ate it, or after he had fire, he cooked and ate it. If he was forgetful or unfortunate with his fire these things amounted to burial or cremation. Or he kept by it, because he had liked the person, expecting it to revive, until it became objectionable, or until he forgot that point of view and felt hungry. At any rate he has left us no graves. Some neolithic men buried their chiefs and great people at any rate. We know that because of the mounds they have left. What became of the common men we do not know. Some neolithic people burnt their dead. Early neolithic mummies are not in evidence to confirm Mr. Grant Allen's theory. The Greeks anciently buried, took to burning, and reverted to burial. There are dozens of adequate reasons and quasi reasons why a tribe should give up burial for burning or *vice versâ*. The idea of an immediate terrestrial millennium substituted burial for burning at the outbreak of Christianity. Hygienic theories are restoring cremation. In a settled community where there is no convenient great river, to eat, bury or burn are the only possible ways of getting rid of a dead body. Exposure is only possible to nomads—some of whom do it. The idea of a world-wide logical and orderly development of opinion about the fate of the dead, affecting, in the most logical manner, the funereal practice of humanity, is *à priori* incredible, and quite unsupported by the facts of the case.

But it is Mr. Grant Allen's merit that he makes his theorising look far more flimsy than it is. This ingenious theory of the three stages is placed in the forefront of the book, and in a remarkably ill-advised preface—Mr. Grant Allen will ruin himself by writing prefaces—attention is especially called to it as a remarkable discovery. Hasty people may be pardoned for an altogether unfavourable judgment. As a matter of fact, in spite of this theory of the Three Stages, his book, read with distrust, is as valuable and suggestive a book as has appeared for many a day. It lacks the solid conviction of Tylor's Primitive Culture,[1] perhaps, but it has much the same quality of imaginative stimulation. If the three-stage theory is bad, the amplification of the thesis of that most valuable and unreadable book, Frazer's "Golden Bough,"[2] is a complete compensation. And the collection of matter about manufactured gods is richly suggestive. For the first time there is placed before the general reader a theory—and a very remarkable theory—of the origin of Christian practices that has hitherto been accessible only to the laborious erudite. That alone makes it necessary to read this book. It is a book to quarrel with perhaps, but certainly it is a book to be read.

Of "The Canon" one can scarcely say as much. It is a forbidding mass of matter, opening gravely with impossible premises. The first sentence propounds its wild assumption: "The failure of all efforts in modern times to discover what constituted the ancient canon of the arts has made this question one of the most hopeless puzzles which antiquity presents." But suppose there was no canón? Who says there was a canon? Before we are over two pages we have it assumed that "the priests are practically the masters of the old world" (*cf.* Maspero),[3] and that there is "an esoteric doctrine of religion" which has come down to us "in unbroken continuity at least from the building of the Great Pyramid." After that it is not surprising to find a suggestion that there is a mystical meaning in Hamlet, for the devotees of the Bacon-Shakespeare cryptogram[4] are of one kin with and the degenerate successors of the Gnostics and Cabalists. But the

[1] The English geologist Edward Tylor (1832-1917) theorized about late prehistorical conditions on earth.

[2] *The Golden Bough* (1890), by Sir James Frazer (1854-1941), is an encyclopedic study of primitive thought generally, and especially primitive religious beliefs.

[3] Gaston Maspero (1846-1916), the French Egyptologist.

[4] Wells alludes to the crankish methods of "deducing" "secret meanings" from Shakespeare's texts. See the Appendix, no. 56.

book is not so wild and whirling as its preliminary assumptions and its lapse towards the esoteric theory of Hamlet suggest. Admit its grounds of action, admit that profoundly wise priesthood with its unaccountable desire to transmit inconclusive science by cryptogrammic means to posterity, and the rest is a sane and laborious effort, not without interest even to the incredulous. The modern mystic is commonly a poor fool, on the verge of entire intellectual disorganization. But the anonymous author of "The Canon" is not of that generation; his work has the unmistakable quality of power. He is three or twelve hundred years out of his generation, which is after all his misfortune rather than his fault. Amidst the Rosicrucians or the Gnostics he would have been a great master. The chapters on the Cabala, The Ark and The Temples, for instance, are really admirable expositions of a method of inquiry that I had thought vanished from the earth. Yet but a little while since, in spite of Montaigne and the vulgar habit of thought, it was the prevailing method among learned and scholarly men. So late as the days of Milton, Comenius was endeavouring to systemise it as the Analogical Method.[5]

The modern method of inquiry, as Bacon described it,[6] was of course a systematised Fetishism, the natural human method in all ages. Shallow unthinking people use the word "Fetishism" as if it were the quintessence of folly instead of the quintessence of common sense. The essential idea of Fetish is that cause follows effect, an idea underlying all rational operations, the fault of the system is that each savage who practises it has to discover for himself for the most part what is adequate fetish for the effect he desires and what is not. He dies before his system has clarified. Bacon's great idea was essentially a systematisation of

---

[5] Comenius' analogical method was a system of teaching conceived of as the analogue of the sun's functioning in the universe. See *The Great Didactic*, ed. M. W. Keatinge (New York: A & C. Black, 1896), especially chapter 9.

[6] Francis Bacon (1561-1626) expounds this method principally in his *Novum Organum* (1620).

Fetish, a permanent record of experiences, the sane correlation of effects and causes, and the elimination of sham
from operative Fetishes. The immense impetus given to
knowledge by the experimental method has now finally
carried scientific certitude in many directions beyond the
reach of experimental verification. But to a certain type
of men and perhaps to all women a purely scientific method
has ever been unsatisfactory; a certain imaginative type
is perpetually reaching out towards some transcendent
parallelism or systematisation of phenomena, irrespective
of the causative relationships of ordinary experience. As
the root of some symbolism and fetish meet in its lower
development, this symbolist type of mind will be found
believing that the shuffling of a pack of cards under certain
conditions will leave the cards arranged in a series symbolical of a series of forthcoming events, or that the creases
in the palm of a man's hand have a symbolical prophetic
relationship to his forthcoming environment. In its higher
it manifests itself in such intensely superstitious science
as the transcendental comparative anatomy of Owen[7] or
in the symbolic system of theology developed in this
present work. Comparative anatomy is always sliding
towards mystic interpretations. In my days of study we
worshipped "nephridia" and were on the verge of believing
the cosmos a "highly modified nephridium."[8] And the
"schematic mollusc" has no ground for contempt of its
elder brother, the microcosm. Yet many of us who reject
each and every transcendentalism that is offered us,
do still find it imperative to believe in spite of the absolute
darkness that the whole of being has an interaction and
correlation beyond the system of causes that the scientific
method reveals.

[7] Wells's view of Sir Richard Owen (see chap. 2) probably comes from T.
H. Huxley, whose essay, "Owen's Position in the History of Anatomical Science,"
was included in *The Life of Richard Owen* written by Owen's son (2 vols. [London:
John Murray, 1894], 2: 273-332).

[8] "Nephridia" and "nephridium" were misprinted in the original review-essay
as "neplindia" and "neplindium"; see Wells's letter to the editor, *SR* 85 (Feb.
26, 1898): 296.

The "Canon" has an indiscreet bickering preface by Mr. Cunninghame Graham.[9] Such a sentence as, "I take it that one of the objects of the author of this work is to sustain that in astronomy, in mathematics, in certain other branches of knowledge, the ancients knew a good deal more than modern men of science dare to admit," not only misrepresents the book, but is a quite unjust libel on the modern man of science. "Men of science understand the need of bold advertisement," he writes. He says nothing of the New Woman, but evidently has that scorn of the modern censor in mind; "Deal with sex problems (pruriently of course), be mystic, moral or immoral, flippant, or best of all be dull, success is sure." The "*à la mode* philosopher" gets swift severe handling. Theosophy is trotted out, as though the ancients had no such rag-tag and bobtail of fools, and there is a vigorous "slanging" of the modern architect. But why Mr. Cunninghame Graham should have used this preface as a fitting occasion to vent his miscellaneous spleen against the age which has intruded upon his lifetime, and to extoll the alleged wisdom of the ancients, does not clearly appear. It does little to recommend a thoughtful and laborious (if wrongheaded) contribution to theological study.

[9] Robert Bontine Cunninghame Graham (1852-1936), Scottish author, politician, and friend of Buffalo Bill (see the *Dictionary of National Biography*).

III. *Revisions of the Future*

> Zoology is, indeed, a philosophy and a literature to those who can read its symbols.
>
> *Text-Book of Biology*[1]

Wells published three drafts of *The Time Machine* prior to the Heinemann edition, which is essentially the final and definitive version.[2] Two of these earlier drafts appeared serially: the first, in seven installments, in the *National Observer* between March and June 1894; the other, in five installments, in William Henley's *New Review* between January and June 1895. An American edition, put out by Henry Holt, certainly antedates Heinemann's and probably also the *New Review* version, which, it can be argued, represents a revision of the manuscript Holt accepted.[3]

---

[1] *Text-Book of Biology*, 2nd ed. (London: W. B. Clive, 1894), part 1, p. 131.

[2] The Atlantic Edition does include some textual alterations, but all of them are minor. In a prefatory note he speaks of having found a copy of *The Time Machine* "in which, somewhen about 1898 or 1899, he marked out a few modifications in arrangement and improvements in expression. Almost all these changes he has accepted." *AtlEd*, 1: xxii.

[3] The Heinemann edition appeared at the end of May 1895. The Library of Congress received copies of the American edition on May 7. The first chapter of the Holt *Time Machine* is much closer to the opening episode in the *National Observer* than it is to either the *New Review* or the Heinemann version, and Holt also lacks the Epilogue common to the latter two—all of which suggests, as Bergonzi argues, that the manuscript version Holt accepted was one which W. E. Henley as editor of the *New Review* asked Wells to revise and expand somewhat. See Bernard Bergonzi, "The Publication of *The Time Machine*, 1894-5," *Review of English Studies*, n.s. 11 (1960): 42-51.

Three earlier drafts, two of which are apparently no longer extant, precede the *National Observer* serial. The first of these, *The Chronic Argonauts*, came out in three installments in the *Science Schools Journal* (in April, May, and June 1888). For the most part this fragment (reprinted as an appendix to Bergonzi's *The Early H. G. Wells*), anticipates *The Invisible Man* (1897)—especially in its use of local color and village humor—much more than it does any

An acquaintance with these various published drafts reveals that the genesis of *The Time Machine* goes back to ideas Wells began working out in some of his earliest writings. The serial versions in particular make it possible to analyze three distinguishable ideational components. Chronologically the last, but most necessary of all is the "invention" itself, in Wells's sense of the term—which is to say, not merely the notion of travelling through time by means of a machine but also its rationale. An apocalyptic biology, the second ideational component, informs the Time Traveller's vision of the future. Finally, proceeding from and relating both these other elements is the metaphysical concept of a complementarity between free choice and predestination.

The rationale behind time-travel receives a great deal of attention in the *National Observer* serial. The first episode Wells devotes largely to a proto-(William) Jamesian demonstration that time is a dimension of consciousness.[4] He has his Philosopher—that is, the Time

---

published version of *The Time Machine*. Of the other two very early drafts, Geoffrey West gives a synopsis (*GW*, pp. 291-92) based on what he was told by Wells's "life-long" friend (*EA*, p. 189), A. Morley Davies. To judge from West's account, the future societies in both these "lost" revisions of *The Chronic Argonauts* resemble the social order in *When the Sleeper Wakes* (1899) much more than they do any in *The Time Machine*.

[4] William James discusses the notion of time as duration—as a dimension of consciousness—in his *Principles of Psychology* (2 vols. [New York: Henry Holt, 1890]), where he remarks, for example: "The unit of composition of our perception of time is *duration*, with a bow and a stern, as it were—a rearward- and a forward-looking end" (1: 609; emphasis in original). Another passage in James's *Principles* expresses a possibility similar to one Wells elaborates in his short story "The New Accelerator" (1903):

Suppose [James writes] we were able, within the length of a second, to note 10,000 events distinctly, instead of barely 10, as now; if our life were then destined to hold the same number of impressions, it might be 1000 times as short.... The motions of organic beings would [in that case] be so slow to our senses as to be inferred, not seen. The sun would stand still in the sky, the moon be almost free from change, and so on. (1: 639)

Wells was no doubt familiar with the above-quoted passage when he wrote "The New Accelerator": his wife Amy had given him a copy of James's *Principles* some years before (this copy, now in the Wells Archive at the University of Illinois, is inscribed with the date November 9, 1898). Whether Wells had read James's book prior to his writing the first episode of the *National Observer Time Machine* is not clear. But psychologistic ideas of time were "in the air"

Traveller—offer an exposition of four-dimensional geometry, which Wells associates with the astronomer and
mathematician Simon Newcomb, a transcription of whose
lecture on the subject he had evidently come upon in
Nature the previous month.[5] Rejecting, however, the notion of "another [spatial] direction at right angles to the
other three," the Philosopher proposes instead that time
is the "fourth dimension"—one through which man should
be able to travel as freely as he does through space. This
paradox serves as the hypothesis which the Philosopher's
journey into the future validates; but it also serves as the
premise for the "voyage" of consciousness into that future.
One paradox logically opens the way to the other: the
imaginative possibility of time-travel leads to the imaginative vision of degeneration. These paradoxes liberate consciousness from the restrictions of preconceived ideas, from
"the thought edifice of space, time and number, that our
forefathers contrived."

Wells seems to have conceived the vision of the future
in the *National Observer Time Machine* simply as an
example appended to an argument against an unimaginative complacency which blinds man to the evolutionary
prospects that may really await him. In answer to the

in the early 1890s. Henri Bergson, for instance, treats time as *la durée* in his
Essai sur les données immédiates de la conscience (1889) and in subsequent
works.

[5] Wells links the idea of a fourth spatial dimension specifically with "Professor
Simon Newcombe" (*sic*). Newcomb (1835-1909), an astronomer and mathematician, outlined the possibility of a four-dimensional geometry as part of a lecture
to the New York Mathematical Society in December 1893. Wells probably came
across a transcription of that lecture published as "Modern Mathematical
Thought" in *Nature* 49 (Feb. 1, 1894): 325-29. The passages dealing with
four-dimensional geometry (pp. 328-29 in *Nature*) Newcomb later expanded
as his Presidential Address to the American Mathematical Society (printed under
the title "The Philosophy of Hyper-Space" in *Science*, n.s. 7 [Jan. 7, 1898]:
1-7).
   The hypothesis of a fourth spatial dimension "at right angles to the other
three" had been put forward almost a decade before Newcomb's first lecture
by C. H. Hinton in "What is the Fourth Dimension?" (1884), reprinted
in his *Scientific Romances, First Series* (London: Swan Sonnenschein, 1886).
Closer to Wells's own conception is Edwin Abbott's *Flatland* (1884), where the
fourth dimension "is really Thoughtland" ([London: Seeley, 1884], p. 90).

smug supposition that "the drift of sanitary science" makes it inevitable "that . . . humanity will breed and sanitate itself into human Megatheria," the Time Traveller gives an account of two degenerate species he encountered in the year 12,203; but the Eloi (unnamed in the *National Observer*) and the Morlocks never come into contact with each other. They function merely as illustrations the Philosopher cites in response to the objections from his audience which continually interrupt his narrative. In fact, the structure of the *National Observer* serial, like that of most of Wells's early essays, consists of paradox and confirming example (though not always in that order). The vision itself has no shape of its own. The penultimate paragraph of the last *National Observer* episode—with its mention of a distant future when "this planet" will share "the plight of Mercury, with one face turned always to the sun"—hints at the conclusion of "The Further Vision" in Wells's later drafts, and in that respect anticipates his "revised" emphasis on the controlling influence of cosmic laws. But in the *National Observer* there is no "Further Vision" to give form to the Time Traveller's "prophecy" by outlining a pattern of devolution tending towards extinction,[6] and the role of evolutionary dynamics in determining the degenerative processes whose result the Time Traveller observes remains a matter of the barest suspicion.

The near total absence of a sense of cosmic determinism conforms to Wells's insistence in the *National Observer Time Machine* on the openness of human choice and on human responsibility for the consequences. Man can use his mind to risk liberating himself: though it may seem paradoxical, time-travel, the Philosopher maintains, is a logical extension of human consciousness, entailing the freeing of consciousness from temporal restriction. Man can also imprison himself in the safe confines of "sanitary"

[6] For a discussion of the devolutionary pattern in *The Time Machine*, see R. M. Philmus, "*The Time Machine*; or, The Fourth Dimension as Prophecy," *PMLA* 84 (1969): 530-32.

ideas, in which case civilization, as epitomized by "sanitary science," will eventually destroy "the forces that begat it."

Wells argues for liberation, for innovation in the "principles of thought and symbolism on which our minds travel." The *National Observer Time Machine* assaults "the thought edifice of space, time and number, that our forefathers contrived" and proposes instead the concept of "the unique," as Wells called it. Perception of the uniqueness of phenomena is not available to the "rigid," anthropocentric mind, which, unaware of its enculturated limitations, imposes its "thought edifice" on the universe, thereby reducing everything to a "clockwork" uniformity of "rigid reasonableness." To escape that kind of "rigid reasonableness" and rediscover the "unique," the human mind must become conscious of itself and its true capacities—and in consequence become free, that is, self-determining. This is the ultimate implication of the "possibility or paradox" with which the *National Observer Time Machine* opens.

The *New Review Time Machine* begins wih the "opposite" (in Wells's usage, "complementary") idea. In place of the Philosopher's paradoxical proof of how human consciousness can free itself from time, the Time Traveller offers an exposition of the Wellsian idea of a "Universe Rigid." Wells had submitted an essay bearing that title to the *Fortnightly* and it was scheduled to be printed shortly after "The Rediscovery of the Unique"; but, as Wells reports in *Experiment in Autobiography*, Frank Harris became exasperated at the incomprehensibility of "The Universe Rigid" and destroyed the galleys.[7] Whether a manuscript version still exists or not, the gist of Wells's idea indubitably appears in the *New Review* as the metaphysical basis for time travel:

> I propose [says the Time Traveller] a wholly new view
> of things based on the supposition that ordinary

[7] Cf. the discussion and notes on the Rigid Universe in chapter 1.

human perception is an hallucination. I'm sorry to drag in predestination and free-will, but I'm afraid those ideas will have to help. Look at it in this way. . . . Suppose you knew fully the position and the properties of every particle of matter, of everything existing in the universe at any particular moment of time: suppose, that is, that you were omniscient. Well, that knowledge would involve the knowledge of the condition of things at the previous moment, and at the moment before that, and so on. If you knew and perceived the present perfectly, you would perceive therein the whole of the past. If you understood all natural laws the present would be a complete and vivid record of the past. Similarly, if you grasped the whole of the present, knew all its tendencies and laws, you would see clearly all the future. To an omniscient observer there would be no forgotten past—no piece of time as it were that had dropped out of existence—and no blank future of things yet to be revealed. Perceiving all the present, an omniscient observer would likewise perceive all the past and all the inevitable future at the same time. Indeed, present and past and future would be without meaning to such an observer: he would always perceive exactly the same thing. He would see, as it were, a Rigid Universe filling space and time—a Universe in which things were always the same. He would see one sole unchanging series of cause and effect to-day and to-morrow and always. If "past" meant anything, it would mean looking in a certain direction; while "future" meant looking the opposite way. . . .

. . . From the absolute point of view the universe is a perfectly rigid unalterable apparatus, entirely predestinate, entirely complete and finished . . . from the absolute standpoint—which is the true scientific standpoint—time is merely a dimension, quite analogous to the three dimensions in space. Every particle of matter has length, breadth, thickness, and—duration.[8]

This neo-Laplacean notion of a Rigid Universe might seem to contradict the argument of the *National Observer Time Machine*, but actually the two are complementary. The Philosopher's demonstration in the *National Observer* purports to validate time-travel from the standpoint of human consciousness as a possibility of human consciousness. The Time Traveller in the *New Review*, on the other hand, intends to give cognitive reality to time future as an object of human consciousness, and this requires that the future exist—a proposition that is true only from the cosmic or "absolute" standpoint. The qualifying "absolute" is essential also in differentiating the "Universe Rigid" from the "rigid reasonableness" Wells rejects in "The Rediscovery of the Unique." Whereas the "mind-forg'd manacles" of an unomniscient "rigid reasonableness" would constrain free will and deny any cognition of a unique movement "from things that are past and done with for ever to things that are altogether new," "the absolute standpoint" does not impinge on the human sense of freedom, nor does it impugn as delusive a human consciousness of change.

The metaphysical shift to the "Universe Rigid" in the *New Review* directs the focus away from the possibilities of human choice and control and towards the operation of cosmic laws in bringing about a devolutionary future.[9]

[8] From "The Inventor." Compare Wells's later recollection of the substance of "The Universe Rigid," quoted in chapter 1.

[9] For the Holt edition of *The Time Machine*, Wells used as an epigraph two lines from Robert Browning's poem *Rabbi Ben Ezra* (1864), which perhaps signal his transition to the cosmic determinism implicit in the *New Review*, but which also anticipate a Wellsian kind of complementarity. The lines in question—"Fool! All that is, at all/ Lasts ever, past recall" (XXVII, ll. 157-58)—in their Browningesque context allow man's power to accept his past. Thus, like the lines following shortly thereafter—"He [God] *fixed* thee 'mid this dance/ Of *plastic* circumstance,/ This Present, thou, forsooth, wouldst fain arrest" (XXVIII, 11: 163-65; emphasis added)—they seek to reconcile free will with destiny. Out of context, however, the notion that the past "Lasts ever" quite readily falls in with the quasi-Laplacean idea of a Universe Rigid (but not so readily with the *National*

In accordance with this transition in complementary standpoints, from human to cosmic, Wells concentrates on the prophetic vision itself, enlarging its temporal scope. His revision postpones the discovery of the Eloi and the Morlocks from 12,203 to 802,701. The *relative* nearness of the former date conforms to Wells's focus in the *National Observer* on the influence of present human concerns and endeavors on the prospects for the human species; the astronomical "distance" between the present age and 802,701 affords the time for cosmic laws, more than human effort, to determine the future. Between 802,701 and 30 million years hence, the Time Traveller witnesses a Darwinian struggle between predator and prey in an ever-devolving series moving inexorably towards cosmic destruction. The Eloi and the Morlocks; the animals resembling "rabbits or some breed of kangaroo" and the gigantic centipedes; "a thing like a huge white butterfly" and "a monstrous crab-like creature"—all prepare for the solar eclipse that prefigures the end of the world.[10]

Though the epilogue in the *New Review* looks briefly backwards to the distant past, the direction of vision is otherwise forwards, towards a future where the inexorable logic of cosmic laws points to devolution and extinction as the inevitable conclusions of degeneration. Replacing the *National Observer*'s argumentative dialogue concerning the meaning of the vision are the Time Traveller's various speculations on what present-day human tendencies would permit control over man's destiny to fall entirely to the laws of the cosmos. Although the Time Traveller's explanations are all tentative, they all suppose that what is envisioned is the "logical conclusion,"[11] directed by the laws of nature, of tendencies existing at the present time.

If the principal defect of the *National Observer Time*

Observer's phenomenological argument for time-travel, which the American edition retains).

[10] Behind this vision are Wells's early speculations on man's precarious future in the universe, for which see chapter 5.

[11] *New Review Time Machine*, p. 338; Heinemann, p. 84.

Machine is the shapelessness and insubstantiality of its prophecy, that of the *New Review* is its failure to dramatize the contributory human causes of devolution. The Heinemann *Time Machine* fuses the two serialized versions into a self-sufficient unity. By reinstating, in revised form, the *National Observer*'s introductory argument about time as a dimension of consciousness, Wells reaffirms the possibilities for human will in a Rigid Universe and thus juxtaposes the cosmic and human standpoints. The final revision implies that a narrow scope of consciousness is responsible for cosmic catastrophe, that what the Time Traveller foresees is the ultimate result of the unimaginative complacency—the "rigid reasonableness"—exemplified by his audience. Apart from this significant revision, the Heinemann edition differs from the *New Review* almost solely in matters of chapter divisions and in its omission of the episode wherein the Time Traveller stuns or kills the rabbitlike "grey animal, or grey man, whichever it was." Retention of that episode in the Heinemann version would obviously have confused the moral issues in *The Time Machine*'s human standpoint: after all, the "grey animal, or grey man" is presumably a descendant of the Eloi, whose part the Time Traveller takes against the Morlocks.[12]

The Heinemann *Time Machine*, then, brings together in an aesthetic synthesis ideas that Wells had previously dealt with separately, by and large. It represents the confluence of the "invention" of time-travel, an apocalyptic theory of evolution, and the metaphysical complementarity between human and cosmic standpoints which connects the rationale for time-travel with the prophetic vision thereby achieved.

[12]According to Bergonzi, in his essay on *The Time Machine* (see note 3), Wells originally added the episode concerning the rabbits and the centipedes to pad out an installment in Henley's *New Review* (Wells himself gives some confirmation to that notion in his prefatory remarks to the Atlantic Edition, 1: xxi-xxii). But while this theory is sufficient to account for why the episode initially was included, it is not sufficient as an explanation of why Wells later decided it should be left out of the final version.

The *National Observer Time Machine* is reprinted here in its entirety. From the *New Review* are included the opening paragraphs of the first chapter (those which Wells dropped from the Heinemann edition) and all of "The Further Vision" (to afford the full context of the subsequently omitted episode concerning the "rabbits" and "centipedes").

TIME TRAVELLING

Possibility or Paradox

The Philosophical Inventor was expounding a recondite matter to his friends. The fire burnt brightly, and the soft radiance of the incandescent lights in the lilies of silver, caught the bubbles that flashed and passed in our glasses of amber fluid. Our chairs, being his patents, embraced and caressed us rather than submitted to be sat upon, and there was that luxurious after-dinner atmosphere, when thought runs gracefully free of the trammels of precision. And he put it to us in this way, as we sat and lazily admired him and his fecundity.

'You must follow me carefully here. For I shall have to controvert one or two ideas that are almost universally accepted. The geometry, for instance, they taught you at school is founded on a misconception.'

'Is not that rather a large thing to expect us to begin upon?' said the argumentative person with the red hair.

'I do not mean to ask you to accept anything without reasonable ground for it. But you know of course that a mathematical line, a line of thickness *nil*, has no real existence. They taught you that. Neither has a mathematical plane. These things are mere abstractions.'

'That is all right,' said the man with the red hair.

'Nor can a cube, having only length, breadth, and thickness, have a real existence.'

'There I object,' said the red-haired man. 'Of course a solid body may exist. All real things—'

'So most people think. But wait a moment. Can an *instantaneous* cube exist?'

'Don't follow you,' said the red-haired man.

"Time Travelling"
National Observer, n.s. 11 (March 17, 1894): 446-47. [Signed] These first seven selections are from the *National Observer Time Machine*.

'Can a cube that does not last for any time at all, have a real existence?'

The red-haired man became pensive.

'Clearly,' the Philosophical Inventor proceeded; 'any real body must have extension in *four* directions: it must have length, breadth, thickness, and—duration. But through a natural infirmity of the flesh, which I will explain to you in a moment, we incline to overlook the fact. There are really four dimensions, three which we call the three planes of space, and a fourth, time. There is, however, a tendency to draw an unreal difference between the former three and the latter, because it happens that our consciousness moves intermittently in one direction along the latter from the beginning to the end of our lives.'

'That,' said the very young man, making spasmodic efforts to relight his cigar over the lamp; 'that [is] very clear, indeed.'

'Now it is very remarkable that this is so extensively overlooked,' continued the Philosophical Inventor with a slight accession of cheerfulness. 'Really this is what is meant by the fourth dimension, though some people who talk about the fourth dimension do not know they mean it. It is only another way of looking at time. *There is no difference between time and any of the three dimensions of space except that our consciousness moves along it.* But some foolish people have got hold of the wrong side of that idea. You have all heard what they have to say about this fourth dimension.'

'*I* have not,' said the provincial mayor.

'It is simply this. That space, as our mathematicians have it, is spoken of as having three dimensions, which one may call length, breadth, and thickness, and is always definable by reference to three planes, each at right angles to the others. But some philosophical people have been asking why *three* dimensions particularly—why not another direction at right angles to the other three?—and have even tried to construct a four-dimensional geometry. Professor Simon Newcombe [*sic*] was expounding this to the New York Mathematical Society only a month or so ago. You know how on a flat surface which has only two dimensions we can represent a figure of a three-dimensional solid, and similarly they think that by models of three dimensions they could represent one of four—if they could master the perspective of the thing. See?'

'I think so,' murmured the provincial mayor, and knitting his brows he lapsed into an introspective state, his lips moving as one who repeats mystic words. 'Yes, I think I see it now,' he said after some time, brightening in a quite transitory manner.

'Well, I do not mind telling you I have been at work upon this geometry of four dimensions for some time, assuming that the fourth dimension is time. Some of my results are curious. For instance, here is a portrait of a man at eight years old, another at the age of fifteen, another seventeen, another of twenty-three, and so on. All these are evidently sections, as it were, three-dimensional representations of his four-dimensioned being, which is a fixed and unalterable thing.'

'Scientific people,' proceeded the philosopher after the pause required for the proper assimilation of this, 'know very well that time is only a kind of space. Here is a popular scientific diagram, a weather record. This line I trace with my finger shows the movement of the barometer. Yesterday it was so high, yesterday night it fell, then this morning it rose again, and so gently upward to here. Surely the mercury did not trace this line in any of the dimensions of space generally recognised? But certainly it traced such a line, and that line, therefore, we must conclude was along the time-dimension.'

'But,' said the red-haired man, staring hard at a coal in the fire; 'if time is really only a fourth dimension of space, why is it, and why has it always been, regarded as something different? And why cannot we move about in time as we move about in the other dimensions of space?'

The philosophical person smiled with great sweetness. 'Are you so sure we can move freely in space? Right and left we can go, backward and forward freely enough, and men always have done so. I admit we move freely in two dimensions. But how about up and down? Gravitation limits us there.'

'Not exactly,' said the red-haired man. 'There are balloons.'

'But before the balloons, man, save for spasmodic jumping and the inequalities of the surface, had no freedom of vertical movement.'

'Still they could move a little up and down,' said the red-haired man.

'Easier, far easier, down than up.'

'And you cannot move at all in time, you cannot get away from the present moment.'

'My dear sir, that is just where you are wrong. That is just where the whole world has gone wrong. We are always getting away from the present moment. Our consciousnesses, which are immaterial and have no dimensions, are passing along the time-dimension with a uniform velocity from the cradle to the grave. Just as we should travel *down* if we began our existence fifty miles above the earth's surface.'

'But the great difficulty is this,' interrupted the red-haired man. 'You *can* move about in all directions of space, but you cannot move about in time.'

'That is the germ of my great discovery. But you are wrong to say that we cannot move about in time. For instance, if I am recalling an incident very vividly I go back to the instant of its occurrence, I become absent-minded as you say. I jump back for a moment. Of course we have no means of staying back for any length of time any more than a savage or an animal has of staying six feet above the ground. But a civilised man knows better. He can go up against gravitation in a balloon, and why should he not be able to stop or accelerate his drift along the time-dimension; or even turn about and travel the other way?'

'Oh, *this*,' began the common-sense person, 'is all—'

'Why not?' said the Philosophical Inventor.

'It's against reason,' said the common-sense person.

'What reason?' said the Philosophical Inventor.

'You can show black is white by argument,' said the common-sense person; 'but you will never convince me.'

'Possibly not,' said the Philosophical Inventor. 'But now you begin to see the object of my investigations into the geometry of four dimensions. I have a vague inkling of a machine—'

'To travel through time!' exclaimed the very young man.

'That shall travel indifferently in any direction of space and time as the driver determines.'

The red-haired man contented himself with laughter.

'It would be remarkably convenient. One might travel back, and witness the Battle of Hastings!'

'Don't you think you would attract attention?' said the red-haired man. 'Our ancestors had no great tolerance for anachronisms.'

'One might get one's Greek from the very lips of Homer and Plato!'

'In which case they would certainly plough you for the little-go. The German scholars have improved Greek so much.'

'Then there is the future,' said the very young man. 'Just think! one might invest all one's money, leave it to accumulate at interest, and hurry on ahead!'

'To discover a society,' said the red-haired man, 'erected on a strictly communist basis.'

'It will be very confusing, I am afraid,' said the common-sense person. 'But I suppose your machine is hardly complete yet?'

'Science,' said the philosopher, 'moves apace.'

THE TIME MACHINE

'The last time I saw you, you were talking about a machine to travel through time,' said the red-haired man.

The common-sense person groaned audibly. 'Don't remind him of *that*,' he said.

'My dear Didymus,[1] it is finished,' said the Philosophical Inventor.

With violence, the red-haired man wanted to see it, and at once.

'There is no fire in the workshop,' said the Philosophical Inventor, becoming luxuriously lazy in his pose; 'and besides, I am in my slippers. No; I had rather be doubted.'

'You are,' said the red-haired man. 'But tell us: Have you used it at all?'

'To confess the simple truth, even at my own expense, I have been horribly afraid. But I tried it, nevertheless. The sensations are atrocious—atrocious.'

His eye rested for a moment on the very young man, who with a moist white face was gallantly relighting the cigar the German officer had offered him.

'You see, when you move forward in time with a low velocity of (say) thirty in one, you get through a full day of twenty-four hours in about forty-eight minutes. This means dawn, morning, noon, evening, twilight, night, at about ordinary stage pace. After a few days are traversed, the alternations of light and gloom give one the sensations of London on a dismal day of drifting fog. Matters get very much worse as the speed is increased. The maximum of inconvenience is about two thousand in one; day and night in less than a minute. The sun rushes up the sky at a sickening pace, and the moon with its changing phases makes one's brain reel. And you get a momentary glimmer of the swift stars swinging in circles round the pole. After

"Time Machine"
National Observer, n.s. 11 (March 24, 1894): 472-73.
    [1] That is, "Doubting Thomas."

that, the faster you go the less you seem to feel it. The sun goes hop, hop, each day; the night is like the flapping of a black wing; the moon opens and shuts—full to new and new to full; the stars trace at last faint circles of silver in the sky. Then the sun, through the retention of impressions by the eye, becomes a fiery band in the heavens, with which the ghostly fluctuating belt of the moon interlaces, and the tint of the sky becomes a flickering deep blue. At last even the flickering ceases, and the only visible motion in all the universe is the swaying of the sun-belt as it dips towards the winter solstice and rises again to the summer. The transitory sickness is over. So under the burning triumphal arch of the sun, you sweep through the ages. One has all the glorious sensations of a swooping hawk or a falling man—for one of those trapeze fellows told me the sense of falling is very delicious—and much the same personal concern about the end of it.'

The Philosophical Inventor stopped abruptly, and began to knock the ashes out of the filthy pipe he smokes.

'Not a bad description of the Cosmic Clock with the pendulum taken off,' said the very young man after an interval.

'Plausible so far,' said the red-haired man; 'but we have to come to earth now. Or were you entirely engaged by the heavenly bodies?'

'No,' said the Inventor; 'I noticed a few things. For instance, when I was going at a comparatively slow pace, Mrs. Watchet came into the workshop by the door next to the house and out by the one into the yard. Really she took a minute or so, I suppose, to traverse the room, but to me she appeared to shoot across like a rocket. And so soon as the pace became considerable, the apparent velocity of people became so excessively great that I could no more see them than a man can see a cannon-ball flying through the air.'

The common-sense person shivered and drew the air in sharply through his teeth.

'Then it is odd to see a tree grow up, flash its fan of green at you for a few score of summers, and vanish—all in the space of half an hour. Houses too shot up like stage buildings, stayed a while, and disappeared, and I noticed the hills grow visibly lower through the years with the wear of the gust and rain.'

'It is odd,' said the red-haired man, pursuing a train of thought, 'that you were not interfered with by people. You see, you have been, I understand, through some hundred thousand years or so'—the Philosopher nodded— 'and all that time you have been on one spot. People must have noticed you, even if you did not notice them. A gentleman in an easy attitude, dressed in anachronisms, and meditating fixedly upon the celestial sphere, must in the course of ages, have palled upon the species. I wonder they did not try to remove you to a museum or make you . . .'

This amused the German officer very much. Without warning he filled the room with laughter, and some of it went upstairs and woke the children. '*Sehr gut*! Ha, ha! You are axplodet, mein friendt!'

'The same difficulty puzzled me—for a minute or so,' said the Philosopher, as the air cleared. 'But it is easily explained.'

'Gott in Himmel!' said the German officer.

'I don't know if you have heard the expression of "presentation below the threshold." It is a psychological technicality. Suppose, for instance, you put some red pigment on a sheet of paper, it excites a certain visual sensation, does it not? Now halve the amount of pigment, the sensation diminishes. Halve it again, the impression of red is still weaker. Continue the process. Clearly there will always be *some* pigment left, but a time will speedily arrive when the eye will refuse to follow the dilution, when the stimulus will be insufficient to excite the sensation of red. The presentation of red pigment to the senses is then said to be "below the threshold." Similarly my rapid passage through time, traversing a day in a minute fraction of a second, diluted the stimulus I offered to the perception of these excellent people of futurity far below . . .'

'Yes,' said the red-haired man, interrupting after his wont. 'You have parried that. And now another difficulty. I suppose while you were slipping thus invisibly through the ages, people walked about in the space you occupied. They may have pulled down your house about your head and built a brick wall in your substance. And yet, you know, it is generally believed that two bodies cannot occupy the same space.'

'What an old-fashioned person you are!' said the Philosophical Inventor. 'Have you never heard of the Atomic Theory? Don't you know that every body, solid, liquid, or gaseous, is made up of molecules with empty spaces between them? That leaves plenty of room to slip through a brick wall, if you only have momentum enough. A slight rise of temperature would be all one would notice and of course if the wall lasted too long and the warmth became uncomfortable one could shift the apparatus a little in space and get out of the inconvenience.' He paused.

'But pulling up is a different matter. That is where the danger comes in. Suppose yourself to stop while there is another body in the same space. Clearly all your atoms will be jammed in with unparalleled nearness to the atoms of the foreign body. Violent chemical reactions would ensue. There would be a tremendous explosion. Hades! how it would puzzle posterity! I thought of this as I was sailing away thousands of years ahead. I lost my nerve. I brought my machine round in a whirling curve and started back full pelt. And so I pulled up again in the very moment and place of my start, in my workshop, and this afternoon. And ended my first time journey. Valuable, you see, chiefly as a lesson in the method of such navigation.'

'Will you go again?' said the common-sense person.

'Just at present,' said the Philosophical Inventor; 'I scarcely know.'

A.D. 12,203

A Glimpse of the Future

He rose from his easy chair and took the little bronze lamp in his hand, when we reverted to the topic of his Time Machine. He smiled, 'I know you will never believe me,' he said, 'until you see it with your own eyes.' So speaking he led us down the staircase and along the narrow passage to his workshop. 'I have had another little excursion since I saw you last,' he remarked over his shoulder.

'It is an ill thing if one stop it too suddenly,' said he as he stood holding the lamp for us to see; 'though my life was happily spared.'

'What happened?' said the sceptical man, staring suspiciously at the squat framework of aluminium, brass and ebony, that stood in the laboratory. It was an incomprehensible interlacing of bars and tubes, oddly awry, heeling over into the black shadows of the corner as if to elude our scrutiny. By the side of the leather saddle it bore, were two dials and three small levers curiously curved.

'You see how this rail is bent?' said the philosopher.

'I see you have bent it.'

'And that rod of ivory is cracked.'

'It is.'

'The thing fell over as I stopped and flung me headlong.'

He paused but no one spoke. He seemed to take it as acceptance, and proceeded to narrative.

'There was the sound of a clap of thunder in my ears. I may have been stunned for a moment. A pitiless hail was hissing around me, and I was sitting on soft turf beside the overturned Time Machine. I was on what seemed to be a little lawn in a garden, surrounded by rhododendron bushes, and I noticed that their mauve and purple blos-

"A.D. 12,203"
National Observer, n.s. 11 (March 31, 1894): 499-500.

soms were dropping in a shower under the beating of the hailstones. Over the machine, the rebounding dancing hail hung in a little cloud, and it drove along the ground like smoke. In a moment I was wet to the skin. "Fine hospitality," said I, "to a man who has travelled innumerable years to see you." I stood up and looked round me. A colossal figure, carved apparently of some white stone, loomed indistinctly beyond the bushes through the hazy downpour. But all else of the world was invisible.'

'H'm,' said the sceptic, 'this is interesting. May I ask the date?'

Our host pointed silently to the little dials.

'*Years*, ten—these divisions are thousands? I see now. Ten thousand, three hundred and nine,' said the commonsense person, reading. '*Days*, two hundred and forty-one. That is counting from now?'

'From now,' said the Inventor. The common-sense person seemed satisfied by these figures, and the flavour of intelligent incredulity that had survived even the Inventor's exhibition of the machine, began to fade from his expression.

'Go on,' said the doubter, looking hard into the machine.

'My sensations would be hard to describe. As the columns of hail grew thinner I saw the white figure more distinctly. It was very large, for a silver birch tree touched its shoulder. It was of white marble, in shape something like a winged sphinx, but the wings instead of being carried vertically over the back were spread on either side. It chanced that the face was towards me, the sightless eyes seemed to watch me. There was the faint shadow of a smile on the lips. I stood looking into this enigmatical countenance for a little space, half a minute, perhaps, or half an hour. As the hail drove before it, denser or thinner, it seemed to advance and recede. At last I tore my eyes far away from it for a moment, and saw that the hail curtain had worn threadbare, and that the sky was lightening with the promise of the sun. I looked up again at

the crouching white shape, and suddenly the full temerity
of my voyage came upon me. What might appear when
that hazy curtain was altogether withdrawn? What might
not have happened to men? What if cruelty had grown
into a common passion? What if in this interval the race
had lost its manliness, and had grown into something
inhuman, unsympathetic and overwhelmingly powerful?
To them I might seem some old-world savage animal only
the more dreadful and disgusting for my likeness to themselves, a foul creature to be incontinently slain. I was seized
with a panic fear. Already I saw other vast shapes, huge
buildings with intricate parapets, and a wooded hillside
dimly creeping in upon me through the lessening storm.
I turned in frantic mood to the Time Machine, and strove
hard to readjust it.

'As I did so the shafts of the sun smote through the
thunder-storm. The grey downpour was swept aside, and
vanished like the trailing garments of a ghost. Above me
was the intense blue of the summer sky with some faint
brown shreds of cloud whirling into nothingness. The great
buildings about me now stood out clear and distinct,
shining with the wet of the thunderstorm and picked out
in white by the unmelted hailstones piled along their
courses. I felt nakedly exposed to a strange world. I felt
as perhaps a bird may feel in the clear air, knowing the
hawk wings above and will swoop. My fear grew to frenzy.
I took a breathing space, set my teeth, and again grappled
fiercely, wrist and knee, with the machine. It gave under
my desperate onset and turned over. My chin was struck
violently. With one hand on the saddle and the other on
this lever I stood, panting heavily, in attitude to mount
again.

'But with this recovery of a prompt retreat my courage
recovered. I looked more curiously and less fearfully at
this world of the remote future. In a circular opening high
up in the wall of the nearer house I saw a group of figures,
clad in robes of rich soft colour. They had seen me, and

their faces were directed towards me. From some distant point behind this building a thin blade of colour shot into the blue air and went skimming in a wide ascending curve overhead. A white thing, travelling crow-fashion with a rare flap of the wings, may have been a flying machine. My attention was called from this to earth again by voices shouting. Coming through the bushes by the white sphinx could be seen the heads and shoulders of several men running. One of these emerged in a pathway leading straight to the little lawn upon which I stood with my machine. His was a slight figure clad in a purple tunic, girdled at the waist with a leather belt. A kind of sandals or buskins seemed to be upon his feet—I could not clearly distinguish which. His legs were bare to the knees, and his head was bare. For the first time I noticed how warm the air was. He struck me as being a very beautiful and graceful figure, but indescribably frail. His flushed face reminded me of the more beautiful kind of consumptive, that hectic beauty of which we used to hear so much . . .'

'That,' said the medical man, 'entirely discredits your story.' He was sitting on the bench near the circular saw. 'It is so absolutely opposed to the probabilities of our hygienic science—'

'That you disbelieve an eye witness!' said the Philosophical Investigator.

'Well, you must admit the suggestion of pthisis, coupled with a warm climate—'

'Don't interrupt,' said the red-haired man. 'Have we not this battered machine here to settle our doubts?'

I turned to the Philosopher again, but he had taken the lamp and stood as if he would light us back through the passage. Apparently he was offended at the attempt to dispose of his story from internal evidence. The curtain fell abruptly upon our brief glimpse of A.D. 12,203, and the rest of the evening passed in an unsuccessful attempt on the part of the doctor to show that the physique of civilised man was better than that of the savage. I agreed with a remark of the Philosopher's: that even if this were the case, it was a slender inference that the improvement would continue for the next ten thousand years.

THE REFINEMENT OF HUMANITY

A.D. 12,203

This man, who said he had travelled through time, refrained, after our first scepticism, from any further speech of his experiences, and in some subtle way his silence, with perhaps a certain change we detected in his manner and in his expressed opinion of existing things, won us at last to a doubt of our own certain incredulity. Besides, even if he had not done as he said, even if he had not, by some juggling along the fourth dimension, glimpsed the world ten thousand years ahead, yet there might still be a sufficiently worthy lie wasting in his brain. So that some conversational inducements began to be thrown towards him, and at last he partially forgave us and produced some few further fragments of his travel story.

'Of the fragile beauty of these people of the distant future,' said he, 'I bear eye-witness, but how that beauty came to be, I can only speculate. You must not ask me for reasons.'

'But did they not explain things to you?' asked the red-haired man.

'Odd as it may seem, I had no cicerone. In all the narratives of people visiting the future that I have read, some obliging scandal-monger appears at an early stage, and begins to lecture on constitutional history and social economy, and to point out the celebrities. Indeed so little had I thought of the absurdity of this that I had actually anticipated something of the kind would occur in reality. In my day-dreams, while I was making the machine, I had figured myself lecturing and being lectured to about the progress of humanity, about the relations of the sexes,

"Refinement of Humanity"
National Observer, n.s. 11 (April 21, 1894): 581-82.

and about capital and labour, like a dismal Demological Congress. But they didn't explain anything. They couldn't. They were the most illiterate people I ever met.

'Yes, I was disappointed. On the other hand there were compensations. I had been afraid I might have to explain the principles of the Time Machine, and send a perfected humanity on experimental rides, with some chance of having my apparatus stolen or lost centuries away from me. But these people took it for granted I was heaven-descended, a meteoric man, coming as I did in a thunderstorm, and so soon as they saw me appear ran violently towards me, and some prostrated themselves and some knelt at my feet. "Come," said I, as I saw perhaps fifty of these dainty people engaged in this pleasing occupation; "this at least is some compensation for contemporary neglect." A feeling of fatherly exaltation replaced the diffidence of my first appearance. I made signs to them that they should rise from the damp turf, and therewith they stood smiling very fearlessly and pleasantly at me. The height of them was about four feet, none came much higher than my chest, and I noticed at once how exquisitely fine was the texture of their light garments, and how satin smooth their skins. Their faces—I must repeat—were distinctly of the fair consumptive type, with flushed cheeks, and without a trace of fulness. The hair was curled.'

The medical man fidgeted in his chair. He began in a tone of protest: 'But *à priori*—'

The Philosophical Investigator anticipated his words. 'You would object that this is against the drift of sanitary science. You believe the average height, average weight, average longevity will all be increased, that in the future humanity will breed and sanitate itself into human Megatheria. I thought the same until this trip of mine. But, come to think, what I saw is just what one might have expected. Man, like other animals, has been moulded, and will be, by the necessities of his environment. What keeps men so large and strong as they are? The fact that if any drop below a certain level of power and capacity for competition, they die. Remove dangers, render physical exertion no longer a necessity but an excrescence upon life, abolish competition by limiting population: in the long run—'

'But,' said the medical man, 'even if man in the future no longer need strength to fight against other men or beasts, he will still need a sufficient physique to resist disease.'

'That is the queer thing,' said the Time Traveller; 'there was no disease. Somewhen between now and then your sanitary science must have won the battle it is beginning now. Bacteria, or at least all disease causing bacteria, must have been exterminated. I can explain it in no other way.

'Certainly there had been a period of systematic scientific earth culture between now and then. Gnats, flies, and midges were gone, all troublesome animals, and thistles and thorns. The fruits of this age had no seeds, and the roses no prickles. Their butterflies were brilliant and abundant, and their dragonflies flying gems. It must have been done by selective breeding. But these delicious people had kept no books and knew no history. The world, I could speedily see, was perfectly organised—finished. It was still working as a perfect machine, had been so working for ages, but its very perfection had abolished the need of intelligence. What work was needed was done out of sight, and modesty, delicacy, had spread to all the necessary apparatus of life. The inquiries about their political economy I subsequently tried to make by signs, and by so much of their language as I learnt, were not understood or were gently parried. I saw no one eating. Indeed for some time I was in the way of starvation till I found a furtive but very pleasant and welcome meal of nuts and apples provided me in an elegant recess. They were entirely frugivorous, I found—like the Lemuridae. There was no great physical difference in the sexes, and they dressed exactly alike.'

The medical man would have demurred again.

'You are so unscientific,' said the Philosophical Inventor. 'The violent strength of a man, the distinctive charm and relative weakness of a woman, are the outcome of a period when the species survived by force and was ever in the face of danger. Marriage and the family were militant necessities before the world was conquered. But humanity has passed the zenith of its fierceness, and with an intelligent and triumphant democracy, willing to take over the care of offspring and only anxious to save itself from suffocation by its own increase, the division of a community into so many keenly competitive households elbowing one another for living room must sooner or later cease. And even now there is a steady tendency to assimilate the pursuits of the sexes. A very little refinement in our thinking, and even we should see that distinctive costume is an indelicate advertisement of facts it is the aim of all polite people to ignore.

'The average duration of life was about nineteen or twenty years. Well—what need of longer? People live nowadays to threescore and ten because of their excessive vitality, and because of the need there has been of guarding, rearing, and advising a numerous family. But a well-organised civilisation will change all that. At any rate, explain it as you will, these people about the age of nineteen or twenty, after a period of affectionate intercourse, fell into an elegant and painless decline, experienced a natural Euthanasia, and were dropped into certain perennially burning furnaces wherein dead leaves, broken twigs, fruit peel, and other refuse were also consumed.

'Their voices, I noticed, even at the outset, were particularly soft and their inflections of the tongue, subtle. I did a little towards learning their language.' He made some peculiar soft cooing sounds. 'The vocabulary is not very extensive.'

The red-haired man laughed and patted his shoulder.

'But I am anticipating. To return to the Time Machine.

I felt singularly reassured by the aspect of these people and by their gentle manner. Many of them were children, and these seemed to me to take a keener interest in me than the fully grown ones. Presently one of these touched me, at first rather timidly, and then with more confidence. Others followed his or her example. They were vastly amused at the coarseness of my skin and at the hair upon the back of my hands, particularly the little ones. As I stood in the midst of a small crowd of them, one came laughing towards me, carrying a chain of some beautiful flowers altogether new to me, and put it about my neck. The idea was received with melodious applause; and presently they were running to and fro for flowers, and laughingly flinging them upon me until I was almost smothered with blossom. You, who have never seen the like, can scarcely imagine what delicate and wonderful flowers ten thousand years of culture had created. A flying machine, with gaily painted wings, came swooping down, scattering the crowd right and left, and its occupant joined the throng about me. Then someone suggested, it would seem, that their new plaything should be exhibited in the nearest building; and so I was beckoned and led and urged, past the Sphinx of white marble, towards a vast grey edifice of fretted stone. As I went with them, the memory of my confident anticipations of a profoundly grave and intellectual posterity came, with irresistible merriment, to my mind.'

THE SUNSET OF MANKIND

'We have no doubt of the truth of your story,' said the red-haired man to him that travelled through time; 'but there is much in it that is difficult to understand.'

'On the surface,' said the Time Traveller.

'For instance, you say that the men of the year twelve thousand odd were living in elaborate luxury, in a veritable earth garden; richly clothed they were and sufficiently fed. Yet you present them as beautiful—well!—idiots. Some intelligence and some labour, some considerable intelligence I should imagine, were surely needed to keep this world garden in order.'

'They had some intelligence,' said the Time Traveller, 'and besides—'

'Very little though; they spoke with a limited vocabulary, and foolishly took you and your Time Machine for a meteorite. Yet they were the descendants of the men who had organised the world so perfectly, who had exterminated disease, evolved flowers and fruits of indescribable beauty, and conquered the problem of flying. Those men must have had singularly powerful minds—'

'You confuse, I see, original intelligence and accumulated and organised knowledge. It is a very common error. But look the thing squarely in the face. Were you to strip the man of to-day of all the machinery and appliances of his civilisation, were you to sponge from his memory all the facts which he knows simply as facts, and leave him just his coddled physique, imperfect powers of observation, and ill-trained reasoning power, would he be the equal in wit or strength of the paleolithic savage? We do, indeed, make an innumerable multitude of petty discoveries nowadays, but the fundamental principles of thought and symbolism upon which our minds travel to these are

"Sunset of Mankind"
National Observer, n.s. 11 (April 28, 1894): 606-08.

immeasurably old. We live in the thought edifice of space, time and number, that our forefathers contrived. Look at it fairly: we invent by recipe, by Bacon's patent method for subduing the earth. The world is moving now to comfort and absolute security, not so much from its own initiative as from the impetus such men as he gave it. Then the more we know the less is our scope for the exercise of useful discovery, and the more we advance in civilisation the less is our need of a brain for our preservation. Man's intelligence conquers nature, and in undisputed empire is the certain seed of decay. The energy revealed by security will run at first into art—or vice. Our descendants will give the last beautifying touch to the edifice of this civilisation with the last gleam of their waning intelligences. With perfect comfort and absolute security, the energy of advance must needs dwindle. That has been the history of all past civilisation, and it will be the history of all civilisations. Civilisation means security for the weak and indolent, panmyxia[1] of weakness and indolence, and general decline. The tradition of effort that animates us will be forgotten in the end. What need for education when there is no struggle for life? What need of thought or strong desires? What need of books, or what need of stimulus to creative effort? As well take targe and dirk and mail underclothing into a City office. Men who retain any vestige of intellectual activity will be restless, irked by their weapons, inharmonious with the serene quiescence which will fall upon mankind. They will be ill company with their mysterious questionings, unprosperous in their

[1] "Panmyxia" is Weismann's coinage; it denotes suspension of natural selection in organs that have no use (e.g., the eyes of cave fish) and consequent degeneration of these organs (August Weismann, *Essays upon Heredity and Kindred Biological Problems*, ed. Edward B. Poulton et al., 2d ed. rev., 2 vols. [Oxford: Clarendon Press, 1891-1892], 1: 90-91).

Though the mechanism of panmixia was Weismann's reply to the Lamarckian (use-disuse inheritance) explanation of the same phenomena, Wells evidently combines the two, perhaps partly following the lead of G. J. Romanes, who accepted panmixia but rejected its Weismannian corollary, germ-plasm (see the lengthy Spencer-Romanes-Weismann debate in the *Contemporary Review* 63, 64, 66 [1893, 1894] and also note 3 to "The Biological Problem of Today").

love-making, and will leave no offspring. So an end comes at last to all these things.'

'I don't believe that,' said the common-sense person; 'I don't believe in this scare about the rapid multiplication of the unfit, and all that.'

'Nor do I,' said the Time Traveller. 'I never yet heard of the rapid multiplication of the unfit. It is the fittest who survive. The point is that civilisation—any form of civilisation—alters the qualifications of fitness, because the organisation it implies and the protection it affords, discounts the adventurous, animal, and imaginative, and puts a premium upon the mechanical, obedient, and vegetative. An organised civilisation is like Saturn, and destroys the forces that begat it.'

'Of course that is very plausible,' said the common-sense person, in the tone of one who puts an argument aside, and proceeded to light a cigar without further remark.

'When do you conceive this civilising process ceased?' asked the red-haired man.

'It must have ceased for a vast period before the time of my visit. The great buildings in which these beautiful little people lived, a multitude together, were profoundly time-worn. Several I found collapsed through the rusting of the iron parts, and abandoned. One colossal ruin of granite, bound with aluminium, was not very distant from the great house wherein I sheltered, and among its precipitous masses and confusion of pillars were crowded thickets of nettles—nettles robbed of their stinging hairs and with leaves of purple brown. There had been no effort apparently to rebuild these places. It was in the dark recesses of this place, by-the-by, that I met my first morlock.'

'*Morlock*! What is a morlock?' asked the medical man.

'A new species of animal, and a very peculiar one. At first I took it for some kind of ape—'

'But you slip from my argument,' interrupted the red-haired man. 'These people were clothed in soft and beautiful raiment, which seems to me to imply textile manufactures, dyeing, cutting out, skilled labour involving a certain amount of adaptation to individual circumstance.'

'Precisely. Skilled labour of a certain traditional sort— you must understand there were no changes of fashion— skill much on the level of that required from a bee when it builds its cell. That occurred to me. It puzzled me very much at first to account for it. I certainly found none of the people at any such work. But the explanation—that is so very grotesque that I really hesitate to tell you.'

He paused, looked at us doubtfully. 'Suppose you imagine machines—'

'Put your old shoes in at one end and a new pair comes out at the other,' laughed the red-haired man. 'Franken- stein Machines that have developed souls, while men have lost theirs! The created servant steals the mind of its creator; he puts his very soul into it, so to speak. Well, perhaps it is possible. It is not a new idea, you know. And you have said something about flying-machines. I suppose they were repaired by similar intelligent apparatus. Did you have a chat with any of these machine-beasts?'

'That seems rather a puerile idea to me,' said the Time Traveller, 'knowing what I do. But to realise the truth, you must bear in mind that it is possible to do things first intelligently and afterwards to make a habit of them. Let me illustrate by the ancient civilisation of the ants and bees. Some ants are still intelligent and originative; while other species are becoming mere automatic crea- tures, to repeat what were once intelligent actions. The working bees, naturalists say, are almost entirely auto- matic. Now, among these men—'

'Ah, these morlocks of yours!' said the red-haired man. 'Something ape-like! Human neuters! But—'

'Look here!' suddenly interrupted the very young man. He had been lost in profound thought for some minute or so, and now rushed headlong into the conversation, after his manner. 'Here is one thing I cannot fall in with. The sun, you say, was hotter than it is now, or at any rate the climate was warmer. Now the sun is really supposed to be cooling and shrinking, and so is the earth. The mean temperature ought to be colder in the future. And besides this, the Isthmus of Panama will wear through at last, and the Gulf Stream no longer impinge upon our shores with all its warmth.'

'There,' said the Time Traveller, 'I am unable to give you an explanation. All I know is that the climate was very much warmer than it is now, and that the sun seemed brighter. There was a strange and beautiful thing, too, about the night, and that was the multitude of shooting stars. Even during the November showers of our epoch I have never seen anything quite so brilliant as an ordinary night of this coming time. The sky seemed alive with them, especially towards midnight, when they fell chiefly from the zenith. Besides this the brilliance of the night was increased by a number of luminous clouds and whisps, many of them as bright or brighter than the Milky Way; but, unlike the Milky Way, they shifted in position from night to night. The fall of meteorites, too, was a comparatively common occurrence. I think it was the only thing these delightful people feared, or had any reason to fear. Possibly this meteoric abundance had something to do with the increased warmth. A quantity of such bodies in the space through which the solar system travelled might contribute to this in two ways: by retarding the tangential velocity of the earth in its orbit, and so accelerating its secular approach to the sun, and by actually falling into the sun and so increasing its radiant energy.[2] But these are guesses of mine. All I can certainly say is that the

[2] Lord Kelvin developed a theory that the sun was constantly being "refuelled" by the impacting of meteorites into its surface; by 1860 he had abandoned this notion of solar heat conservation because it required planetary orbital accelerations contrary to observed fact (see Agnes M. Clerke, *A Popular History of Astronomy during the Nineteenth Century*, 4th ed. rev. [London: A. & C. Black, 1902], pp. 310-311). By introducing a meteoric cloud, Wells both reinstates Kelvin's old theory and links it with a planetary slowdown whereby the "Golden Age" is a function of the earth's gradually falling into the sun (see note 3 to "The Time-Traveller Returns").

climate was very much warmer, and had added its enervating influence to their too perfect civilisation.'

'Warmth and colour, ruins and decline,' said the red-haired man. 'One might call this age of yours the Sunset of Mankind.'

IN THE UNDERWORLD

'I have already told you,' said the Time Traveller, 'that it was customary on the part of the delightful people of the upper world to ignore the existence of these pallid creatures of the caverns, and consequently when I descended among them I descended alone.

'I had to clamber down a shaft of perhaps two or three hundred yards. The descent was effected by means of hooks projecting from the sides of the well, and since they were adapted to the needs of a creature much smaller and lighter than myself I was speedily cramped and fatigued by the descent. And not simply fatigued. My weight suddenly bent one of the hooks and almost swung me off it into the darkness beneath. For a moment I hung by one hand, and after that experience I did not dare to rest again, and though my arms and back were presently acutely painful, I continued to climb with as quick a motion as possible down the sheer descent. Glancing upward I saw the aperture a mere small blue disc above me, in which a star was visible. The thudding sound of some machine below grew louder and more oppressive. Everything save that minute circle above was profoundly dark. I was in an agony of discomfort. I had some thought of trying to get up the shaft again, and leave the underworld alone. But while I turned this over in my mind I continued to descend.

'It was with intense relief that I saw very dimly coming up a foot to the right of me a long loophole in the wall of the shaft, and, swinging myself in, found it was the aperture of a narrow horizontal tunnel in which I could lie down and rest. My arms ached, my back was cramped, and I was trembling with the prolonged fear of falling. Besides this the unbroken darkness had a distressing effect

"Underworld"
National Observer, n.s. 12 (May 19, 1894): 14-15.

upon my eyes. The air was full of the throbbing and hum of machinery.

'I do not know how long I lay in that tunnel. I was roused by a soft hand touching my face. Starting up in the darkness I snatched at my matches, and, hastily striking one, saw three grotesque white creatures similar to the one I had seen above ground in the ruin, hastily retreating before the light. Living as they did, in what appeared to me impenetrable darkness, their eyes were abnormally large and sensitive, just as are the eyes of the abyss fishes or of any purely nocturnal creatures, and they reflected the light in the same way. I have no doubt that they could see me in that rayless obscurity, and they did not seem to have any fear of me apart from the light. But so soon as I struck a match in order to see them, they fled incontinently, vanishing up dark gutters and tunnels from which their eyes glared at me in the strangest fashion.

'I tried to call them, but what language they had was apparently a different one from that of the overworld people. So that I was left to my own unaided exploration.

'Feeling my way along this tunnel of mine, the confused noise of machinery grew louder, and presently the wall receded from my hand, and I felt I had come to an open space, and striking another match saw I had entered an arched cavern, so vast that it extended into darkness at last beyond the range of my light. Huge machines with running belts and whirling fly-wheels rose out of the obscurity, and the grey bodies of the Morlocks dodged my light among the unsteady shadows. Several of the machines near me were disused and broken down. They appeared to be weaving machines, and were worked by leather belts running over drums upon great rotating shafts that stretched across the cavern. I could not see how the shafts were worked. And very soon my match burned out.'

'That was a pity,' said the red-haired man.

'I was afraid to push my way down this avenue of throbbing machinery in the dark, and with my last glimpse I discovered that my store of matches had run low. It had never occurred to me until that moment that there was any need to economise them, and I had wasted almost half the box in astonishing the above-ground people, to whom fire was a novelty. I had four left then. As I stood in the dark a hand touched mine, then some lank fingers came feeling over my face. I fancied I detected the breathing of a number of these little beings about me. I felt the box of matches in my hand being gently disengaged, and other hands behind me plucking at my clothing.

'The sense of these unseen creatures examining me was indescribably unpleasant. The sudden realisation of my ignorance of their ways of thinking and possible actions came home to me very vividly in the darkness. I shouted at them as loudly as I could. They started away from me, and then I could feel them approaching me again. They clutched at me more boldly, whispering odd sounds to each other. I shivered violently and shouted again, rather discordantly. This time they were not so seriously alarmed, and made a queer laughing noise as they came towards me again.

'I will confess I was frightened. I determined to strike another match and escape under its glare. Eking it out with a scrap of paper from my pocket, I made good my retreat to the narrow tunnel. But hardly had I entered this when my light was blown out, and I could hear them in the blackness rustling like wind among leaves, and pattering like rain as they hurried after me. In a moment I was clutched by several hands again, and there was no mistake now that they were trying to draw me back. I struck another light and waved it in their dazzled faces. You can scarcely imagine how nauseatingly unhuman those pale chinless faces and great pinkish grey eyes seemed as they stared stupidly, suddenly blinded by the light.

'So I gained time and retreated again, and when my

second match had ended struck my third. That had almost burnt through as I reached the opening of the tunnel upon the well. I lay down upon the edge, for the throbbing whirl of the air-pumping machine below made me giddy, and felt sideways for the projecting hooks. As I did so, my feet were grasped from behind, and I was tugged violently backwards. I lit my last match ... and it incontinently went out. But I had my hand on the climbing bars now, and, kicking violently, disengaged myself from the clutches of the Morlocks, and was speedily clambering up the shaft again. One little wretch followed me for some way, and captured the heel of my boot as a trophy.'

'I suppose you could show us that boot without the heel,' said the red-haired man, 'if we asked to see it?'

'What do you think they wanted with you?' asked the common-sense person.

'I don't know. That was just the beastliness of it.'

'And is that all you saw of the Morlocks?' said the very young man.

'I saw some once again. Frankly, I was afraid of them. I did not even look down one of those wells again.'

'Have you no explanation to offer of those creatures?' said the red-haired man. 'What were they really? In particular, what was their connection with the upper-world people, and how had they been developed?'

'I am a traveller, and I tell you a traveller's tale. I am not an annotated edition of myself.'

'Cannot you hazard something? I am puzzled by your statement, that human beings will differentiate into two species without any separation. Would not intermarriage prevent this?'

'Oh no! a species may split up into two without any separation into different districts. This matter has been worked out by Gulick. He uses the very convenient word "segregation" to express his idea.[1] Imagine, for instance,

[1] John Thomas Gulick (1832-1923), American naturalist, published a number of papers arguing that the isolation or segregation of individuals is the cause

the more refined and indolent class of people to intermarry mainly among themselves, and the operative or business class—the class of operatives aspiring to rise to business influence and finding their interests mainly in the satisfaction of a taste for industrial and business pursuits—also marrying mainly in their own class. Might there not be a widening separation? Indeed, since this time-journey of mine I have fancied that there is such a split going on even now in our English society, a split that began some two hundred and fifty years ago or more. I do not mean any split between working people and rich—families drop and rise from toil to wealth continually—but between the sombre, mechanically industrious, arthimetical, inartistic type, the type of the Puritan and the American millionaire and the pleasure-loving, witty, and graceful type that gives us our clever artists, our actors and writers, some of our gentry, and many an elegant rogue. Conceive such types drifting away from one another each in its own direction. Along the former line we should get at last a colourless love of darkness, dully industrious and productive, and along the latter, brilliant weakness and gay silliness. But this is a mere theory of mine. The fact remains that humanity had differentiated into two very distinct species in the coming time, explain it as you will. Such traditional industries as still survived remained among the Morlocks, but the sun of man's intelligence had set and the night of humanity was creeping on apace.'

---

of new species diverging from the old. In his essay on "Divergent Evolution through Cumulative Segregation" (*Annual Report of the Board of Regents of the Smithsonian Institution* [1891]), he contends, on the basis of his study of the colors of snail shells in the Sandwich Islands, that there exists a universal principle of "segregational evolution" which, applied to man, must eventuate in the evolutionary fissioning of *homo sapiens* if "free intergeneration" comes to an end as a result of "segregation" along national, linguistic, caste, penal, sanitary, educational, or industrial lines (pp. 334-335).

THE TIME-TRAVELLER RETURNS

'After my glimpse of the underworld my mind turned incessantly towards this age again. The upper-world people, who had at first charmed me with their light beauty, began to weary and then to irritate me by their insubstantiality. And there was something in the weird inhumanity of the undermen that robbed me of my sense of security. I could not imagine that they regarded me as their fellow creature, or that any of the deep reasonless instincts that keep man the servant of his fellow man would intervene in my favour. I was to them a strange beast. When I thought of the soft cold hands clutching me in the subterranean darkness I was filled with horrible imaginings of what might have been my fate.

'Then these creatures, being now aware of my existence, and possessing far more curiosity than the upper-world people, began to trouble my nights. Their excessive sensibility to light kept me safe from them during the days, but after the twilight I found it advisable to avoid the deep shadows of the buildings and to sleep out under the stars. And even in the open, when the sky was overcast, these pallid little monsters ventured to approach me.

'I could see very dimly their grey forms approaching through the black masses of the bushes, and could hear the murmuring noises that stood to them in the place of articulate speech.

'I think they were far more powerfully attracted by the Time Machine than by myself. Their minds were essentially mechanical. That, indeed, was one of the dismal thoughts that came to me—that possibly they would try to take me to pieces and investigate my construction. The only thing that kept me in that future age after I had begun to realise what had happened to humanity was my

"Time-Traveller Returns"
National Observer, n.s. 12 (June 23, 1894): 145-46.

interest in the present one. I was reluctant to go until I had seen enough to tell you some definite facts about your descendants. But the near approach of these Morlocks was too much for me. As one came forward in the obscurity and laid his hand upon the bars of the Time Machine, I cried aloud and vaulted into the saddle, and in another moment that strange world of the future had swept into nothingness, and I was reeling down the time dimension to this age of ours again. And so my visit to the year 12,203 came to an end.'

He paused. For some minute or so there was silence.

'I do not like your vision,' said the common-sense person.

'It seems to me just the Gospel of Despair,' said the financial journalist.

The Time Traveller lit a cigar.

'Why there should be any particular despair for you in the contemplation of a time when our kind of beast—' he glanced round the room with a faint smile—'has ceased to exist, I fail to see.'

'We have always been accustomed to consider the future as in some peculiar way ours,' said the red-haired man. 'Your story seems to rob us of our birthright.'

'For my part I have always believed in a steady Evolution towards something Higher and Better,' said the common-sense person; and added, 'and I still do.'

'But still essentially human in all respects?' asked the Time Traveller.

'Decidedly,' said the common-sense person.

'In the past,' said the Time Traveller, 'the evolution has not always been upward. The land animals, including ourselves, zoologists say, are the descendants of almost amphibious mudfish that were hunted out of the seas by the ancestors of the modern sharks.'

'But what will become of Social Reform? You would make out that everything that ameliorates human life tends to human degeneration.'

'Let us leave social reform to the professional philanthropist,' said the Time Traveller. 'I told you a story; I am not prepared to embark upon a political discussion. The facts remain . . .'

'*Facts*!' said the red-haired man *sotto voce*.

'That man has been evolved from the inhuman in the past—to go no further back, even the paleolithic men were practically inhuman—and that in the future he must sooner or later be modified beyond human sympathy.'

'Leaving us,' said the red-haired man, 'a little island in time and a little island in space, the surface of the little globe out of all the oceans of space, and a few thousands of years out of eternity.'

'The limits are still large enough for me to be mean in,' said the Time Traveller.

'And after man?' said the medical man.

'A world with a continually longer day and a continually shorter year, so the astronomers tell us. For the drag of the tides upon the spin of the earth will bring this planet at last to the plight of Mercury, with one face turned always to the sun.[1] And the gradual diminution of the centrifugal component of the earth's motion due to inter-planetary matter[2] will cause it to approach the sun slowly and surely as the sun cools, until the parent body has recovered its offspring again. During the last stages of the sunward movement over those parts of the earth that are sunward there will be an unending day, and a vast red sun growing ever vaster and duller will glow motionless in the sky. Twice already it will have blazed into a transient period of brilliance as the minor planets, Mercury and Venus, melted back into its mass.[3] On the further

---

[1] The coincidence of Mercury's day and year (discovered by Schiaparelli in 1889) supported G. H. Darwin's theory of solar tidal drag (Clerke, *History of Astronomy*, pp. 319-320; see also note 3 to "'Cyclic' Delusion"). Here Wells foreshortens a condition of the very far future: the day the earth turns a single face to the sun must occur incomparably more distant in time than the day the earth reaches a like tidal stasis with respect to the much stronger tidal drag of the moon.

[2] On "interplanetary matter," see note 2 to "Sunset of Mankind."

[3] As late as 1890, Camille Flammarion (*Popular Astronomy: A General*

side of the earth will be perpetual night and the bitterest cold, and between these regions will be belts of twilight, of perpetual sunset, and perpetual afternoon. Whether there will be any life on the earth then we can scarcely guess. Somewhere in the belts of intermediate temperature, it may be, that strange inconceivable forms of life will still struggle on against the inevitable fate that awaits them. But an end comes. Life is a mere eddy, an episode, in the great stream of universal being, just as man with all his cosmic mind is a mere episode in the story of life—'

He stopped abruptly. 'There is that kid of mine upstairs crying. He always cries when he wakes up in the dark. If you don't mind, I will just go up and tell him it's all right.'

Description of the Heavens, trans. J. Ellard Gore [New York: D. Appleton, 1894], p. 298) perpetuated Lord Kelvin's tables (1854; see note 2 to "Sunset of Mankind") showing the quantity of heat each planet would generate by falling into the sun. Mercury and Venus would maintain the solar furnace for a bit more than 90 years; if the sun absorbed the entire solar system, it would have fuel for less than 46,000 years.

I. THE INVENTOR

The man who made the Time Machine—the man I shall call the Time Traveller—was well known in scientific circles a few years since, and the fact of his disappearance is also well known. He was a mathematician of peculiar subtlety, and one of our most conspicuous investigators in molecular physics. He did not confine himself to abstract science. Several ingenious and one or two profitable patents were his: very profitable they were, these last, as his handsome house at Richmond testified. To those who were his intimates, however, his scientific investigations were as nothing to his gift of speech. In the after-dinner hours he was ever a vivid and variegated talker, and at times his fantastic, often paradoxical, conceptions came so thick and close as to form one continuous discourse. At these times he was as unlike the popular conception of a scientific investigator as a man could be. His cheeks would flush, his eyes grow bright; and the stranger the ideas that sprang and crowded in his brain, the happier and the more animated would be his exposition.

Up to the last there was held at his house a kind of informal gathering, which it was my privilege to attend, and where, at one time or another, I have met most of our distinguished literary and scientific men. There was a plain dinner at seven. After that we would adjourn to a room of easy chairs and little tables, and there, with libations of alcohol and reeking pipes, we would invoke the God. At first the conversation was mere fragmentary chatter, with some local *lacunæ* of digestive silence; but towards nine or half-past nine, if the God was favourable, some particular topic would triumph by a kind of natural selection, and would become the common interest. So it was, I remember, on the last Thursday but one of all—the

"I. The Inventor"
New Review 12 (Jan. 1895): 98-101. [Signed] These two selections are from the *New Review Time Machine*.

Thursday when I first heard of the Time Machine.

I had been jammed in a corner with a gentleman who shall be disguised as Filby. He had been running down Milton—the public neglects poor Filby's little verses shockingly; and as I could think of nothing but the relative status of Filby and the man he criticised, and was much too timid to discuss that, the arrival of that moment of fusion, when our several conversations were suddenly merged into a general discussion, was a great relief to me.

"What's that is nonsense?" said a well-known Medical Man, speaking across Filby to the Psychologist.

"He thinks," said the Psychologist, "that Time's only a kind of Space."

"It's not thinking," said the Time Traveller; "it's knowledge."

"Foppish affectation," said Filby, still harping upon his wrongs; but I feigned a great interest in this question of Space and Time.

"Kant," began the Psychologist—

"Confound Kant!" said the Time Traveller. "I tell you I'm right. I've got experimental proof of it. I'm not a metaphysician." He addressed the Medical Man across the room, and so brought the whole company into his own circle."It's the most promising departure in experimental work that has ever been made. It will simply revolutionise life. Heaven knows what life will be when I've carried the thing through."

"As long as it's not the water of Immortality I don't mind," said the distinguished Medical Man. "What is it?"

"Only a paradox," said the Psychologist.

The Time Traveller said nothing in reply, but smiled and began tapping his pipe upon the fender curb. This was the invariable presage of a dissertation.

"You have to admit that time is a spatial dimension," said the Psychologist, emboldened by immunity and addressing the Medical Man, "and then all sorts of remarkable consequences are found inevitable. Among others, that it becomes possible to travel about in time."

The Time Traveller chuckled: "You forget that I'm going to prove it experimentally."

"Let's have your experiment," said the Psychologist.

"I think we'd like the argument first," said Filby.

"It's this," said the Time Traveller: "I propose a wholly new view of things based on the supposition that ordinary human perception is an hallucination. I'm sorry to drag in predestination and free-will, but I'm afraid those ideas will have to help. Look at it in this way—this, I think, will give you the gist of it: Suppose you knew fully the position and the properties of every particle of matter, of everything existing in the universe at any particular moment of time: suppose, that is, that you were omniscient. Well, that knowledge would involve the knowledge of the condition of things at the previous moment, and at the moment before that, and so on. If you knew and perceived the present perfectly, you would perceive therein the whole of the past. If you understood all natural laws the present would be a complete and vivid record of the past. Similarly, if you grasped the whole of the present, knew all its tendencies and laws, you would see clearly all the future. To an omniscient observer there would be no forgotten past—no piece of time as it were that had dropped out of existence—and no blank future of things yet to be revealed. Perceiving all the present, an omniscient observer would likewise perceive all the past and all the inevitable future at the same time. Indeed, present and past and future would be without meaning to such an observer: he would always perceive exactly the same thing. He would see, as it were, a Rigid Universe filling space and time—a Universe in which things were always the same. He would see one sole unchanging series of cause and effect to-day and to-morrow and always. If 'past' meant anything, it would mean looking in a certain direction; while 'future' meant looking the opposite way."

"H'm," said the Rector, "I fancy you're right. So far."

"I know I am," said the Time Traveller. "From the absolute point of view the universe is a perfectly rigid unalterable apparatus, entirely predestinate, entirely complete and finished. Now, looking at things, so far as we can, from this standpoint, how would a thing like this box appear? It would still be a certain length and a certain breadth and a certain thickness, and it would have a definite mass; but we should also perceive that it extended back in time to a certain moment when it was made, and forward in time to a certain moment when it was destroyed, and that during its existence it was moved about in space. An ordinary man, being asked to describe this box, would say, among other things, that it was in such a position, and that it measured ten inches in depth, say, three in breadth, and four in length. From the absolute point of view it would also be necessary to say that it began at such a moment, lasted so long, measured so much in time, and was moved here and there meanwhile. It is only when you have stated its past and its future that you have completely described the box. You see, from the absolute standpoint—which is the true scientific standpoint—time is merely a dimension, quite analogous to the three dimensions in space. Every particle of matter has length, breadth, thickness, and—duration."

"You're perfectly right," said the Rector. "Theologians threshed all that out ages ago."

"I beg your pardon," said the Psychologist, "nothing of the sort. Our first impression, the very foundation of our mental life, is order in time. I am supported—"

"I tell you that psychology cannot possibly help us here," said the Time Traveller, "because our minds do not represent the conditions of the universe—why should they?—but only our necessities. From my point of view the human consciousness is an immaterial something falling through this Rigid Universe of four dimensions, from the direction we call 'past' to the direction we call 'future.' Just as the sun is a material something falling through the same universe towards the constellation of Hercules."

"This is rather abstruse," said Filby under his breath to me.

"I begin to see your argument," said the Medical Man. "And you go on to ask, why *should* we continue to drift in a particular direction? Why *should* we drive through time at this uniform pace? Practically you propose to study four-dimensional geometry with a view to locomotion in time."

"Precisely. *Have* studied it to that end."

"Of all the wild extravagant theories!" began the Psychologist.

"Yes, so it seemed to me, and so I never talked of it until—"

"Experimental verification!" cried I. "You are going to verify *that*?"

"The experiment!" cried Filby, who was getting brain-weary.

"Let's see your experiment anyhow," said the Psychologist, "though it's all humbug, you know."

The Time Traveller smiled round at us. Then, still similing faintly, and with his hands deep in his trousers pockets, he walked slowly out of the room, and we heard his slippers shuffling down the long passage to his laboratory.

XIII. THE FURTHER VISION

"I have already told you of the sickness and confusion that comes with time travelling. And this time I was not seated properly in the saddle, but sideways and in an unstable fashion. For an indefinite time I clung to the machine as it swayed and vibrated, quite unheeding how I went, and when I brought myself to look at the dials again I was amazed to find where I had arrived. One dial records days, another thousands of days, another millions of days, and another thousands of millions. Now, instead of reversing the levers I had pulled them over so as to go forward with them, and when I came to look at these indicators I found that the thousands hand was sweeping round as fast as the seconds hand of a watch—into futurity. Very cautiously, for I remembered my former headlong fall, I began to reverse my motion. Slower and slower went the circling hands until the thousands one seemed motionless and the daily one was no longer a mere mist upon its scale. Still slower, until the grey haze around me became distincter and dim outlines of an undulating waste grew visible.

"I stopped. I was on a bleak moorland, covered with a sparse vegetation, and grey with a thin hoarfrost. The time was midday, the orange sun, shorn of its effulgence, brooded near the meridian in a sky of drabby grey. Only a few black bushes broke the monotony of the scene. The great buildings of the decadent men among whom, it seemed to me, I had been so recently, had vanished and left no trace, not a mound even marked their position. Hill and valley, sea and river—all, under the wear and work of the rain and frost, had melted into new forms. No doubt, too, the rain and snow had long since washed out the Morlock tunnels. A nipping breeze stung my hands

"XIII. Further Vision"
New Review 12 (May 1895): 577-83. [Signed]

and face. So far as I could see there were neither hills, nor trees, nor rivers: only an uneven stretch of cheerless plateau.

"Then suddenly a dark bulk rose out of the moor, something that gleamed like a serrated row of iron plates, and vanished almost immediately in a depression. And then I became aware of a number of faint-grey things, coloured to almost the exact tint of the frost-bitten soil, which were browsing here and there upon its scanty grass, and running to and fro. I saw one jump with a sudden start, and then my eye detected perhaps a score of them. At first I thought they were rabbits, or some small breed of kangaroo. Then, as one came hopping near me, I perceived that it belonged to neither of these groups. It was plantigrade, its hind legs rather the longer; it was tailless, and covered with a straight greyish hair that thickened about the head into a Skye terrier's mane. As I had understood that in the Golden Age man had killed out almost all the other animals, sparing only a few of the more ornamental, I was naturally curious about the creatures. They did not seem afraid of me, but browsed on, much as rabbits would do in a place unfrequented by men; and it occurred to me that I might perhaps secure a specimen.

"I got off the machine, and picked up a big stone. I had scarcely done so when one of the little creatures came within easy range. I was so lucky as to hit it on the head, and it rolled over at once and lay motionless. I ran to it at once. It remained still, almost as if it were killed. I was surprised to see that the thing had five feeble digits to both its fore and hind feet—the fore feet, indeed, were almost as human as the fore feet of a frog. It had, moreover, a roundish head, with a projecting forehead and forward-looking eyes, obscured by its lank hair. A disagreeable apprehension flashed across my mind. As I knelt down and seized my capture, intending to examine its teeth and other anatomical points which might show human characteristics, the metallic-looking object, to which I have already alluded, reappeared above a ridge in the moor, coming towards me and making a strange clattering sound as it came. Forthwith the grey animals about me began to answer with a short, weak yelping—as if of terror—and bolted off in a direction opposite to that from which this new creature approached. They must have hidden in burrows or behind bushes and tussocks, for in a moment not one of them was visible.

"I rose to my feet, and stared at this grotesque monster. I can only describe it by comparing it to a centipede. It stood about three feet high, and had a long segmented body, perhaps thirty feet long, with curiously overlapping greenish-black plates. It seemed to crawl upon a multitude of feet, looping its body as it advanced. Its blunt round head, with a polygonal arrangement of black eye spots, carried two flexible, writhing, horn-like antennae. It was coming along, I should judge, at a pace of about eight or ten miles an hour, and it left me little time for thinking. Leaving my grey animal, or grey man, whichever it was, on the ground, I set off for the machine. Halfway I paused, regretting that abandonment, but a glance over my shoulder destroyed any such regret. When I gained the machine the monster was scarce fifty yards away. It was certainly not a vertebrated animal. It had no snout, and its mouth was fringed with jointed dark-coloured plates. But I did not care for a nearer view.

"I traversed one day and stopped again, hoping to find the colossus gone and some vestige of my victim; but, I should judge, the giant centipede did not trouble itself about bones. At any rate both had vanished. The faintly human touch of these little creatures perplexed me greatly. If you come to think, there is no reason why a degenerate humanity should not come at last to differentiate into as many species as the descendants of the mud fish who fathered all the land vertebrates. I saw no more of any insect colossus, as to my thinking the segmented creature must have been. Evidently the physiological difficulty that at present keeps all the insects small had been surmounted at last, and this division of the animal kingdom had arrived at the long awaited supremacy which its enormous energy and vitality deserve. I made several attempts to kill or capture another of the greyish vermin, but none of my missiles were so successful as my first; and, after perhaps a dozen disappointing throws, that left my arm aching, I felt a gust of irritation at my folly in coming so far into futurity without weapons or equipment. I resolved to run on for one glimpse of the still remoter future—one peep into the deeper abysm of time—and then to return to you and my own epoch. Once more I remounted the machine, and once more the world grew hazy and grey.

"As I drove on, a peculiar change crept over the appearance of things. The unwonted greyness grew lighter; then —though I was travelling with prodigious velocity—the blinking succession of day and night, which was usually indicative of a slower pace, returned, and grew more and more marked. This puzzled me very much at first. The alternations of night and day grew slower and slower, and so did the passage of the sun across the sky, until they seemed to stretch through centuries. At last a steady twilight brooded over the earth, a twilight only broken now and then when a comet glared across the darkling sky. The band of light that had indicated the sun had long since disappeared; for the sun had ceased to set—it simply rose and fell in the west, and grew ever broader and more red. All trace of the moon had vanished. The circling of the stars, growing slower and slower, had given place to creeping points of light. At last, some time before I stopped, the sun, red and very large, halted motionless upon the horizon, a vast dome glowing with a dull heat, and now and then suffering a momentary extinction. At one time it had for a little while glowed more brilliantly again, but it speedily reverted to its sullen red-heat. I perceived by this slowing down of its rising and setting that the work of the tidal drag was done. The earth had come to rest with one face to the sun, even as in our own time the moon faces the earth.

"I stopped very gently and sat upon the Time Machine, looking round. The sky was no longer blue. North-eastward it was inky black, and out of the blackness shone brightly and steadily the pale white stars. Overhead it was a deep indian red and starless, and south-eastward it grew brighter to a glowing scarlet where, cut by the horizon, lay the huge red motionless hull of the sun. The rocks about me were of a harsh reddish colour, and all the trace of life that I could see at first was the intensely green vegetation that covered every projecting point on its south-eastern side. It was the same rich green that one sees on forest moss or on the lichen in caves: plants which like these grow in a perpetual twilight.

"The machine was standing on a sloping beach. The sea stretched away to the south-west, to rise into a sharp bright horizon against the wan sky. There were no breakers and no waves, for not a breath of wind was stirring. Only a slight oily swell rose and fell like a gentle breathing, and showed that the eternal sea was still moving and living. And along the margin where the water sometimes broke was a thick incrustation of salt—pink under the lurid sky. There was a sense of oppression in my head, and I noticed that I was breathing very fast. The sensation reminded me of my only experience of mountaineering, and from that I judged the air to be more rarefied than it is now.

"Far away up the desolate slope I heard a harsh scream, and saw a thing like a huge white butterfly go slanting and fluttering up into the sky and, circling, disappear over some low hillocks beyond. The sound of its voice was so dismal that I shivered and seated myself more firmly upon the machine. Looking round me again, I saw that, quite near, what I had taken to be a reddish mass of rock, was moving slowly towards me. Then I saw the thing was really a monstrous crab-like creature. Can you imagine a crab as large as yonder table, with its many legs moving slowly and uncertainly, its big claws swaying, its long antennae, like carters' whips, waving and feeling, and its stalked eyes gleaming at you on either side of its metallic front? Its back was corrugated and ornamented with ungainly bosses, and a greenish incrustation blotched it here and there. I could see the many palps of its complicated mouth flickering and feeling as it moved.

"As I stared at this sinister apparition crawling towards me, I felt a tickling on my cheek as though a fly had lighted there. I tried to brush it away with my hand, but in a moment it returned, and almost immediately went another by my ear. I struck at this, and caught something thread-like. It was drawn swiftly out of my hand. With a frightful qualm, I turned, and saw that I had grasped the antenna of another monster crab that stood just behind me. Its evil eyes were wriggling on their stalks, its mouth was all alive with appetite, and its vast ungainly claws, smeared with an algal slime, were descending upon me. In a moment my hand was on the lever, and I had placed a month between myself and these monsters. But I was still on the same beach, and I saw them distinctly now as soon as I stopped. Dozens of them seemed to be crawling here and there, in the sombre light, among the foliated sheets of intense green.

"I cannot convey the sense of abominable desolation that hung over the world. The red eastern sky, the north-ward blackness, the salt Dead Sea, the stony beach crawl-ing with these foul, slow-stirring monsters, the uniform poisonous-looking green of the lichenous plants, the thin air that hurts one's lungs: all contributed to an appalling effect. I moved on a hundred years, and there was the same red sun—a little larger, a little duller—the same dying sea, the same chill air, and the same crowd of earthy crustacea creeping in and out among the green weed and the red rocks. And in the westward sky I saw a curved pale line like a vast new moon.

"So I travelled, stopping ever and again, in great strides of a thousand years or more, drawn on by the mystery of the earth's fate, watching with a strange fascination the sun grow larger and duller in the westward sky, and the life of the old earth ebb away. At last, more than thirty million years hence,[1] the huge red-hot dome of the sun had come to obscure nearly a tenth part of the darkling heavens. Then I stopped once more, for the crawling multitude of crabs had disappeared, and the red beach, save for its livid green liverworts and lichens, seemed lifeless. And now it was flecked with white. A bitter cold assailed me. Rare white flakes ever and again came eddying down. To the north-eastward, the glare of snow lay under the starlight of the sable sky, and I could see an undulating crest of hillocks pinkish-white. There were fringes of ice along the sea margin, with drifting masses further out; but the main expanse of that salt ocean, all bloody under the eternal sunset, was still unfrozen.

"I looked about me to see if any traces of animal-life remained. A certain indefinable apprehension still kept me in the saddle of the machine. But I saw nothing moving, in earth or sky or sea. The green slime on the rocks alone testified that life was not extinct. A shallow sandbank had appeared in the sea and the water had receded from the beach. I fancied I saw some black object flopping about upon this bank, but it got motionless as I looked at it, and I judged that my eye had been deceived, and that the black object was merely a rock. The stars in the sky were intensely bright and seemed to me to twinkle very little.

"Suddenly I noticed that the circular westward outline

[1] On the false compression of astrophysical time on the part of Lord Kelvin and other nineteenth-century physicists, see Loren Eiseley, *Darwin's Century* (Garden City: Doubleday, 1958), chapter 9; also the reference cited in note 11, chapter 1. As Wells later remarked, the 1890s believed that the Second Law of Thermodynamics would bring about the "'inevitable' freezing up of the world . . . in a million years or less" (Preface to *The Time Machine* [New York: Random House, 1931], pp. ix-x).

of the sun had changed; that a concavity, a bay, had appeared in the curve. I saw this grow larger. For a minute perhaps I stared aghast at this blackness that was creeping over the day, and then I realised that an eclipse was beginning. Either the moon or the planet Mercury was passing across the sun's disc. Naturally, at first I took it to be the moon, but there is much to incline me to believe that what I really saw was the transit of an inner planet passing very near to the earth.

"The darkness grew apace; a cold wind began to blow in freshening gusts from the east, and the showering white flakes in the air increased in number. From the edge of the sea came a ripple and whisper. Beyond these lifeless sounds the world was silent. Silent? It would be hard to convey the stillness of it. All the sounds of man, the bleating of sheep, the cries of birds, the hum of insects, the stir that makes the background of our lives—all that was over. As the darkness thickened, the eddying flakes grew more abundant, dancing before my eyes; and the cold of the air more intense. At last, one by one, swiftly, one after the other, the white peaks of the distant hills vanished into blackness. The breeze rose to a moaning wind. I saw the black central shadow of the eclipse sweeping towards me. In another moment the pale stars alone were visible. All else was rayless obscurity. The sky was absolutely black.

"A horror of the great darkness came on me. The cold, that smote to my marrow, and the pain I felt in breathing overcame me. I shivered and a deadly nausea seized me. Then like a red-hot bow in the sky appeared the edge of the sun. I got off the machine to recover myself. I felt giddy and incapable of facing the return journey. As I stood sick and confused I saw again the moving thing upon the shoal—there was no mistake now that it was a moving thing—against the red water of the sea. It was a round thing, the size of a football perhaps, or, it may be, bigger, and tentacles trailed down from it; it seemed black against the weltering blood-red water, and it was hopping fitfully about. Then I felt I was fainting. But a terrible dread of lying helpless in that remote and awful twilight sustained me while I clambered upon the saddle."

IV. *The Opposite Idea*

... there is almost always associated with the suggestion of
advance in biological phenomena an opposite idea, which is its
essential complement.

"Zoological Retrogression"[1]

Opposite ideas—in the simplest sense, notions running
counter to currently accepted opinion—always attracted
Wells. Typically, he begins an essay by outlining a commonly held belief and in the course of his exposition
suggests that "There is a consideration affecting the discussion ... that, oddly enough, has passed almost unnoticed" ("The Rate of Change in Species"). He then proceeds to explain this "consideration," the significance of
which (as he develops it) either controverts a popular
conception or renders it paradoxical. Through the dialectic
of his argument, Wells seeks to make human consciousness
"plastic," imaginatively open and thus conformable to the
nature of things—adaptable to a universe of irreducible
"uniques." Nothing in the cosmos is strictly like anything
else: the mind perceives an identity among phenomena
only "by an unconscious or deliberate disregard of an
infinity of small differences" ("The Rediscovery of the
Unique")—and by obliviousness to the essential reality,
change.

"The 'Cyclic' Delusion" (1894), for example, remarks on
the human tendency, biologically "woven into the texture
of our being," to perceive every process as circular, a
repetition of what has happened before. But exact recur-

---

[1] "Zoological Retrogression," reprinted in chapter 5.

rence, Wells points out, is illusory. The phenomena which come within the purview of, say, astronomers or biologists may appear to behave cyclically, but really most of them do not. "Every day is—though by an imperceptible amount —longer"; offspring are "not *quite* like the parent"; the rhythm of the heart may seem to be perpetually the same, but one day this muscle ceases to pulse; and so on. With allowances made for local exceptions, "the main course" of the universe "is forward, from the things that are past and done with for ever to things that are altogether new." This means that change is real, not delusive; so that regardless of whether the future will appear progressive or retrogressive "according to present ideals" ("Zoological Retrogression"), it will not simply reiterate what has gone before.

"We discover ... apparent cycles ... only through the limitation of our observation." For a similar reason, says Wells, astronomers do not discover changes taking place in the moon. Although it is plausible, for instance, that lunar volcanic eruptions occur, no such upheavals have been noticed, nor has any consequent transformation of the lunar surface. This is not only because changes of that kind would be less noticeable on the moon than on earth, but also because "the eye that watched [the moon] was set against the expectation of change" ("The Visibility of Change in the Moon" [1895]). Observers expect not to find alterations in the lunar landscape; therefore, they do not see any.

Now and again, however, scientists do come upon the unexpected. Witness the discovery that oxygen responds in more than one way to spectroscopic analysis. This fact supports the hypothesis that "there are two kinds of oxygen, one with an atom a little heavier than the other," which in turn "opens one's eyes to an amazing possibility ... that, after all, atoms might not be all exactly alike, that they might have individuality, just as animals have." "The Possible Individuality of Atoms" (1896) thus restates a metaphysical notion congenial to Wells, one which he is convinced science confirms: that "*All being is unique, or, nothing is strictly like anything else*" ("The Rediscovery of the Unique").

It is his predilection for this notion of the uniqueness of things that disposes him to argue for lunar transformations and against cyclical recurrence.[2] In "The Biological Problem of To-Day" (1894), he rejects August Weismann's theory of germ-plasm precisely because it seems to make evolutionary change improbable.[3] To Wells's mind, Weismann's insistence on the immortality and immutability of germ cells implies a metaphysics akin to the mystical idea of the "pre-formation" of all life at the beginning of time. Indeed, it is true that Weismann so respected the conservative nature of the mechanism of heredity that he posited perfect replication of the parent stock in the offspring, replication qualified only by allowance for the recombining and reordering of parental traits in the progeny as a result of sexual reproduction.[4] In the absence of a theory of mutation (still some decades away), Wells is quite right in objecting that such a hypothesis cannot adequately account for the rise of what Darwin calls "variations" in species or (consequently) for the emergence of new species.

Wells also perceptively recognized the importance of "the *rate* of change in species" as an evolutionary determinant. Contrary to popular conceptions—shared even by many biologists of the time—about what characteristics best fit a species to survive, he reasoned that the potential

[2] The connection Wells saw between "the Unique" (and "individuality") and change (moving on "to things that are altogether new") also accounts for his abiding interest in the future.

[3] On Wells's changing views towards, and final acceptance of, Weismannism, see the discussions in chapters 1 and 6.

[4] See Weismann, "The Continuity of the Germ-Plasm as the Foundation of a Theory of Heredity" and "The Significance of Sexual Reproduction in the Theory of Natural Selection," in *Essays upon Heredity and Kindred Biological Problems*, ed. Edward B. Poulton et al., 2d ed. rev., 2 vols. (Oxford: Clarendon Press, 1891-1892), 1: 163-254, 257-342.

"plasticity," or adaptability, of species must vary in direct proportion to their fecundity and the time span between generations. Although the popular conception of "Nature, red in tooth and claw"[5] stressed strength and cunning as best equipping a species in the struggle for existence, Wells concluded otherwise: "The true heirs of the future"—the ultimate victors in the struggle for existence—"are the small, fecund, and precocious creatures" whose capacity for multiplying and maturing rapidly enables them to develop quickly variations conformable to environmental changes ("The Rate of Change in Species" [1894]).

Opposite ideas of this sort very much depend upon the "standpoint" taken. From the standpoint of evolution, survival of the species is of paramount importance; the individual is expendable. This is the paradox Wells stresses in "The Duration of Life" (1895). "The business of the animal"—and of man under natural conditions—"seems to be, not to live its own life, but to reproduce its own kind, and the term of life at its disposal is adjusted accurately to the special difficulties of this purpose."

From the cosmic biological perspective, then, the death of the individual has no significance. "Death," Wells argues, "is not inherent in living matter. Protoplasm may live forever." Nevertheless, "mortal man and the immortal protozoa have the same barren immortality; the individuals perish, living on only in their descendants . . . ; the type alone persists" ("Death" [1895]). Nature is therefore indifferent to individualistic human effort, which it tragically—or comically—counterpoints.

The laws of the cosmos do not accord with human desires or expectations. Indeed, nature, if viewed anthropomorphically (that is, falsely) seems to oppose man and resist his explanations. Skeletons, for instance, cannot be accounted for simply in terms of their utility as "support

[5] *In Memoriam* (1850), LVI, l. 15. Though Tennyson's poem antedates *On the Origin of Species* (1859), his became a popular catch-phrase, like Herbert Spencer's "struggle for existence." See Gertrude Himmelfarb, *Darwin and the Darwinian Revolution* (New York: Norton, 1968), pp. 230-32.

and armature." If support were its purpose, a skeleton of silica would be preferable to one of phosphate and carbonate of lime, silica being sturdier and more durable. For armature, an exoskeletal structure such as crustaceans possess would seem to offer more protection than the skeletons of the "higher" animals. And why a rigid and brittle skeleton at all when some species of fish manage perfectly well with a "skeleton of gristle" ("Concerning Skeletons" [1896])?

Biochemistry, Wells suggests, may one day be able to answer these questions. In the meantime, one may speculate as to whether there may be "another basis for life" altogether. No reason prevents the supposition that life could be built upon compounds that are not organic: "silicon-aluminium organisms" could have existed "in the past history of our planet" or may now exist on some other planet whose temperatures are much higher than those on earth at present ("Another Basis for Life" [1894]).

Overt or tacit in all these speculations, as elsewhere in Wells's writings, is an attack on human "rigidity" in any form. The moral lesson that nature surely teaches is that fixity is fatal. Man himself, when he becomes rigid in his thinking, impervious to the "opposite idea," also becomes incapable of change, loses his adaptability, and verges towards extinction.

THE "CYCLIC" DELUSION

Nothing is more deeply impressed upon the human mind than the persuasion of a well-nigh universal cyclic quality in things, of an inevitable disposition to recur in the long run to a former phase. In great things and in small we see it; we are, indeed, like men in a workshop full of whirling machinery, who, wherever they turn, see a wheel, until at last this rotation is so dinned into the texture of our minds that the whole world spins. Every moment the heart goes through its cycle from dilatation to contraction and so back to dilatation; for every four heart-beats the lungs expand and contract; then hunger comes, is satisfied, recurs; the sun rises and sets, and sleep follows activity. Other bodily functions run in longer periods, as the moon changes from new to full and from full to new, and spring-tide follows neap; in still larger circles spins the succession of seed-time and harvest. Yet larger again is the circle of the lifetime from birth to begetting, and so again to birth. The planetary cycles accomplish themselves in still longer periods, and, greatest and slowest of all, the pole of the earth completes its gigantic precessional revolution through the constellations.

It is scarcely wonderful if the human mind is inclined to look for, and ready to discover, the circle—the recurrence—in everything it deals with. A few years ago that happily departed phrase, "the inevitable reaction," was alive to witness to the facility of this persuasion. We find it in history, in poetry, in mathematics. A straight line is an arc of a circle of infinite radius, says the mathematician; and a ring is the world-wide symbol of eternity. This idea lies implicitly at the base of countless scientific researches and theories. Numerous investigators are looking for a weather cycle, and a sun-spot cycle wobbles

"'Cyclic' Delusion"
SR 78 (Nov. 10, 1894): 505-06. [*GW, GR*]

restlessly in the hands of its discoverer. Then Professor Chandler has, with infinite pains, disentangled a Chandlerian cycle of variation in latitude.[1] In geological literature the idea that Glacial periods have occurred time after time is constantly cropping up, in spite of the absence of any satisfactory corroboration. It is one of the commonest employments of the modern astronomer to discover pairs of stars revolving round one another. And both the meteoric and the nebular hypotheses—really theories of the material universe—are cyclic theories, in which cold dark bodies, moving through space, collide, are rendered gaseous and incandescent by the heat of the collision, and slowly revert by radiation to the cold dark condition again.

A remarkable instance of the power of this predisposition towards the cyclic view of things is the case of the double star in the Swan, known to astronomers as 61 Cygni. Mr. Mann and Dr. Peters separately observed this star, and *calculated the orbits of its constituents!* Their calculations were entirely fallacious, as subsequent inquiry showed. Then Professor Newcomb suggested the constituents revolved round a common centre, but sufficient reasons, too complex to treat with here, have been adduced to rebut this suggestion. The attitude of the astronomical mind at present might be expressed by the question, "Then what *do* they revolve round?" The recent work of Dr. Wilsing shows only that the two constituents approach and recede in a spasmodic fashion. Yet, in a recent article by that well-known astronomer Miss Clerke,[2] discussing this work of his, the cyclic nature of these movements is still tacitly in evidence.

Now, it is a curious and suggestive speculation to investigate the sources of this cyclic predisposition. In the end one is surprised by the narrowness of the base upon which

[1] Seth Carlo Chandler, the American astronomer, published "On the Variation of Latitude" in several installments (1891-1893) in the *Astronomical Journal,* which he also edited.

[2] Agnes M. Clerke ("A Double Star," *Knowledge* 17 [Nov. 1, 1894]: 257-258) states substantially what Wells says about Mann, Peters, Newcomb, and Wilsing and star 61 Cygni.

this extraordinary conception has arisen. In the first place, the planetary motions, the lunar phases, the tides, the alternation of day and night, and the sequence of seasons, cease in the light of scientific analysis to be corroboratory evidence. For both the generally accepted theories of the origin of the solar system suppose a nebulous cloud rotating on its axis to begin with, from the central mass of which the planets were torn by centrifugal force, and sent spinning in widening orbits round the central sun, throwing off satellites as they spun; on which view these instances of cyclic recurrence are really only special aspects of one and the same case, consequences of an eddying motion in the original nebula. The periodicity of many animal functions, waking and sleep and the reproductive seasons, for instance, are very conceivably correlated with these.

And, with further examination, we discover that these apparent cycles seem cyclic only through the limitation of our observation. The tidal drag upon the planets slowly retards their rotation, so that every day is—though by an imperceptible amount—longer. "As certain as that the sun will rise" is a proverb for certainty, but one day the sun will rise for the last time, will become as motionless in the sky as the earth is now in the sky of the moon. According to Professor G. H. Darwin, the actual motion of a satellite is spiral; it recedes from its source and primary until a maximum distance is attained, and thence it draws nearer again, until it reunites at last with the central body.[3] Moreover, the recurrence of living things is also illusory. The naturalist tells us that the egg hatches into a hen not *quite* like the parent hen; that if we go back along the pedigree we shall come at last to creatures not hens, but to the ancestral forms of the hen. Take only a few generations, and the cycle seems perfect enough; but, as

[3] Sir George Howard Darwin (1845-1912), astronomer son of Charles Darwin, advanced a Theory of Tidal Evolution, which in part hypothesized that should tidal forces retard planetary rotation, any satellite of that planet would eventually be drawn back to that parent body.

more and more are taken, we drift further and further from the starting point—drift steadily, without any disposition to return.

Then the beating of the heart, the breathing, the rhythm of muscular motion, all the physiological sequences spring probably out of one common necessity, the impossibility—or, at least, the great inconvenience—of living tissue acting and feeding at the same time, of loading and discharging the gun simultaneously. We have activity, fatigue, and nutritive pause, activity again; for only half its beat is the heart actively working, the remaining period is a pause during which the repair of the muscular tissue occurs. It is at least a plausible speculation that the musical sequences appeal to us as they do because of the rhythmic quality of our physiological organization. And, though one heart-beat seems to follow the next truly enough, yet a time comes when the pitcher goes no longer to the well.

So it may be that this cyclic quality that is so woven into the texture of our being, into the fundamentals of our thought, is, after all, a prejudice, the outcome of two main accidents of our existence. We live in an eddy; are, as it were, the creatures of that eddy. But the great stream of the universe flows past us and onward. Here and there is a backwater or a whirling pool, a little fretful midge of life spinning upon its axis, or a gyrating solar system. But the main course is forward, from the things that are past and done with for ever to things that are altogether new.

THE VISIBILITY OF CHANGE IN THE MOON

The absolute quiescence of the lunar crust is a commonplace of popular science; it is, however, open to doubt whether the belief in the permanence of the lunar surface has all the justification its wide acceptance might lead us to expect. This conclusion has been drawn from the absence of any perceptible change in the forms of lunar contours, and of any visible eruptive phenomena. But it must be remembered that fairly extensive changes of contour may have occurred before the epoch of lunar photography, and that even now the displacement of relatively large masses has a very fair chance of escaping notice. As Mr. Elger has pointed out, objects as large as Monte Nuovo or Jorullo might come into existence in many regions without anyone being the wiser,[1] and a catastrophe as extensive as the destruction of Herculaneum and Pompeii might still escape detection. And few people outside astronomical circles probably appreciate the peculiar consequences the physical conditions of our satellite's surface would have upon the phenomena of volcanic eruption.

The most striking features of a typical volcanic eruption upon our planet are certainly the tumultuous noises of the outbreak, and the enormous clouds of steam and pumiceous ashes that rush out of the vent and spread over the country encircling the volcano. These cloudy masses form a background to reflect and exaggerate whatever incandescence may be visible within the crater. But upon the moon all this pomp of smoke and flame would be absent, because upon the moon there is no atmosphere to buoy up the finely divided products of the eruption,

"Visibility of Change"
Knowledge 18 (Oct. 1895): 230-31. [Signed]
[1] Thomas Gwyn Elger, *The Moon: A Full Description and Map of its Principal Physical Features* (London: G. Philip & Son, 1895), p. 37. Wells quotes verbatim. Readers of *Knowledge* would have recognized Elger as a frequent contributor.

and whatever the volcano threw out would, so soon as the velocity of its projection was lost, fall back at once upon the lunar surface. The uprush of flames, which is another striking accompaniment of terrestrial outbreaks, would also be absent, since a flame rushes upward only because it is specifically lighter than the air through which it rushes. The intense cold of the lunar surface, together with the absence of atmospheric pressure, would also conspire to rob any incandescent gas of its visibility, for so soon as it was released at the vent it would expand and cool, and so elude our observation. A momentary disclosure of incandescence is all we can anticipate under the most favourable circumstances, and in the bright glare of the lunar day—and it is only the lunar day we are accustomed to observe—it is conceivable that the equivalent of the most violent terrestrial eruptions might be going on in the field of our largest telescope without attracting attention.

Even could one stand upon the moon itself near the vent, the phenomena of an eruption in progress would still be far less awe-inspiring than upon this planet. In a profound silence and in the unmitigated glare of the sunlight we should see the molten rock creeping sluggishly from the lips of the crater, and in the place of the explosive escape of volumes of steam the surface of the lava flow would merely be agitated by the bubbling out of what would immediately become a frosty garment of snow and carbon-dioxide. It would be little more terrific than the squeezing of paint from a tube. The forcible and sustained ejection of scoriæ and ashes on a terrestrial volcano is due largely to the effervescent escape of superheated steam from the molten magma; but if the lunar surface is, as is generally supposed, somewhere near the absolute zero of temperature, then the isotherm of the freezing point of water must be some considerable distance beneath the crust, and the boiling point isotherm still deeper. In which case the expansive force of the contained water may be much less in a lunar than in a terrestrial crater, and indeed it may be insufficient to spray up or even vesiculate the more viscous lava flow. On the other hand, however, the feebler gravitational energy of the moon and the absence of a superincumbent atmosphere would enable a much smaller expansive force to project masses to a considerable altitude, and a far smaller force of upheaval to rupture a much greater thickness of overlying crust. The lunar eruption would be therefore, one may think, more of the nature of one violent explosion like the discharge of a gun, and nothing more, rather than the sustained pyrotechnic display of a terrestrial outbreak.

Taken altogether, these considerations point to the conclusion that a lunar eruption, if such a thing is still possible, would consist essentially of two phases; the first, the very transient one of breaking through the crust, would eject any obstacle in the vent to an enormous altitude, the ejected rock or rocks, in a more or less pulverized condition, raining back *immediately* about the volcanic vent, and then might follow an inconspicuous and noiseless bubbling and guttering out of snow and frozen gas, and (less probably) lava within the lips of the crater. The former scarcely more than the latter could be expected to be visible from this planet.

But it must be borne in mind that these are purely speculative suggestions, involving finally the groundless implication that the moon has differences of internal temperature, and so some lingering vestiges of internal energy. There is plausibility in the belief that at the absolute zero of temperature matter will have lost all its inter-molecular energy, and, among other things, that it will not be able to contract further. If we assume that not only the unilluminated surface of the moon, but its very centre also, has sunk to that final static state, then the volcanic forces due to the contraction of a cooler exterior upon a warmer nucleus do not come into play. But along another line the grounds for anticipating lunar changes are less hypothetical. There must still be superficial displacements due to the expansions and contractions which the monthly passage of the solar heat-wave must cause, and there is not only periodic heating and cooling of the lunar surface, but since no matter is perfectly rigid, there must also be a tidal deformation due to the sun's attraction. These influences, at any rate, whatever we may think of the volcanic possibility, *must* produce tiltings and instabilities, and in the tremendous impact of meteorites—for the moon, unlike the earth, has no pneumatic protection from such jars—we have a force more than adequate to start landslips and overthrow the tottering summits of cliffs. Altogether there is plentiful *a priori* ground for denying that the moon is indeed an immutable dead world beyond all further indignities of change.

And this is not merely an *a priori* proposition, for about twenty years ago there is every reason to suppose that a black spot appeared near Hyginus, and in 1866 a certain amount of discussion centred about the crater Linné. The floor of Plato has also been suspect, but without any very decisive results. Assuredly there can be no more promising field of observation for the amateur astronomer in possession of a fairly powerful telescope than a detailed study of some definite portion of the lunar disc, and an exhaustive comparison with the accumulating collection of photographic charts that have been made during the past decade. To see the side of some mighty crater suddenly slide and crumble into ruin, or some gaping chasm opening in a dazzling slope of white, has so far been the lot of no terrestrial observer. Yet it may be that already such change has happened in the field of some watching telescope, and only escaped observation because the eye that watched was set against the expectation of change. And even as this is written some happy mortal may be detecting the faint stirring, the scarcely perceptible movement that marks the still living forces that have so far been hidden from our eyes. But the chances are that whatever changes may be proceeding will be detected in a less dramatic way—by the systematic measurement and comparison of photographic charts extending over a considerable period of years.

THE POSSIBLE INDIVIDUALITY OF ATOMS

The recent excitement over Helium and Argon has distracted attention from some very remarkable and significant work recently published by Mr. Baly upon the twofold spectra exhibited by oxygen and nitrogen.[1] The implications of his paper are of something more than technical interest,and, as the reader will speedily see, we have ample excuse for transposing them from the dialect of chemistry into the common language. The popular persuasion is that all the atoms of any particular element are exactly alike, that one atom of oxygen is identically similar to another. It is a thing we learn in our very first lessons in chemistry and retain for the rest of our lives. But these experiments throw very considerable doubt upon this widely accepted view. Let us consider the nature of them.

The elementary fact upon which spectrum analysis depends, that the light from an incandescent solid body decomposes into a continuous rainbow-hued band when passed through a prism, is known to everyone. In the case of a solid or liquid body the molecules are not free to vibrate, and their interference with one another produces light of all qualities, from the darkest red to the deepest violet. But gaseous molecules are free to move in any direction. When, therefore, gas or vapour is rendered luminous—which can easily be done by passing an electric spark through it—unlike an incandescent solid or liquid, it does not give a continuous strip of colour in the spectroscope, but a number of bright lines at intervals separated by dark gaps. And if, while these bright lines are being

"Possibile Individuality"
SR 82 (Sept. 5, 1896): 256-57. [*GW, GR*]
[1] Edward C. C. Baly ("A Possible Explanation of the Two-Fold Spectra of Oxygen and Nitrogen," *Royal Society Proceedings* 57 [March 21, 1895]: 468-469) gives the findings mentioned by Wells, including the tie-in with J. J. Thomson Wells makes later on.

observed, a beam from an electric light or limelight is directed towards the spectroscope, they are at once seen as dark lines upon the ribbon of variegated colour which distinguishes the light of an incandescent solid. The change is supposed to be due to the absorption by the molecules of the gas of light of certain definite wave-lengths. Just as each wire of a piano has a particular note to which it will respond, so each bright ray in the spectrum of a luminous gas absorbs the vibrations at a particular point in the gamut of colour. The wave-length, or the vibration frequency, of each tint of light blotted out from the continuous band of colour by the gas is the same as that emitted when the gas is made luminous, precisely as, in the case of the piano, the wire which sounds middle C when struck is that which vibrates when the same note is sung. To carry the analogy still further, many gases which have in their spectra a line at a certain wave-length have another line at the octave above in the light scale. Hydrogen, for instance, has all its lines connected by a simple harmonic relation.

And now comes a curious thing that has long been known. Many gases—the new Argon is one, and oxygen and nitrogen are older instances—have variable spectra, according to the conditions under which they are made luminous. How are these changes caused? Do the molecules or atoms twist differently in some way under the different influences that make them luminous? Do they, to use a rough expression, vibrate lengthways-on and emit or interfere with one particular set of vibrations under this stimulation and "endways-on" under that? Or does the difference of the light mark some more profound difference of condition in the gas under the different circumstances? The former (up to the last month) was decidedly the favourite theory. For no one thought—except, perhaps, those who had considered Professor J. J. Thomson's experiments upon the electrical decomposition of steam[2]—that the gas under treatment underwent any perceptible change. But Mr. Baly's observations go to show that the latter possibility is after all the more probable one. For the gas that collects about the point whence the sparks leap across the containing vessel, he has found, after a little while is slightly denser or lighter (it depends upon the length of the spark) than that at the other.

This is really a very remarkable result indeed. Unless some experimental error has been overlooked, one of two things must follow. Either *oxygen is not an element* (nor nitrogen, nor argon), and the electric spark decomposes it, or there are two kinds of oxygen, one with an atom a little heavier than the other. And this opens one's eyes to an amazing possibility. The suggestion was made some years ago that, after all, atoms might not be all exactly alike, that they might have individuality just as animals have.[3] The average man weighs (let us say) twelve stone, but some men are down to seven and others up to eighteen. Taken haphazard, however, you can safely say that a million men will weigh (with the minutest margin of error) twelve million stone. Take, however, some force to sort out your men—say, for instance, the stress of economic forces—and take one sample of a million coal-heavers and another of a million clerks, and one will be above the average and another below. Now it may be the electric spark traversing the gas has an analogous selective action. Your heavier atoms or molecules get driven this or that way with slightly more force. Clearly the oxygen in one direction will become a little denser than that in another. It is at least an odd suggestion (for which Mr. Baly must not be held guilty). We offer it merely as a dream. This is indeed a time for dreaming. There cannot be the slightest

---

[2] Joseph John Thomson (1856-1940), English physicist, whose *Notes on Recent Researches in Electricity and Magnetism* contains the experimental results of passing current through various gases (see previous note).
[3] See "The Rediscovery of the Unique."

doubt that we are at last in the dawn of a period of profound reconstructions in the theory of chemistry. And where the threescore and ten "Elements" will be at the end of it even our speculative enterprise hesitates to guess.

THE BIOLOGICAL PROBLEM OF TO-DAY

Two hundred years ago interpretations of the embryological development of plants and animals frankly involved the miraculous. Naturalists found within the stem of a growing shoot of corn a miniature of the ear; or, breaking the shell of an egg incubated for a few hours under a hen, revealed therein a tiny organism, hardly visible, but pulsating with life. They were content with the conclusion that the process of development was the mere growth into visibility and then into adult size of a miniature of the adult. Following our human craving for a rounded interpretation of nature they held that, germ within germ, like a nest of Indian puzzle-boxes, all the descendants of each original animal and plant had been placed within each other by the Creator at the beginning of the world. The course of the generations of animals and plants was a true evolution, or unrolling of these series of miniatures; each generation was the blossoming into life of the outermost surviving member; each when it withered or died left behind the still surviving members folded one within the other in the seed or egg.

The methods and the habit of observation in those days alike were imperfect; yet in 1759 Caspar Friedrich Wolff,[1] in his *Theoria Generationis,* confronted the prevailing doctrine with observations showing that young embryos were not miniatures of the adult. On the contrary, he asserted that young embryos were masses of tissue practically unformed, and that change after change was induced upon them until the characters of the adult were attained.

As is the habit of prevailing doctrines, this old theory of evolution did not succumb to observed truth: the generalization of Wolff found little favour among the

"Biological Problem"
SR 78 (Dec. 29, 1894): 703-04. [*GW, GR*]

[1] Kaspar Friedrich Wolff (1733-1794), German biologist and pioneer in embryology.

biologists of his day. But, from then till now, a slow accumulation of observations has established his main contention, and, with our modern appliances, it could be demonstrated to any one within an hour that the successive stages passed through by embryos resembled neither one another nor the adult. Nowadays, every one knows that man, for instance, begins individual existence as a single cell of microscopic size; that this simple beginning on its upward path passes through stages corresponding first to the simplest and then to worm-like invertebrates, and that it puts on the vertebrate type in the guise of a lowly, fish-like creature. The gill-apertures close, the limbs appear, and it slowly creeps up through stages recalling the ranks of the mammals, until at birth scarcely has it concealed its identity with the man-like apes.

The microscope shows this slow metamorphosis to consist in the multiplication of cells—the living units of which all organisms are composed—and in the deploying of the sheets and masses of cells to their ordered places in the cell community. The recognition of the cellular nature of organisms, and of embryological growth as cell-multiplication and cell-arrangement, and of many diseases and abnormalities of organisms as vagaries of cell-growth, is not the least of the advances of the science of to-day. It has disposed permanently of the crude dogma of evolution that Wolff attacked; but it has merely changed the *venue* of the old controversy from the gross realities of visible matter to the invisible structure of living matter. Miraculous preformation of the adult in the egg, disproved for masses of cells, has betaken itself to masses of molecules.

Weismann is the high priest of this temple rebuilded, and the only thing more astonishing than his theory is the vogue it enjoys. Correlating with the research of others some patient and beautiful investigations of his own upon the branching polyps of the sea, Weismann put forward the idea that seeds or eggs contained a peculiar substance, different in kind from the prevailing living protoplasm of plants and animals, and that they could arise only from those parts of the body in which resided a stock of the peculiar material originally derived from the parent. In its first inception this idea was neither novel nor unlikely; an increasing body of opinion in England and Germany supports the view that the resemblances of heredity are associated with the transmission from parent to child of a definite material substance. But the idea grew in Weismann's fertile imagination until it bore the exotic fruits with which his name is associated. First, he insisted on the complete separation between the hereditary material and the material of the tissues of the body. A portion was used in the formation of the new organism; the remainder was secluded in the tissues of the organism undisturbed and uninfluenced by all the shaping and moulding influences that affected the organism during life, and was handed on unaltered to the next generation. Translated into intelligible terms this metaphysical conception implied that acquired characters are not inherited; that, for instance, however a man's habits and vices and education may write their marks upon his bodily frame, his children come into the world exactly as if his experiences had been the stuff that dreams are made of. But a development still more surprising was to come. It is agreed that the material bearer of inherited qualities (named by Weismann the germ-plasm) resides in cells, almost certainly in the special organ of the cell known as the nucleus. Weismann would now have us suppose that the germ-plasm is composed of a number of separate pieces, each piece being a veritable microcosm corresponding to some separate ancestor, and each being composed of innumerable particles. These are the ultimate living units, and they are arranged in a definite and extremely complicated architecture. The mystery of development is that as the organism grows by the division of cells, these cells arrange themselves in the proper places and assume the proper characters. "It is no mystery," says

Weismann, "for I have imagined my architecture of the pieces of germ-plasm to be such that at each cell-division the architecture partially disintegrates, and to the cells resulting from the division there are handed on different and appropriate groups of particles corresponding to different qualities. When the organism is fully formed, the architecture of the germ-plasm is disintegrated completely, and each cell contains only the particles corresponding to its individual characters." Naturally such cells are incapable of giving rise to anything but cells of their own order. New organisms can arise only because a number of the complete ancestral pieces of the germ-plasm were preserved with their architecture untouched.

It is a charming instance of the invention of a tortoise to support the elephant that carries the earth. But, apart from its purely imaginative character, it rests upon a supposition regarding cell-division which Oscar Hertwig, than whom no one living knows more about cells, has recently shown to be unproved and improbable. The supposition is that there exists a kind of cell-division in which the qualities of the parent cell are distributed unequally between the daughter-cells. In the stages of division of cells, as seen under the microscope, nothing is more striking than what one may call the elaborate precautions taken to secure that a fair half shall be handed to each daughter-cell. In the vast assemblage of organisms the bodies of which consist each of a single cell, the most familiar method of reproduction is by simple division. Yet in these the daughter organisms become like each other and like the parent cell. Among higher animals and plants there are known innumerable instances showing that each cell or group of cells contains the characters of the whole organism, although only such characters are active at any time as are required by the situation of the cell or group of cells. Many plants may be chopped in pieces, and each piece, placed in damp earth, will reproduce the whole. A piece of begonia leaf, part of the twig of a willow, pieces cut out of many worms and polyps, under suitable conditions, will reproduce the whole organism. But still more definite are some recent experiments upon the early stages of developing embryos. Hertwig and Driesch and Wilson have succeeded in shaking apart the cells of young embryos; upon which the separate cells did not give rise to parts of the embryo but, recommencing from the beginning, proved that they contained the qualities of the whole by giving rise to the whole.[2] It were tedious iteration to detail these facts which are known to every biologist. But it is worth while to point out that while the public have been devouring the fruit of the tree of Weismannism, spite of the warnings of Herbert Spencer and Romanes that it is bitter,[3] Dr. Oscar Hertwig has cut the tree across at the roots.

[2] Wilhelm August Oscar Hertwig (1849-1922), Hans Adolf Eduard Driesch (1867-1941), and Edmund Beecher Wilson (1856-1939) all disagreed, for empirical reasons, with Weismann's contention (quoted by Wells in the previous paragraph) that cell division in the embryo in and of itself produces qualitative differences in the cells resulting from that division. A report of Hertwig's theories by Peter Chalmers Mitchell ("Hertwig's 'Preformation or New Formation,' " *Natural Science* 5 [August-Oct. 1894]: 132-134, 184-194, 292-297) ties together these names and their experimental data just as Wells does. Doubtless also, this essay of Mitchell's is the source of Wells's outline of the history of the "preformation" vs. "new formation" controversy from Wolff to Weismann.

[3] Though both Spencer and Romanes rejected Weismann's germ-plasm theory, Spencer championed the inheritance of acquired characteristics, concerning which Romanes was sceptical (see note 1 to "Sunset of Mankind").

THE RATE OF CHANGE IN SPECIES

There is a consideration affecting the discussion of Natural Selection that, oddly enough, has passed almost unnoticed by biologists, though any one might think it, when plainly stated, an obvious matter. This neglected consideration is the relation that must exist between the age of maturity in a species and the rapidity with which that species will undergo modification. Let us illustrate by a simple instance. Conceive an animal, A, which, if it be fortunate, and, as an individual, well adapted to its conditions, arrives at sexual maturity and begets offspring in the space of a year. Thereupon this offspring comes under the action of natural selection; the ill-equipped mostly perish, the fitter individuals survive. Next year these survivors reproduce, and the process of selection is repeated. So, in ten years, external conditions have, as it were, picked over ten successive generations of our species A, it has been through the assay ten times, had ten tries to meet the requirements of its environment, each time with the rejection of unsuitable variations, and with encouragement and increase of any improvement in the pattern submitted. But, in the same space of time, an animal of a species B, that only came to sexual maturity in ten years, would merely have begun to submit its first set of samples, its first generation, to the action of natural selection. Clearly the species A must have a capacity for change ten times that of B, if the number of offspring and other conditions are equal.

Now the actual differences in the animal and vegetable kingdoms are far wider than this: on the one hand is man, who rarely, even in tropical countries, becomes the head of a household before the sixteenth or seventeenth year; while, on the other, we have microscopic organisms that

"Rate of Change"
SR 78 (Dec. 15, 1894): 655-56. [*GW, GR*]

are actively reproductive within a few hours of their birth. And this difference in the plasticity of species is further accentuated by the fact that among the lower organisms the number of offspring per parent, the choice of patterns, that is, submitted to natural selection, is far greater than among the higher. Indeed, it is no exaggeration to say that there are organisms which in the course of one year turn over as many generations as mankind has done in the whole period of written history, and which in the space of a human lifetime are as capable of as much modification—if changing circumstances require it—as the human animal has undergone since the hairy cave-dweller made his celebrated sketch of a mammoth with a flint upon a bone.

The fact that man had scarcely changed at all, at least anatomically, in the space of many thousand years was one of the crushing arguments adduced by Cuvier against St.-Hilaire;[1] but evidently in such a slow-breeding creature the evolutionary process must be almost stagnant, so far as the natural selection of non-acquired variations goes. Where we should look for perceptible modification, where, if anywhere, De Varigny's suggestion of experimental evolution[2] should be carried out, is among the rapidly breeding and abundantly breeding smaller organisms. And there it is, indeed, that we find the clearest suggestion of evidence in favour of the mutability of species.

On our supposition that we must count the stages of evolution in generations rather than years, no type of living thing should undergo specific alteration so rapidly as the bacteria, and as a matter of fact there is excellent ground

[1] Georges Cuvier opposed catastrophism to the evolutionism of Etienne Geoffroy St.-Hilaire and Lamarck, and he showed (but not in debating St.-Hilaire) that the descendants of Egyptian human and animal mummies are biologically identical to their forebears (*A Discourse on the Revolutions of the Surface of the Globe and the Changes Thereby Produced in the Animal Kingdom*, trans. anonymous [Philadelphia: Carey & Lea, 1831], pp. 84, 222-246).

[2] Henry Crosnier de Varigny, *Experimental Evolution (Lectures Delivered in the 'Summer School of Art and Science,' University Hall, Edinburgh, August, 1891)* (London: Nature Series, 1892).

129

for believing that the zymotic diseases, whose ravages give us the only means of tracing these organisms beyond our own time, have undergone a secular variation of considerable magnitude in virulence and symptom, even within the historical period. And our inference that large slow-breeding animals are virtually incapable of specific change in harmony with changing conditions affords a clue to a feature of the fossil record that has been remarked upon by palæontologists again and again. The fact is that the large forms of one group are never succeeded in a subsequent epoch by their own descendants, but are ousted by some previously insignificant group, that each leading type of animal has worked out its structure in obscurity, risen in its day to supremacy, stamped itself upon the fossil record, and passed away. The large labyrinthodonta[3] of the coal measure, for instance, are replaced by alien groups of reptiles in the secondary rocks, which again do not develop into, but disappear before, the rising mammals, and the subdivisions of these again manifest the same phenomena.

The explanation is plain enough. Imagine in our own time some far-reaching change effected in the conditions of life on this planet, an increase in humidity, perhaps, or a change in the composition of the air effected speedily—say in a hundred years or so. In that time the small organisms, with their prompt fecundity, would have followed the change, come round to the drift, altered and survived. But the larger ones, driving on the old course by virtue of the inertia of their too extensive lives, would have scarcely changed in the century, and, being no longer fitted to the conditions around them, would dwindle and—if no line of retreat offered itself—become extinct. A group of large animals (such as the elephants and the hoofed herbivora) is a group that has, as it were, staked its existence upon the permanence of the current conditions;

---

[3] A class of large amphibians of the Triassic period having teeth of labyrinthine structure.

has become powerful, massive, and slow-breeding; and so has purchased the lordship of the present at the price of the remote future. The kingdom of life is the very reverse of hereditary. The dominant animal spends its inheritance in reigning. Its reign may be brief or long; but, brief or long, at the end of it, awaiting it, is the absolute certainty of death.

The true heirs of the future are the small, fecund, and precocious creatures; those obscure, innumerable plastic species that die in myriads and yet do not diminish, that change this way or that as the pressure of necessity guides. The large predominant species flourish so long as the fight suits them, but when the battle turns against them they do not retreat, they perish. Man, for instance, is indisputably lord of the world as it is, and especially of the temperate zone; but, face to face with the advance of a fresh glacial epoch, or a sudden accession of terrestrial temperature, or the addition of some new constituent to the atmosphere, or a new and more deadly disease bacillus, he would remain obstinately man, with the instincts, proclivities, weaknesses, and possibilities that he has now. His individual adaptability and the subtlety of his contrivance are no doubt great, but his capacity for change as a species is, compared with that of a harvest mouse or a green-fly, infinitesimal. He would very probably go before the majority of such slight and flexible creatures. No doubt man is lord of the whole earth of to-day, but the lordship of the future is another matter. To give him that argues a confidence in the permanence of terrestrial conditions which has no justification either in geological or astronomical science. No doubt he is the heir of all the ages, but the herring, the frog, the Aphis, or the rabbit, it may be, is the residuary legatee.

THE DURATION OF LIFE

An essay of Weismann,[1] charming and profound, and written before the obsession of a logical theory had carried him into arid metaphysics, discusses the duration of life in men and animals. To many, perhaps to most living things, death comes unexpectedly, with an ironical indifference to the period of the animal's life, or to its business of the moment. The man may be preparing to be merry, the bird may be a-building, the butterfly not yet dry from the chrysalis, when they are fallen upon by blind mischance, by enemies intent only on dinner, or by unthinking microbes. Confronted by such extrinsic accidents, men cry out after their kind; the poet attuning an ineffectual lamentation, the moralist preaching, the pagan urging to the day of pleasure; but the naturalist must be dumb. His opportunity comes with the animals that avoid or escape colliding fates, and that yet, after a fixed period, run down like a clock. The seeds of death, apparently, have been lying inert in the body and come to fatal maturity after a lapse of time that varies little among individuals of the same species, but that is widely different among different kinds of animals.

Threescore and ten is the natural period of man's life. The elephant will live two hundred years, the horse but half a century. Singing-birds and fowls and pheasants will live for nearly twenty years, but parrots, eagles, falcons, and swans are known to survive their century. Some live through nearly two centuries. Queen-ants and worker-ants may live for years; Sir John Lubbock[2] kept a queen-ant

"Duration of Life"
SR 79 (Feb. 23, 1895): 248. [GW, GR]
    [1] See Weismann's "The Duration of Life," in *Essays upon Heredity*, 1: 3-66. This is Wells's basis throughout, save for his closing sentences about early man.
    [2] Ibid., p. 52, and editorial notes by Poulton, pp. 19, 52. Sir John Lubbock, First Baron Avebury (1834-1913), as a naturalist specialized in the study of ants. His books include *On the Origin and Metamorphosis of Insects* (1874); *Ants, Bees, and Wasps* (1882); and *On the Senses, Instincts, and Intelligence of Animals* (1888).

alive for thirteen years, during all which period she continued to lay fertile eggs; but the males live only a few days. Queen-bees live two or three years; workers and drones a few months, although, indeed, in one sense the death of the latter is unnatural, as the workers drive them away from the stores of food, so that they perish of starvation. Among insects generally, the period of adult life varies greatly. Many, like the May-flies, dance in the sun only for a few hours: the sexes meet, the eggs are deposited, and the creatures die before nightfall. Many butterflies and moths are unprovided with feeding organs, and live only a few hours, others for many days. Some snails and shell-fish are annual, maturing in spring, growing and breeding through the summer, and leaving their eggs to maintain the species during the cold of winter. Others are biennial, others, again, live for many years, growing to gigantic size.

Leaving out of count certain minor factors, like the time required for growing to a large size, and the slower growth of animals that must waste time and energy in capturing living food, it is certain that there is an intimate connection all through the animal kingdom between the duration of life and the reproductive habits. Animals, in one sense, are like the bright and fragrant flowers of plants; since, when their function is accomplished, when seeds are formed, they wither and perish. The business of the animal seems to be, not to live its own life, but to reproduce its own kind, and the term of life at its disposal is adjusted accurately to the special difficulties of this purpose. Weismann and Alfred Russel Wallace[3] suggest that death comes as soon as possible after the due number of successors has been produced, in order that each species may always be represented by a full tale of young and vigorous individuals. Natural selection acts like a contractor who has undertaken to keep a window-box gay with fresh blossoms: each plant must be removed almost before its flowers fade.

[3]See Weismann, *Essays upon Heredity,* 1:23-24.

But our present concern is with the fact rather than with explanation of the fact. Taking the needs of reproduction as a master-key, we find it unlocking the secret of inequalities in life. The May-flies live only a few hours, but their eggs are produced abundantly, and have only to be dropped into the pools from which the parents, leaving their chrysalids, sprang into the sunny air. The short-lived moths and butterflies similarly are untroubled by family cares. When the eggs have to be deposited on common and abundant food-plants, the females need and possess few hours in which to accomplish their easy task. The males, on the other hand, have to fly about seeking and sometimes fighting for possession of the females, and to them a longer life is allotted. Butterflies and moths that live for more than a few days are those whose caterpillars require a rarer food-plant, a more carefully chosen nursery and feeding-ground. The females have to fly about seeking convenient spots for their offspring, and the eggs, instead of ripening and being deposited simultaneously, are laid from day to day until the full tale be accomplished. In many tribes of bees, the males play their part but once, and that during the nuptial flight of the queen; immediately afterwards they die, or shortly after are killed by the workers. The queens, secluded in the middle of the hive, produce crops of workers year after year, and so their lives are prolonged.

Among the birds and beasts, parental cares have brought length of days with them. The small singing-birds are rapid breeders, sometimes producing five or six nestlings twice a year; but their enemies are equally numerous, and, despite the constant attention of male and female, play such havoc with the young that hardly in twenty years will a pair rear up young enough to maintain the species. Birds like pheasants and fowls are still more prolific, but old and young alike are preyed upon by a multitude of enemies. The birds of prey are slow breeders; their active flight makes it impossible that the females should carry with them a burden of developing eggs, and, in their long lives, they leave behind them no more progeny than quicker-breeding, shorter-lived creatures.

All the mammals survive the time at which they bring forth their young, and among them, as among birds, habits of feeding and living determine their prolificness; and the rate at which they reproduce their young determines their length of days. The elephant must roam over great tracts of country in search of food for his vast framework. The mother carries her young for nearly two years, the young take twenty years to become mature, and thus the elephant may live through many generations of quicker-breeding animals. Among men living in communities, and resorting to infanticide or to emigration, the conditions are artificial; and we know little of the length of days in the savage populations that keep in equilibrium with their environment. But we know how races that become parents while they are yet children, are senile when more slowly maturing races are in the vigour of adult life. Again we know how among polygamous races the males are shorter-lived, producing like horses more progeny in a shorter time. As the qualities of tenderness and pity and love are the race's reward for parental cares, so its males, long-lived from ancient monogamous habit, have been able to acquire and transmit the traditional lore that is the origin of all our wisdom and our arts.

DEATH

In a recent essay,[1] natural death was presented as a careful gardener, weeding out the old that there might be room for the new, and not as a casual intruder scattering wanton destruction. In order that each regiment of animals and plants may be kept full of creatures resplendent with young and vigorous life, an age is fixed at which the battered veterans must retire. In some regiments the notice is short and sharp; individuals are hustled out of the ranks the moment their business is accomplished. In others there is a retiring allowance of life, and individuals drift through senility towards their end. The nature of the end we conceive from our knowledge of it in man and the higher animals, and conceive it erroneously. For with the higher animals what we call death is a sudden cessation of the gross functions of the body. There is a moment at which the watchers say "this, that was alive, is now dead." Death has come by one of the *atria mortis*, the three gates; by failure of the heart, or the lungs, or the brain, the mechanism has broken down and stops suddenly and visibly. Even in old age when there has been a slow degeneration of all the organs, the final arrest of their functions comes sharply, at a particular moment. But this suddenness is no part of the real nature of the event. The point of time varies with the skill of the surgeon, and with the appliances at his disposal. It is not until long after the moment at which it seems to us that the spirit has left the body that the tissues are dead. For hours afterwards the skin remains alive, the hairs grow, the sweat-glands are in repulsive activity, while the muscles respond

"Death"
SR 79 (March 23, 1895): 376-77. [*GW, GR*]
    [1] Wells alludes to his "The Duration of Life," to which "Death" is a sequel (both pieces are unsigned). As in the earlier essay, his starting point is Weismann's "The Duration of Life" (essay 1 in *Essays upon Heredity*) and this leads into an original meditation founded upon Weismann's essay 3, "Life and Death," *Essays upon Heredity*, 1:107-161.

to electrical stimulation by nightmare contortions. The body of a man is a highly integrated structure; each organ has a communion so intimate with every other organ that failure of any part is reflected upon the whole, and the breakdown of heart, or lungs, or brain brings slow but irremediable disaster upon the whole body. In this we have to distinguish two things: what we call death—the sudden arrest that is an accident of the complex harmony of the body, as when a steamship is stopped in mid-ocean by the rupture of a valve—and the actual death of the living protoplasm of the cells and tissues.

In the descending scale of animal life, the relations between the organs are less and less intimate, and the misleading suddenness of the arrest of their machinery fades away. The heart of a turtle, from which the brain has been removed, will continue to beat for days. A worm or a star-fish may be cut in pieces, and each piece remains alive, sometimes even reproducing the whole. Who shall name the point of death of an oyster, or of a sea-anemone? No stoppage of a single organ causes sudden and conspicuous change in the whole; when protoplasmic death of a part occurs, either the part is sloughed away and replaced, or the ripples of destructive change spread slowly from cell to cell, each unaffected part remaining active to the last. In the simplest animals of all, organisms that consist each of a single cell, death may be seen at its lowest terms. There is no composite multicellular body, no bodily mechanism to break down, no possibility of the failure of one set of cells gradually creeping upon others. Each organism is alive or dead as its protoplasm is alive or dead.

Here, in their simplest forms, are life and death; and here, asking if death be inherent in living matter, we find surprising answer. Violence of heat and cold, mechanical forces and the assaults of chemical affinities may destroy these single particles of life; but if not overthrown by rude accident, and if provided with food and drink, their protoplasm lives for ever. Each particle feeds, until, outgrowing a convenient size, it cleaves asunder and the one life becomes two lives. So far as reason and observation can inform us, the living particles in the ponds and seas of to-day have descended in a direct continuity of living material from the first dawn of life. No other solution is open, save the possibility of a spontaneous generation of living matter so continual and so common that it could not have eluded the search of science. This is that "immortality of the protozoa" hinted at by Lankester in England,[2] blazoned into fame by Weismann.

Whether or no the protoplasm of the tissues of higher organisms be potentially immortal, can be only a matter of inference. The reproductive cells, indeed, form a living chain, binding the animals and plants of the present with the animals and plants of the remotest past. This reproductive protoplasm is immortal in precisely the same sense as the protoplasm of single cells is immortal, and there seems no reason to believe with Weismann that the protoplasm of the other tissues has acquired mortality, and is different in kind. It dies, but only because it is part of a complex structure. The machinery of the body is not regulated to last for ever; on the other hand, it is to the advantage of the race that it should break down when reproduction has been accomplished, and its breakdown results in the ruin of its component parts. There is no reason to suppose that the protoplasm itself grows old. A slip cut from a tree many centuries old, may be grafted on a young tree and so enter on a new lease of life. Were the process to be continued, a continuity of protoplasmic life might be maintained. So far as we can tell, death is not inherent in living matter. Protoplasm may live for ever, as a flame shielded from the wind and fed from an endless store would burn for ever.

Interesting as it may be, this triumph over death is barren and formal in the sense that affects us most. The

---

[2] Sir Edwin Ray Lankester (1847-1929) did research on protozoa, particularly the parasitic varieties.

life that endures is life only in an abstract sense. It is individual life that appeals to our emotions, individual death that broods over our joys. Even among the protozoa, the individuals that come into being are new individuals, the parent divided in two is as surely dead as if a corruptible body were left behind. Mortal man and the immortal protozoa have the same barren immortality; the individuals perish, living on only in their descendants, creatures of their body, separated pieces of their undying protoplasm; the type alone persists.

CONCERNING SKELETONS

There are certain questions that, in our present state of physiological knowledge, scientific men, perhaps, do well not to touch, and yet that display as we turn them over such strange uncertain glitterings of suggestion, that it is hard for an irresponsible writer to leave them altogether alone. And one very curious set of unanswered interrogations centre around all these harder parts of skeletal structure that we speak of as shells or bone. *Quo bono?*—if we may ask as much. We refer not so much to bars of gristle as to the skeleton of ordinary language, the hard, brittle structures of phosphate of lime and carbonate of lime. The answer every schoolboy knows with assurance, and every biological student knows it to be anything but satisfactory. Such bars form a framework for the physiological mechanism, an attachment for muscles, a protection for the most vital parts, and so forth. But that does not explain quite a number of little objections of which the schoolboy does not dream.

In the first place, why is it almost always, in the main, phosphate or carbonate of lime? Every animal that is more than microscopic—except some sponges—favours this basis of lime, when it indulges in a hard brittle skeleton at all; and so do most plants that have definite skeletal structure. All the big land animals have it within their bones; the crustacea, mollusca, and brachiopods have it, as a rule, outside on their shells; the coral is enthroned on it; and the large majority of those vertebrates that possess only a tough gristly skeleton within have plates of bony substance on the exterior. Yet there seems to be a competing substance—*silica*, the substance of rock crystal and flint—that forms the light and very beautiful skeleton of the glassy sponges, and of those exquisite "objects for the

"Concerning Skeletons"
SR 81 (June 27, 1896): 646-47. [*GW*, *GR*]

microscope," the Radiolarians and Diatoms. Why do we find no large skeletons of silica? It has many advantages. It is harder than the lime salts, almost twice as hard, rather harder than glass in fact, but not so brittle; it is lighter, and is less amenable to solvents. For teeth, in particular, it is to be recommended—consider the advantages of teeth of flint! Regarding the matter from the point of view of structure, a man would be hardy to deny that the body of a higher vertebrate would not be improved mechanically by the substitution. One may urge that it is not obtainable; but the bamboo gets enough from soil-water to make its canes turn a clasp knife, and from the sea-water, at any rate, the sponge can weave a very handsome and substantial skeleton. This remarkable preference for the salts of lime, softer, heavier, soluble, and more easily fractured, is certainly a puzzling fact.

And next; why is this hard substance, apart from its nature, present at all? You may suggest it gives a rigidity necessary for the animal mechanism, and otherwise unattainable. But an important section of the fishes—the powerful dog-fish, the shark, the lamprey, are examples—has a fine efficient musculature on a skeleton of gristle. Where this happens, then, usually the lime salts appear upon the exterior in tooth-like scales; but this is not the case with the lamprey. And with rigidity comes brittleness. When it is outside, as it is in many molluscs, one can understand its presence better on the plea of armour. But the coral and cuttlefish defy explanation. The former lives not inside its cup and protected by it, but overlapping the top like the froth in a full tankard of porter. Its massive calcareous cup is no protection, no basis for muscles, no bodily support. And the cuttlefish manages all the practical needs of its body with a very admirable skeleton of gristle, and then—has a big lump of calcareous matter imbedded along the upper side of its body. The allied Nautilus and the extinct Ammonites display enormous chambered shells of absolutely mysterious import. Then the Foraminifera, those delicate organisms of the deep sea, have the most exquisite little shells of carbonate of lime floating about in the living slime of their bodies.

Through the animal and vegetable kingdom it is surprising the enormous preponderance of species containing at some point of their organism accumulations of salts of lime. The medical student will recall at once the patches of crystal under the backbone of the frog, and the little crystals and needles of the rhubarb leaf and the bluebell stem; and the vast, needlessly clumsy skeletons of many of the earlier mammals and reptiles (*Brontosaurus* and *Titanotherium e.g.*), and the unwieldy fossil shells (*Hippurites e.g.*), which occur in the secondary strata, will come back at once into the memory of the palæontologist. The general reader will be reminded of the turtle's carapace. One might think that some fundamental vital principle was involved, that in some quite unknown way lime had to come into the organism, and that, once in, it was exceedingly hard to remove any excess of it again. It is well to note that in many cases the lime salts overflow the skeleton, may even do so fatally, as in ossification of the heart. No one can consider the facts of the case and go on believing that all these shells and bones of lime salts are simply explicable as a response to the need of support and armature. In the first place, there was an apparently more convenient material to hand, and in the next, calcareous accumulations turn up again and again where, if anything, so far as our knowledge of the mechanism goes, they would be better absent.

So we find shells and bones repeating in the same vague terms the lesson that the study of animal coloration has in a dim, indecisive way suggested; the lesson that the line of advance in biology lies now along the path of physiological chemistry. What are accidental and what are essential, what substance may replace this constituent and what that, among all the vast complex of compounds that stream into and then stream out again from that

wonderful eddy, that dark tumult of synthesis and decomposition that is—from the physical standpoint—life? is now
the prominent question awaiting attack in this science.
Biological philosophy drifts steadily from that popular
view that every isolated feature in an animal's anatomy
has a precise and complete relation to external necessities,
and that the vein of "pedigree" morphology still contains
abundant ore. From the consideration of the relations of
species to species, of a species to its surroundings, attention
shifts to the general laws that govern the relations of this
set of organs in an animal to that. What determinate
balance may exist between the relative development of
the liver and the pigmentation of an animal, or between
its teeth and its pancreas? are sample questions that will
convey the character of the series of problems zoology
must sooner or later systematically undertake.

ANOTHER BASIS FOR LIFE

Very attractive is the question whether life extends beyond the limits of this little planet of ours. The latest contribution to this branch of speculation is that made by Sir Robert Ball,[1] who, like his predecessors, starts from the hypothesis that the phenomena of life are inseparably associated with certain complex combinations of the chemical elements carbon, nitrogen, hydrogen, and oxygen, and proceeds to search space for these elements under conditions of temperature that admit of vitality. Undeniably, so far as our assured knowledge goes, this association is forced upon us; protoplasm, the common basis of all terrestrial life, is a highly unstable and complicated grouping mainly of the atoms of these four elements and sulphur, and all the phenomena we call vital, up to and including the processes of mind, are associated with the decomposition of some of this substance and the oxidation of carbon and hydrogen. Yet it is certainly open to question whether this connexion of life with the five elements specified above is absolutely inevitable, whether there are not other groups to be found which may be conceived of as running through a series of combinations and decompositions that would afford the necessary material basis for a quasi-conscious and even mental superstructure.

The life that depends upon the interplay of carbon, nitrogen, hydrogen, oxygen, and sulphur is limited by comparatively narrow bounds in the scale of temperature. It does not seem to be possible above the boiling-point of water or far below the freezing-point. Within these limits the net result of vital processes—from the point of view of material science—is the oxidation of a certain amount

"Another Basis"
SR 78 (Dec. 22, 1894): 676-77. [*GW, GR*]

[1] Sir Robert Stawell Ball (1840-1913), mathematician and astronomer and popularizer of astronomical concepts, published "The Possibility of Life in Other Worlds" in the *Fortnightly Review* 56 (Nov. 1894): 718-729. Wells reviewed his *Story of the Sun* for the *PMG* (see the Appendix, no. 28).

of previously unoxidized material and the formation of stable and inert substances. On the supposition, accepted by all scientific men, that the earth is undergoing a steady process of cooling, there was formerly a phase in its existence when life, as we know it, was impossible because of the excessive temperature; and in the future it will again become impossible when the temperature is such that the products of vital activity (of which the principal are carbon-dioxide and water) become solid at the moment of formation, and can no longer be thrown off by the living substance. In that remote future we may anticipate that the former basis of life will form under the chilly atmosphere a lifeless covering to the dead earth, and that if we could travel forward in time we should find above the present rocks layers of ice, solid ammonium carbonate, solid carbon-dioxide, a large series of compounds of carbon with its former contributors to the vital process, once quasi-fluid and active, but now solid and inert.

The crust of the earth, so far as we have been able to investigate it, contains a vast assembly of compounds of the elements silicon and aluminium, with various metals. Clay consists of these two and the elements of water; ordinary sand and the quartz of granite are two forms of an oxide of silicon quite parallel with carbon dioxide; all the other constituents of granite, moreover, contain silicon and aluminium. The whole science of mineralogy, indeed, turns upon silicon and aluminium, and, excepting the carbon and nitrogen compounds, we can find nowhere else such an extensive variety of groupings, such a ringing of the changes of combination, as we have in the case of these two elements. But under existing conditions of temperature, all the innumerable mineral species are mere inert oxidized matter, stable, static, and dead.

Rather more than a year ago Professor Emerson Reynolds[2] pointed out that at very much higher temperatures

[2] James Emerson Reynolds (1844-1920), English chemist, spent the latter part of his life studying silicon compounds. Wells summarizes a portion of Reynolds's "Opening Address" to the British Association for the Advancement of Science

this immobility of the silicon compounds might be exchanged for a vigorous activity; that at temperatures above the points of decomposition of the majority of the carbon-nitrogen compounds a silicon-aluminium series may conceivably have presented cycles of complicated syntheses, decompositions, and oxidations essentially parallel to those that underlie our own vital phenomena. He then laid stress upon the numberless points in which carbon and silicon resemble each other and differ from the remainder of the elements, their unconquerable solidity and the similarity of the three solid forms of each, the peculiar relation of their atomic weights in Mendelejeff's series,[3] the parallelism of their compounds—normal silicates to carbonates, silica to carbon dioxide, chloroform to silicon chloroform—and so forth. Altogether his case was at least fascinatingly plausible. And if we are to admit the possibility that the chemical accompaniments of life were rehearsed long ago and at far higher temperatures by elements now inert, it is not such a very long step from this to the supposition that vital, sub-conscious, and conscious developments may have accompanied such a rehearsal.

One is startled towards fantastic imaginings by such a suggestion: visions of silicon-aluminium organisms—why not silicon-aluminium men at once?—wandering through an atmosphere of gaseous sulphur, let us say, by the shores of a sea of liquid iron some thousand degrees or so above the temperature of a blast furnace. But that, of course, is merely a dream. The possibility of a material evolution of an analogue to protoplasm in the past history of our planet upon a silicon-aluminium basis is, however, something more than a dream. And in this connexion it is interesting to remark, as bearing upon their relative im-

---

as it was reported in *Nature* 48 (Sept. 14, 1893): 477-481.

[3] Dmitri Mendeleev (1834-1907), the great Russian chemist, originator of the system for classifying chemical elements in periodic sequence on the basis of their atomic weights.

portance in extra-terrestrial space, that silicon is a far more abundant and frequent constituent of meteorites than carbon, and that the photosphere of the sun, which is frequently spoken of as incandescent carbon, is just as probably silicon in the incandescent state.

V. *Precarious Man*

He came straight from England, where Nature is hedged, ditched, and drained into the perfection of submission, and he had suddenly discovered the insignificance of man. ... He began to perceive that man is indeed a rare animal, having but a precarious hold upon this land.

"The Empire of the Ants"[1]

The "opposite idea" which most fascinated Wells and evoked some of his most imaginative work from the late 1880s until at least the turn of the century concerns the precarious position of man in the universe. The threats he envisioned to man's hegemony in the order of nature were many and diverse—threats that might lie in the dark potentialities of the human species itself or in those of some other species as yet undiscovered or overlooked in the "abysses" of this or other worlds. One possibility is that man through his own doing would bring about conditions where the laws of nature would determine his extinction,[2] or that he would be transformed beyond recognition in the course of evolutionary change. The other is that man would be supplanted in a violent struggle for existence by some creature with greater capacity "of appetite, en-

[1] *AtlEd*, 10: 493. On "The Empire of the Ants" (1905) and another of Wells's short stories, "The Sea Raiders" (1896), as parables of the ascendancy of nature over man, see D. Y. Hughes, "H. G. Wells: Ironic Romancer," *Extrapolation* 6 (1965): 32-38.

The chronological order of the *essays* discussed in this introduction is as follows: "Zoological Retrogression" (Sept. 1891); "On Extinction" (Sept. 1893); "The Man of the Year Million" (Nov. 1893); "The Extinction of Man" (Sept. 1894); "Intelligence on Mars" (April 1896). As noted below, two of these essays Wells had reprinted in *CPM* (for which reason they are not anthologized here).

[2] Wells's most thorough exploration of this possibility is to be found in the various versions of *The Time Machine* (see chap. 3).

durance, or destruction" ("Zoological Retrogression") or
with greater intelligence than man at present possesses.[3]

Deriving from Wells's vision of nature moving towards
"things that are altogether new" ("The 'Cyclic' Delusion"), these speculations on the precariousness of man
of course have their basis in, and take their immediate
impetus from, biology. "The long roll of palaeontology is
half filled with the records of extermination" ("On Extinction"). Moreover, fossil evidence also shows that the anni-
hilation of a species often follows a period in which that
species is dominant: "In the case of every other predominant animal [that is, other than man] the world has ever
seen, . . . the hour of its complete ascendency has been
the eve of its entire overthrow."[4] From the temporal
perspective of evolution, Darwinian theory, far from
guaranteeing a species' permanent ascendency, offers only
the alternative of "profound modification" ("Zoological
Retrogression") or extinction.

Resistance to this alternative is the theme of "A Vision
of the Past" (1887). There the narrator dreams of an age
of reptilian monsters—presumably in the mesozoic past—
who are convinced that the earth was made for them, "the
culminating point of all existence, the noblest of all beings
who have ever existed or ever will exist." "This world,"
they think, "is ours for ever, and we must progress for
ever into infinite perfection." When *homo sapiens* declares
to them that "your race will in a few million years . . .
be wholly extinct," they attempt to refute him by an
argumentum ad concoctionem. But he wakes up before
they can eat him. The parallel between the attitude of
these reptilians and that of man becomes explicit by
comparison with the opening sentences of "The Extinction
of Man": "It is part of the excessive egotism of the human
animal that the bare idea of its extinction seems incredible

---

[3] See especially "The Sea Raiders," *The War of the Worlds* (1898), and "The
Empire of the Ants," among Wells's fiction.

[4] "The Extinction of Man," *CPM*, p. 179. The essay is reprinted in *CPM*,
with a slight addition, from the *PMG* 59 (Sept. 25, 1894): 3.

to it. 'A world without *us*!' it says, as a heady young Cephalapsis [a now extinct species of fish] might have said it in the old Silurian sea.'"[5]

Wells again attacks man's complacency about his evolutionary future in "Zoological Retrogression" (1891). Against the popular belief in "Excelsior biology"—that the course of human evolution will forever be straightforwardly onward and upward—Wells advances the "antithesis" that the natural history of evolution includes incidents of devolution. More paradoxical still, devolution is sometimes nature's way of doubling back to take a new trail, is sometimes "a plastic process in nature," a means of adjusting to changing environmental conditions: witness the mud-fish. Who knows if nature will require a similar backsliding on the part of "the last of the mud-fish family, man"? Whether in the future the "profound modification" of the human animal "will be, according to present ideals, upward or downward, no one can forecast."

On the other hand, man's tenure may be cut off altogether. It is not impossible that instead of "the Coming Man," nature is preparing a "Coming Beast" to "sweep *homo* away into the darkness from which his universe arose" ("Zoological Retrogression"). Or, as Wells hints in "On Extinction" (1893), the human species may come to the end Thomas Hood envisions in "The Last Man" (1826). In that poem, the human race has been reduced by plague to two survivors, a hangman and a beggar; the one executes the other so that only one man remains, (in Wells's words) "looking extinction in the face."

But even if man continues to evolve, the species as it is at present may in effect cease to exist. "The coming man," Wells ventures to infer in "The Man of the Year Million," "will clearly have a larger brain, and a slighter body than the present."[6] Indeed, the bodily appendages

---

[5] Ibid., p. 172.

[6] "Of a Book Unwritten" (the title of the revision of an essay which first appeared in the *PMG* 57 [Nov. 6, 1893]: 3, as "The Man of the Year Million") in *CPM*, p. 164.

of the brain may well atrophy and in time disappear, to be replaced by mechanical devices; with the result that future men may resemble "human tadpoles."[7] In that case, the form of "the Coming Man" (who would look something like the giant ganglion that is the Grand Lunar of the Selenites in *The First Men in the Moon* [1901]) would not differ much from that of "the Coming Beast" Wells imagines as a large octopuslike creature in "The Sea Raiders" (1896) and *The War of the Worlds* (1898).[8] Nor would formal characteristics be the only possible point of resemblance: their fates, too, might be similar. The bacteria that destroy the Martians figure in "The Extinction of Man" as the fourth and final cause Wells specifies as conceivably terminating the reign of man in the future.[9]

Thus the man of a million years from now, the being who will emerge from the abyss of the future, may be similar to the creatures that Wells fancies may prove the nemesis of present-day man—creatures perhaps already biding their time in the abysses of the sea or of space. Enough is known about the life that in the ocean deeps "drags out under conditions almost inconceivably unlike our own" "to stimulate the imagination" in this regard, "and not enough to cramp its play" ("Life in the Abyss" [1894]). The only thing one can be sure of, Wells insists,

[7] Ibid., p. 171. In another essay reprinted in *CPM*, "Incidental Thoughts on a Bald Head"·(originally in the *PMG* 60 [March 1, 1895]: 10), Wells from a contemplation of bald-headedness goes on to theorize about "a kind of inherent disposition on the part of your human animal to dwindle" to the point where "at last may [man] not disappear altogether ... and a democracy of honest machinery, neatly clad and loaded up with sound principles of action, walk to and fro in a regenerate world?" (*CPM* pp. 159, 160).

[8] On the connection between "The Sea Raiders" and *The War of the Worlds* and these essays of Wells's, see R. M. Philmus, *Into the Unknown* (Berkeley and Los Angeles: University of California Press, 1970), pp. 29-30.

[9] Wells advances four "suggestions out of a host of others" "against this complacency" man entertains towards his future: aside from bacteria, predatory crabs or huge octopuses or migratory ants may, any one of them, bring about the end of man's dominance. The crabs appear in "The Further Vision" of *The Time Machine*; both the Martians and "the sea raiders" are octopuslike; army ants threaten to overrun first South America, then the world, in "The Empire of the Ants"; and disease bacilli play a part in *The War of the Worlds* and "The Stolen Bacillus" (1894).

is that this "abyssmal life" (*sic*) of the sea or of space will not be akin to man as he is at present. "No phase of anthropomorphism," he writes in "Intelligence on Mars" (1896), "is more naive than the supposition of men on Mars": "granted that there has been an evolution of protoplasm upon Mars," Darwinian theory provides good "reason to think that the creatures on Mars would be different from the creatures of earth, in form and function, in structure and in habit, different beyond the most bizarre imaginings of nightmare."

However bizarre by anthropomorphic standards, the Martians—or Selenites—may foreshadow the men of the future. If so, the alternative seemingly open to man—profound modification or extinction—would ultimately be specious. The convergence, however, emphasizes Wells's intent, which is to point out that present-day man precludes the possibility of real ethical choices about his destiny so long as he complacently refuses to recognize how precarious his future is.

A VISION OF THE PAST

It was a sultry afternoon in July. For three hours had I been toiling along a straight and exceedingly dusty road—Roman in origin, rectitude, and grit—and having reached the foot of a steep hill, and feeling exceedingly weary, I sought some shade where I might rest. Hard by the road I observed a narrow foot-path, and following this I came to a tenebrous pine-forest, and there, lying down to meditate, I presently fell asleep, and lo! I dreamed a dream.

It seemed to me that I was being borne rapidly through a swiftly changing scene, and I heard a voice like the rushing of wind through a forest say, "Come into the past—into the past." And then my flight ceased, and I was let to the ground with some force.

Although still reposing at the foot of a tree, I was no longer in a pine-wood. A vast plain stretched around me to the horizon in all directions save one, where in the distance a volcanic peak rose high into the liquid atmosphere. Between where I lay and this peak was a wide calm lake, across which faint ripples were sweeping before a gentle breeze. The shore nearest me was low and marshy, but on the opposite side there arose steep cliffs from the water's edge. Behind these came a series of low hills, and finally the peak behind all. The plain appeared covered by some kind of moss unknown to me, and clumps of unfamiliar trees were frequent. To the vegetation around me, however, I paid but little heed, as my attention was almost immediately attracted, and powerful emotions awakened, by the sight of a strange living form.

On the marshy border of the lake a reptile-like creature, heavy and ungainly, was slowly moving along. Its head was turned from me; its knees nearly touched the ground;

"Vision of the Past"

Science Schools Journal, no. 7 (June 1887), pp. 206-09. [*GW*; signed "Sosthenes Smith"]

and hence its progressive movements were clumsy in the extreme. In particular I noticed that as it raised its foot preparatory to making a step it turned the sole backwards in a manner ludicrous to behold. After watching its movements for some time without being at all able to comprehend what the object of these movements might be, I began to imagine that its only object must be the making of footmarks in the mud. This appeared to me a strange and useless proceeding.

With the intent to benefit science, I attempted to identify the nature of this creature; but, being only accustomed to identify by means of bones and of teeth, I could not do so in this case, because its bones were hidden by its flesh, and because a certain diffidence, that I now feel inclined to regret, prevented any examination of its teeth.

After a time this uncouth beast began slowly to turn round towards me, and then, indeed, I beheld what appeared to me more surprising than all the other grotesque features I had observed; for this strange beast had three eyes, one being in the centre of its forehead; and it looked at me with all three in such a manner that the strangest feelings of fear and trembling were aroused within me, and I made a vain effort to shift myself back a century or so. I was right glad when at length it turned its weird gaze once more towards the lake. At the same time that it did this it made a noise such as I had never before heard, and I live in the faith and the hope that I never shall hear it again. The auditory impression is ineffaceably impressed upon my memory, but I lack words, and hesitate even to attempt, to convey its horrors to the minds of my readers.

Immediately after this sound the calm waters of the lake were disturbed, and there soon appeared above the surface the heads of numerous creatures like unto the first. These all swam rapidly towards the spot where this one stood, and dragged themselves on to the shore; and then I plainly observed what seemed the very strangest thing of all in these creatures—to wit, that they were able to converse together by means of sounds.

And here, alas! I must tell of the greatest loss to science that there has been for many a year; for when I had recovered from my surprise at hearing these strange creatures converse with one another, there flashed upon my mind a process of reasoning by which one could deduce the possession of speaking powers by these beasts from the characters of their lumbar vertebræ. But, sad to relate! I have tried in vain to recall this train of reasoning, which might have proved so valuable in the investigation of many fossil creatures. Many a sleepless night have I spent in trying to recall it, but in vain. I believe the method was to find something about the spinal cord from the vertebræ, about the brain from the spinal cord, and about language from the brain.

But to return to my dream. I was by this time too accustomed to strange things to be in any degree astonished on finding that I could understand what these creatures said, though whether by telepathy or other means it was that I understood them I know not.

They were plainly engaged in listening to a philosophic discourse by the one I had first seen. They stood (or kneeled, for there was little difference between these two postures) around this one in a semi-circle. He gravely closed his median eye (which I took to be his manner of expressing the feeling of solemnity), and then began thuswise: "O Něm" (which I took to be the name of these creatures), "happy in being Něm, thrice happy in being Něm of Dnalgne" (which I took to be the name of that tribe of Něm to which these belonged), "look at the wondrous world around, and think that it is for our use that this world has been formed. Look at the strata displayed in yon scarped cliff, and the facts which they record of the past history of this earth during the many ages in which it has slowly been preparing itself for the reception of us, the culminating point of all existence, the noblest of all beings who have ever existed or ever will exist." Here all the listeners violently winked their median eye, which I took to be a sign of applause and commendation. "Observe our structure, and see how far removed we are from all other living creatures. Think of the wondrous and complicated structure of our teeth; recollect that we alone of living creatures possess the two methods of breathing at different stages in our life, that our median eye is developed to an extent unknown among all the lower animals. Think of all these things, and be proud" (violent winking of the median eye). "And if such we are at present, what may we not expect the future to have in store for us? During all the vast ages to come we shall continue upon this earth, while lower beings pass away and are replaced. This world is ours for ever, and we must progress for ever unto infinite perfection." (Convulsive working of the median eye, accompanied by strange snorting sounds.)

Hitherto I had listened with great amusement at the absurd claims to such a lofty position, made by a creature so inferior to myself in all respects as this philosophic amphibian; but at this point I could no longer restrain myself, and rushing forward I addressed him thuswise:

"O, foolish creature! Think you yourself the great end of all creation? Know, then, that you are but a poor amphibian; that, far from lasting for ever, your race will in a few million years—a trifle in comparison with the enormous lapses of geological chronology—be wholly extinct; that higher forms than you will, by insensible gradations, spring from you and succeed you; that you are here only for the purpose of preparing the earth for the reception of those higher forms, which in turn will but prepare it for the advent of that glorious race of reasoning and soul-possessing beings, who, through the endless æons of the future, will never cease their onward march towards infinite perfection—a race of which I—" But at this point I began to perceive that my eloquence was not pleasing to my audience, and that they all began to move slowly but surely in directions converging on myself. No one who has not known (and which of my readers has?) the feelings aroused by the consciousness of being gazed at by three eyes appertaining to the same individual can form any conception of my feelings when I found myself so glared at by at least a score of three-eyed creatures, as they slowly crept nearer and nearer. Terror completely paralysed me; I could not move a step nor utter a sound. Slowly—so slowly that they scarcely seemed to move—did these creatures approach me, never for a moment ceasing that intense, awful gaze. Nearer and nearer they came, their huge mouths opened; they seemed ready to crush me between their powerful jaws—until at the moment when they seemed to touch me I made one despairing effort, and—I awoke, and behold! it was a dream.

I rose from my resting-place beneath the trees at once, for the evening was come and the grove had grown cold, and quickly made my way over the hill to the nearest railway station, glad to have safely returned into the more congenial atmosphere of the recent epoch.

ZOOLOGICAL RETROGRESSION

Perhaps no scientific theories are more widely discussed or more generally misunderstood among cultivated people than the views held by biologists regarding the past history and future prospects of their province—life. Using their technical phrases and misquoting their authorities in an invincibly optimistic spirit, the educated public has arrived in its own way at a rendering of their results which it finds extremely satisfactory. It has decided that in the past the great scroll of nature has been steadily unfolding to reveal a constantly richer harmony of forms and successively higher grades of being, and it assumes that this "evolution" will continue with increasing velocity under the supervision of its extreme expression—man. This belief, as effective, progressive, and pleasing as transformation scenes at a pantomime, receives neither in the geological record nor in the studies of the phylogenetic embryologist any entirely satisfactory confirmation.

On the contrary, there is almost always associated with the suggestion of advance in biological phenomena an opposite idea, which is its essential complement. The technicality expressing this would, if it obtained sufficient currency in the world of culture, do much to reconcile the naturalist and his traducers. The toneless glare of optimistic evolution would then be softened by a shadow; the monotonous reiteration of "Excelsior" by people who did not climb would cease; the too sweet harmony of the spheres would be enhanced by a discord, this evolutionary antithesis—degradation.

Isolated cases of degeneration have long been known, and popular attention has been drawn to them in order to point well-meant moral lessons, the fallacious analogy of species to individual being employed. It is only recently,

"Zoological Retrogression"
Gentleman's Magazine 271 (Sept. 1891): 246-53. [Signed]

however, that the enormous importance of degeneration as a plastic process in nature has been suspected and its entire parity with evolution recognised.

It is no libel to say that three-quarters of the people who use the phrase, "organic evolution," interpret it very much in this way:—Life began with the amœba, and then came jelly-fish, shell-fish, and all those miscellaneous invertebrate things, and then *real* fishes and amphibia, reptiles, birds, mammals, and man, the last and first of creation. It has been pointed out that this is very like regarding a man as the offspring of his first cousins; these, of his second; these, of his relations at the next remove, and so forth—making the remotest living human being his primary ancestor. Or, to select another image, it is like elevating the modest poor relation at the family gathering to the unexpected altitude of fountain-head—a proceeding which would involve some cruel reflections on her age and character. The sounder view is, as scientific writers have frequently insisted, that living species have varied along divergent lines from intermediate forms, and, as it is the object of this paper to point out, not necessarily in an upward direction.

In fact, the path of life, so frequently compared to some steadily-rising mountain-slope, is far more like a footway worn by leisurely wanderers in an undulating country. Excelsior biology is a popular and poetic creation—the *real* form of a phylum, or line of descent, is far more like the course of a busy man moving about a great city. Sometimes it goes underground, sometimes it doubles and twists in tortuous streets, now it rises far overhead along some viaduct, and, again, the river is taken advantage of in these varied journeyings to and fro. Upward and downward these threads of pedigree interweave, slowly working out a pattern of accomplished things that is difficult to interpret, but in which scientific observers certainly fail to discover that inevitable tendency to higher and better things with which the word "evolution" is popularly associated.

The best known, and, perhaps, the most graphic and typical, illustration of the downward course is to be found in the division of the *Tunicata*. These creatures constitute a group which is, in several recent schemes of classification, raised to the high rank of a sub-phylum, and which includes, among a great variety of forms, the fairly common Sea Squirts, or *Ascidians,* of our coasts. By an untrained observer a specimen of these would at first very probably be placed in the mineral or vegetable kingdoms. Externally they are simply shapeless lumps of a stiff, semi-transparent, cartilaginous substance, in which pebbles, twigs, and dirt are imbedded, and only the most careful examination of this unpromising exterior would discover any evidence of the living thing within. A penknife, however, serves to lay bare the animal inside this house, or "test," and the fleshy texture of the semi-transparent body must then convince the unscientific investigator of his error.

He would forthwith almost certainly make a fresh mistake in his classification of this new animal. Like most zoologists until a comparatively recent date, he would think of such impassive and, from the human point of view, lowly beings as the oyster and mussel as its brethren, and a superficial study of its anatomy might even strengthen this opinion. As a matter of fact, however, these singular creatures are far more closely related to the vertebrata—they lay claim to the quarterings not of molluscs, but of imperial man! and, like novelette heroes with a birth-mark, they carry their proofs about with them.

This startling and very significant fact is exhibited in the details of their development. It is a matter of common knowledge that living things repeat in a more or less blurred and abbreviated series their generalized pedigree in their embryological changes. For instance, as we shall presently remind the reader, the developing chick or rabbit passes through a fish-like stage, and the human fœtus wears an undeniable tail. In the case of these ascidians, the fertilized egg-cell, destined to become a fresh individual, takes almost from the first an entirely different course from that pursued by the molluscs. Instead, the dividing and growing ovum exhibits phases resembling in the most remarkable way those of the lowliest among fishes, the Lancelet, or *Amphioxus*. The method of division, the formation of the primitive stomach and body-cavity, and the origin of the nervous system are identical, and a stage is attained in which the young organism displays—or else simulates in an altogether inexplicable way—vertebrate characteristics. It has a *notochord*, or primary skeletal axis, the representative or forerunner in all vertebrata of the backbone; it displays gill-slits behind its mouth, as do all vertebrated animals in the earlier stages only or throughout life; and, finally, the origin and position of its nervous axis are essentially and characteristically vertebrate. In these three independent series of structures the young ascidian stands apart from all invertebrated animals, and manifests its high descent. In fact, at this stage it differs far more widely from its own adult form than it does from *Amphioxus* or a simplified tadpole.

Like a tadpole, the animal has a well-developed tail which propels its owner vigorously through the water. There is a conspicuous single eye, reminding the zoologist at once of the Polyphemus eye that almost certainly existed in the central group of the vertebrata. There are also serviceable organs of taste and hearing, and the lively movements of the little creature justify the supposition that its being is fairly full of endurable sensations. But this flush of golden youth is sadly transient: it is barely attained before a remarkable and depressing change appears in the drift of the development.

The ascidian begins to take things seriously—a deliberate sobriety gradually succeeds its tremulous vivacity. L'Allegro dies away; the tones of Il Penseroso become dominant.[1]

---

[1] Wells alludes to Milton's two companion poems, which contrast the active and outgoing life (*L'Allegro*) with the contemplative and confined (*Il Penseroso*).

On the head appear certain sucker-like structures, paralleled, one may note, in the embryos of certain ganoid fishes. The animal becomes dull, moves about more and more slowly, and finally fixes itself by these suckers to a rock. It has settled down in life. The tail that waggled so merrily undergoes a rapid process of absorption; eye and ear, no longer needed, atrophy completely, and the skin secretes the coarse, inorganic-looking "test." It is very remarkable that this "test" should consist of a kind of cellulose—a compound otherwise almost exclusively confined to the vegetable kingdom. The transient glimpse of vivid animal life is forgotten, and the rest of this existence is a passive receptivity to what chance and the water bring along. The ascidian lives henceforth an idyll of contentment, glued, head downwards, to a stone,

The world forgetting, by the world forgot.[2]

Now here, to all who refer nature to one rigid table of precedence, is an altogether inexplicable thing. A creature on a level, at lowest, immediately next to vertebrated life, turns back from the upward path and becomes at last a merely vegetative excrescence on a rock.

It is lower even than the patriarchal amœba of popular science if we take psychic life as the standard: for does not even the amœba crawl after and choose its food and immediate environment? We have then, as I have read somewhere—I think it was in an ecclesiastical biography—a career not perhaps teemingly eventful, but full of the richest suggestion and edification.

And here one may note a curious comparison which can be made between this life-history and that of many a respectable pinnacle and gargoyle on the social fabric. Every respectable citizen of the professional classes passes

---

As Wells makes clear, he is referring to the fact that the individual ascidian in the course of its existence becomes increasingly less mobile and finally "fixes itself . . . to a rock."

[2] Alexander Pope, *Eloisa to Abelard* (1717): "How happy is the blameless Vestal's lot!/ The world forgetting, by the world forgot" (ll. 207-208).

through a period of activity and imagination, of "liveliness and eccentricity," of *"Sturm und Drang."* He shocks his aunts. Presently, however, he realizes the sober aspect of things. He becomes dull; he enters a profession; suckers appear on his head; and he studies. Finally, by virtue of these he settles down—he marries. All his wild ambitions and subtle æsthetic perceptions atrophy as needless in the presence of calm domesticity. He secretes a house, or "establishment," round himself, of inorganic and servile material. His Bohemian tail is discarded. Henceforth his life is a passive receptivity to what chance and the drift of his profession bring along; he lives an almost entirely vegetative excrescence on the side of a street, and in the tranquility of his calling finds that colourless contentment that replaces happiness.

But this comparison is possibly fallacious, and is certainly a digression.

The ascidian, though a pronounced case of degradation, is only one of an endless multitude. Those shelly warts that cover every fragment of sea-side shingle are degraded crustaceans; at first they are active and sensitive creatures, similar essentially to the earlier phases of the life-history of a prawn. Other Cirripeds and many Copepods[3] sink down still deeper, to almost entire shapelessness and loss of organization. The corals, sea-mats, the immobile oysters and mussels are undoubtedly descended from free-living ancestors with eye-spots and other sense-organs. Various sea-worms and holothurians have also taken to covering themselves over from danger, and so have deliberately foregone their dangerous birthright to a more varied and active career. The most fruitful and efficient cause of degradation, however, is not simply cowardice, but that loathsome tendency that is so closely akin to it—an aptness for parasitism. There are whole orders and classes thus pitifully submerged. The *Acarina*, or Mites, include an

---

[3] Two orders of crustaceans: cirripeds (e.g., the sea-barnacle) are free-swimming in the larval stage but become immobile as adults; copepods are minute organisms having four or five pair of oarlike feet and like the cirripeds are often parasitic.

immense array of genera profoundly sunken in this way, and the great majority of both the flat and round worms are parasitic degeneration forms. The vile tapeworm, at the nadir, seems to have lost even common sensation; it has become an insensible mechanism of evil—a multiplying disease-spot, living to that extent, and otherwise utterly dead.

Such evident and indisputable present instances of degeneration alone would form a very large proportion of the catalogue of living animals. If we were to add to this list the names of all those genera the ancestors of which have at any time sunk to rise again, it is probable that we should have to write down *the entire roll of the animal kingdom!*

In some cases the degradation has been a strategic retrogression—the type has stooped to conquer. This is, perhaps, most manifest in the case of the higher vertebrate types.

It is one of the best-known embryological facts that a bird or mammal starts in its development as if a fish were in the making. The extremely ugly embryo of such types has gill-slits, sense-organs, facial parts, and limbs resembling far more closely those of a dog-fish than its own destined adult form. To use a cricketing expression, it is "pulled" subsequently into its later line of advance.

The comparative anatomy of almost every set of organs in the adult body enforces the suggestion of this ovarian history. We find what are certainly modified placoid fish scales, pressed into the work of skull-covering, while others retain their typical enamel caps as teeth. The skull itself is a piscine cranium, ossified and altered, in the most patchy way, to meet the heavier blows that bodies falling through air, instead of water, deliver. The nasal organ is a fish's nasal organ, constructed to smell in water, and the roof of the mouth and front of the skull have been profoundly altered to meet a fresh set of needs in aerial life. The ear-drum, in a precisely similar way, is derived from a gill-slit twisted up to supplement the aquatic internal ear, which would otherwise fail to appreciate the weaker sound-waves in air. The bathymetric air-bladder becomes a lung; and so one might go on through all the entire organisation of a higher vertebrate. Everywhere we should find the anatomy of a fish twisted and patched to fit a life out of water; nowhere organs built specially for this very special condition. There is nothing like this in the case of a fish. There the organs are from the first recognizable sketches of their adult forms, and they develop straightforwardly. But the higher types go a considerable distance towards the fish, and then turn round and complete their development in an entirely opposite direction.

This turning is evidently precisely similar in nature, though not in effect, to the retrogression of the ascidian after its pisciform or larval stage.

If the reader can bear the painful spectacle of his ancestor's degradation, I would ask him to imagine the visit of some bodiless Linnæus[4] to this world during the upper Silurian period. Such a spirit would, of course, immediately begin to classify animated nature, neatly and swiftly.

It would be at once apparent that the most varied and vigorous life was to be found in the ocean. On the land a monotonous vegetation of cryptogams would shelter a sparse fauna of insects, gasteropods, and arachnids; but the highest life would certainly be the placoid fishes of the seas—the ancient representatives of the sharks and rays. On the diverse grounds of size, power, and activity, these would head any classification he planned. If our Linnæus were a disembodied human spirit, he would immediately appoint these placoids his ancestors, and consent to a further analysis of the matter only very reluctantly, and possibly even with some severe remarks

[4] Carolus Linnæus (1707-1778), Swedish botanist and inventor of the system used in classifying plants and animals.

and protests about carrying science too far.

The true forefathers of the reader, however, had even at that early period very probably already left the seas, and were—with a certain absence of dignity—accommodating themselves to the necessities of air-breathing.

It is almost certain that the seasonal differences of that time were very much greater than they are now. Intensely dry weather followed stormy rainy seasons, and the rivers of that forgotten world—like some tropical rivers of to-day —were at one time tumultuous floods and at another baking expanses of mud. In such rivers it would be idle to expect self-respecting gill-breathing fish. Our imaginary zoological investigator would, however, have found that they were not altogether tenantless. Swimming in the pluvial waters, or inert and caked over by the torrid mud, he would have discovered what he would certainly have regarded as lowly, specially-modified, and degenerate relations of the active denizens of the ocean—the *Dipnoi*, or mud-fish. He would have found in conjunction with the extremely primitive skull, axial skeleton, and fin possessed by these Silurian mud-fish, a remarkable adaptation of the swimming-bladder to the needs of the waterless season. It would have undergone the minimum amount of alteration to render it a lung, and blood-vessels and other points of the anatomy would show correlated changes.

Unless our zoological investigator were a prophet, he would certainly never have imagined that in these forms [was] vested the inheritance of the earth, nor have awarded them a high place in the category of nature. Why were they living thus in inhospitable rivers and spending half their lives half baked in river-mud? The answer would be the old story of degeneration again; they had failed in the struggle, they were less active and powerful than their rivals of the sea, and they had taken the second great road of preservation—flight. Just as the ascidian has retired from an open sea too crowded and full of danger to make life worth the trouble, so in that older epoch did the mud-fish. They preferred dirt, discomfort, and survival to a gallant fight and death. Very properly, then, they would be classed in our zoologist's scheme as a degenerate group.

Some conservative descendants of these mud-fish live to-day in African and Australian rivers, archaic forms that have kept right up to the present the structure of Palæozoic days. Others of their children, however, have risen in the world again. The gill-breathing stage became less and less important, and the air-bladder was constantly elaborated under the slow, incessant moulding of circumstances to the fashion of a more and more efficient breathing-organ. Emigrants from the rivers swarmed over the yet uncrowded land. Aldermanic amphibia were the magnates of the great coal measure epoch, to give place presently to the central group of reptiles. From these sprang divergently the birds and mammals, and, finally, the last of the mud-fish family, man, the heir of the ages. He it is who goes down to the sea in ships, and, with wide-sweeping nets and hooks cunningly baited, beguiles the children of those who drove his ancestors out of the water. Thus the whirligig of time brings round its revenges; still, in an age of excessive self-admiration, it would be well for man to remember that his family *was* driven from the waters by fishes, who still—in spite of incidental fish-hooks, seines, and dredges—hold that empire triumphantly against him.

Witness especially the trout; I doubt whether *it* has ever been captured except by sheer misadventure.

These brief instances of degradation may perhaps suffice to show that there is a good deal to be found in the work of biologists quite inharmonious with such phrases as "the progress of the ages," and the "march of mind." The zoologist demonstrates that advance has been fitful and uncertain; rapid progress has often been followed by rapid extinction or degeneration, while, on the other hand, a form lowly and degraded has in its degradation often happened upon some fortunate discovery or valuable discipline and risen again, like a more fortunate Antæos, to victory.[5] There is, therefore, no guarantee in scientific knowledge of man's permanence or permanent ascendency. He has a remarkably variable organisation, and his own activities and increase cause the conditions of his existence to fluctuate far more widely than those of any animal have ever done. The presumption is that before him lies a long future of profound modification, but whether that will be, according to present ideals, upward or downward, no one can forecast. Still, so far as any scientist can tell us, it may be that, instead of this, Nature is, in unsuspected obscurity, equipping some now humble creature with wider possibilities of appetite, endurance, or destruction, to rise in the fulness of time and sweep *homo* away into the darkness from which his universe arose. The Coming Beast must certainly be reckoned in any anticipatory calculations regarding the Coming Man.

   [5] Antæos, or Antæus, mythical giant king of Libya, would challenge any stranger in his realm to a wrestling match to the death. Until Hercules bested and slew him as one of his 12 labors, Antæus had never been defeated; the reason, according to some versions of the myth, was that he renewed his strength from contact with the earth, so that whenever he was thrown he would rise again stronger than before. Wells's analogy seems to signify that a species, through "degradation," might attain the "possibilities of appetite, endurance, or destruction" to overcome (more fortunately than Antæus) even Herculean opposition.

ON EXTINCTION

The passing away of ineffective things, the entire rejection by Nature of the plans of life, is the essence of tragedy.
In the world of animals, that runs so curiously parallel
with the world of men, we can see and trace only too
often the analogies of our grimmer human experiences;
we can find the equivalents to the sharp tragic force of
Shakespeare, the majestic inevitableness of Sophocles, and
the sordid dreary tale, the middle-class misery, of Ibsen.
The life that has schemed and struggled and committed
itself, the life that has played and lost, comes at last to
the pitiless judgment of time, and is slowly and remorse-
lessly annihilated. This is the saddest chapter of biological
science—the tragedy of Extinction.

In the long galleries of the geological museum are the
records of judgments that have been passed graven upon
the rocks. Here, for instance, are the huge bones of the
'Atlantosaurus,' one of the mightiest land animals that
this planet has ever seen. A huge terrestrial reptile this,
that crushed the forest trees as it browsed upon their
foliage, and before which the pigmy ancestors of our
present denizens of the land must have fled in abject terror
of its mere might of weight. It had the length of four
elephants, and its head towered thirty feet—higher, that
is, than any giraffe—above the world it dominated. And
yet this giant has passed away, and left no children to
inherit the earth. No living thing can be traced back to
these monsters; they are at an end among the branchings
of the tree of life. Whether it was through some change
of climate, some subtle disease, or some subtle enemy,
these titanic reptiles dwindled in numbers, and faded at
last altogether among things mundane. Save for the riddle
of their scattered bones, it is as if they had never been.

"On Extinction"
Chambers's Journal 10 (Sept. 30, 1893): 623-24. [*GW*]

Beside them are the pterodactyls, the first of vertebrated animals to spread a wing to the wind, and follow the hunted insects to their last refuge of the air. How triumphantly and gloriously these winged lizards, these original dragons, must have floated through their new empire of the atmosphere! If their narrow brains could have entertained the thought, they would have congratulated themselves upon having gained a great and inalienable heritage for themselves and their children for ever. And now we cleave a rock and find their bones, and speculate doubtfully what their outer shape may have been. No descendants are left to us. The birds are no offspring of theirs, but lighter children of some clumsy 'deinosaurs.' The pterodactyls also have heard the judgment of extinction, and are gone altogether from the world.

The long roll of palæontology is half filled with the records of extermination; whole orders, families, groups, and classes have passed away and left no mark and no tradition upon the living fauna of the world. Many fossils of the older rocks are labelled in our museums, 'of doubtful affinity.' Nothing living has any part like them, and the baffled zoologist regretfully puts them aside. What they mean, he cannot tell. They hint merely at shadowy dead subkingdoms, of which the form eludes him. Index fingers are they, pointing into unfathomable darkness, and saying only one thing clearly, the word 'Extinction.'

In the living world of to-day the same forces are at work as in the past. One Fate still spins, and the gleaming scissors cut. In the last hundred years the swift change of condition throughout the world, due to the invention of new means of transit, geographical discovery, and the consequent 'swarming' of the whole globe by civilised men, has pushed many an animal to the very verge of destruction. It is not only the dodo that has gone; for dozens of genera and hundreds of species, this century has witnessed the writing on the wall.

In the fate of the bison extinction has been exceptionally

swift and striking. In the 'forties' so vast were their multitudes that sometimes, 'as far as the eye could reach,' the plains would be covered by a galloping herd. Thousands of hunters, tribes of Indians, lived upon them. And now! It is improbable that one specimen in an altogether wild state survives. If it were not for the merciful curiosity of men, the few hundred that still live would also have passed into the darkness of non-existence. Following the same grim path are the seals, the Greenland whale, many Australian and New Zealand animals and birds ousted by more vigorous imported competitors, the black rat, endless wild birds. The list of destruction has yet to be made in its completeness. But the grand bison is the statuesque type and example of the doomed races.

Can any of these fated creatures count? Does any suspicion of their dwindling numbers dawn upon them? Do they, like the Red Indian, perceive the end to which they are coming? For most of them, unlike the Red Indian, there is no alternative of escape by interbreeding with their supplanters. Simply and unconditionally, there is written across their future, plainly for any reader, the one word 'Death.'

Surely a chill of solitude must strike to the heart of the last stragglers in the rout, the last survivors of the defeated and vanishing species. The last shaggy bison, looking with dull eyes from some western bluff across the broad prairies, must feel some dim sense that those wide rolling seas of grass were once the home of myriads of his race, and are now his no longer. The sunniest day must shine with a cold and desert light on the eyes of the condemned. For them the future is blotted out and hope is vanity.

These days are the days of man's triumph. The awful solitude of such a position is almost beyond the imagination. The earth is warm with men. We think always with reference to men. The future is full of men to our preconceptions, whatever it may be in scientific truth. In the loneliest position in human possibility, humanity supports us. But Hood, who sometimes rose abruptly out of the most mechanical punning to sublime heights, wrote a travesty, grotesquely fearful, of Campbell's 'The Last Man.'[1] In this he probably hit upon the most terrible thing than man can conceive as happening to man: the earth desert through a pestilence, and two men, and then one man, looking extinction in the face.

[1] On Thomas Hood's poem "The Last Man," see the introductory remarks in chapter 5. Although Hood's poem was apparently evoked by Mary Shelley's novel, Wells sees it as an answer to Thomas Campbell's poem—all bearing the same title. Campbell's poem recounts how the "last man"—that is, man alone in the universe—spiritually commends himself to God.

LIFE IN THE ABYSS

That there was any life at all in the deeper parts of the ocean was still a matter for speculation scarcely more than thirty years ago. But since that time—thanks, perhaps, more than anything else to the accident of a broken telegraph cable and the organisms that were fished up with it—a series of dredging expeditions has been undertaken, culminating in the *Challenger* voyage and its voluminous reports.

This abyssmal life drags out under conditions almost inconceivably unlike our own. Very striking is the fact that there is no light in the deep; it is an everlasting blackness, save for the phosphorescent glow that proceeds from almost all its denizens. In this eternal night either the eyes become abortive and altogether reduced, or they become enormously enlarged, to catch, as it were, the faintest gleam amid the profundity. Organs of touch become large and prominent. Many of the deep-sea fishes, of which some impressive figures are given, have single and double rows of light-emitting organs along their sides that glow like the ports of a ship at night. These features, coupled with a certain unaccountable tendency to slightness and thinness in the skin and protective structures, give the fish and crustaceans that form the aristocracy of the ocean gulf a very distinctive character of their own. But a still more striking condition, upon which Dr. Hickson insists, is the enormous superincumbent pressure in the deep sea. "At a depth of 2,500 fathoms the pressure is, roughly speaking, two and a half tons per square inch—that is to say, several times greater than the pressure exerted by the steam upon the pistons of our most powerful engines. Or to put the matter in other words, the pressure per square inch upon the body of any animal that lives

"Life in the Abyss"
A review of Sydney J. Hickson's *The Fauna of the Deep Sea; PMG* 58 (Feb. 9, 1894): 4. [Ed. Attrib.; unsigned]

at the bottom of the Atlantic Ocean is about twenty-five times greater than the pressure that will drive a railway train." As a consequence of this, the animals brought up by the *Challenger* dredges from a pressure of 370 atmospheres to pressure of only one were usually more or less seriously injured. The gases confined in the body cavities behave after the fashion of the gas compressed in a soda-water bottle when the pressure of the cork is relieved—that is, they expand. The unfortunate creatures were cruelly distended, the eyes starting out, and in the case of the fish the swimming bladder was invariably ruptured. And the mention of this leads Dr. Hickson to notice a peculiar danger to which the deep-sea fauna must be liable. If in pursuit of prey or for any other reason they venture upward into regions of less pressure, their swimming bladders will expand and their buoyancy increase. Within limits they may be able to recover the deep again, but if these limits are exceeded the struggling animal, becoming more and more blown out, will float with continually increasing velocity to the surface. The deep-sea fish, then, are exposed to an absolutely unique danger, that of tumbling *upward* and so getting killed.

Another striking passage in this clever work is that pointing out the probability of still larger fish, cuttlefish and crustacea, yet to be discovered on the ocean floor. The dredges hitherto employed were scarcely adapted to the capture of any but the smaller forms. So that the imaginative person may still look forward to hearing some morning of an unfortunate member of a new species of leviathan bumping violently in an explosive state against some ocean-going keel. Possibly every one, except the strictly scientific person, will hope that it may be a long time before we altogether penetrate the darkness and know in its completeness the mystery of life in the abyss. Just now, as Dr. Hickson presents it, our knowledge is in a very pleasant phase; enough to stimulate the imagination, and not enough to cramp its play.

INTELLIGENCE ON MARS

Year after year, when politics cease from troubling, there recurs the question as to the existence of intelligent, sentient life on the planet Mars. The last outcrop of speculations grew from the discovery by M. Javelle of a luminous projection on the southern edge of the planet.[1] The light was peculiar in several respects, and, among other interpretations, it was suggested that the inhabitants of Mars were flashing messages to the conjectured inhabitants of the sister-planet, Earth. No attempt at reply was made; indeed, supposing our Astronomer-Royal, with our best telescope, transported to Mars, a red riot of fire running athwart the whole of London would scarce be visible to him. The question remains unanswered, probably unanswerable. There is no doubt that Mars is very like the earth. Its days and nights, its summers and winters differ only in their relative lengths from ours. It has land and oceans, continents and islands, mountain ranges and inland seas. Its polar regions are covered with snows, and it has an atmosphere and clouds, warm sunshine and gentle rains. The spectroscope, that subtle analyst of the most distant stars, gives us reason to believe that the chemical elements familiar to us here exist on Mars. The planet, chemically and physically, is so like the earth that, as protoplasm, the only living material we know, came into existence on the earth, there is no great difficulty in supposing that it came into existence on Mars. If reason be able to guide us, we know that protoplasm, at first amorphous and unintegrated, has been guided on this earth by natural forces into that marvellous series of forms

"Intelligence on Mars"
SR 81 (April 4, 1896): 345-46. [*GW*, *GR*]
[1] See the notice of a "strange light" on Mars observed at Nice by M. Javelle, in *Nature* 50 (August 2, 1894): 319, which gave rise to speculations concerning signals from Mars (*Black and White* 8 [August 25, 1894]: 244). See, too, *The War of the Worlds*, *AtlEd*, 3: 216.

and integrations we call the animal and vegetable kingdoms. Why, under the similar guiding forces on Mars,
should not protoplasm be the root of as fair a branching
tree of living beings, and bear as fair a fruit of intelligent,
sentient creatures?

Let us waive objections, and suppose that, beginning
with a simple protoplasm, there has been an evolution
of organic forms on the planet Mars, directed by natural
selection and kindred agencies. Is it a necessary, or even
a probable, conclusion that the evolution would have
culminated in a set of creatures with sense-perception at
all comparable to that of man? It will be seen at once
that this raises a complicated, and as yet insoluble, problem—a problem in which, to use a mathematical phrase,
there are many independent variables. The organs of sense
are parts of the body, and, like bodies themselves and all
their parts, present forms which are the result of an almost
infinite series of variations, selections, and rejections. Geographical isolation, for instance, has been one of the great
modifying agencies. Earth movements, the set of currents,
and the nature of rocks acting together have repeatedly
broken up land-masses into islands, and, quite independently of other modifying agencies, have broken up groups
of creatures into isolated sets, with the result that these
isolated sets have developed in diverging lines. He would
be a bold zoologist who should say that existing animals
and plants would have been as they are to-day had the
distribution of land and water in the cretaceous age been
different. Since the beginning of the chalk, all the great
groups of mammals have separated from the common
indifferent stock, and have become moulded into men and
monkeys, cats and dogs, antelopes and deer, elephants and
squirrels. It would be the wildest dream to suppose that
the recurrent changes of sea and land, of continent and
islands, that have occurred since the dawn of life on the
earth, had been at all similar on Mars. Geographical
distribution is only one of a vast series of independently

varying changes that has gone to the making of man. Granted that there has been an evolution of protoplasm upon Mars, there is every reason to think that the creatures on Mars would be different from the creatures of earth, in form and function, in structure and in habit, different beyond the most bizarre imaginings of nightmare.

If we pursue the problem of Martian sensation more closely, we shall find still greater reason for doubting the existence of sentient beings at all comparable with ourselves. In a metaphysical sense, it is true, there is no external world outside us; the whole universe from the furthest star to the tiniest chemical atom is a figment of our brain. But in a grosser sense, we distinguish between an external reality and the poor sides of it that our senses perceive. We think of a something not ourselves, at the nature of which we guess; so far as we smell, taste, touch, weigh, see, and hear. Are these senses of ours the only imaginable probes into the nature of matter? Has the universe no facets other than those she turns to man? There are variations even in the range of our own senses. According to the rate of its vibrations, a sounding column of air may be shrilled up, or boomed down beyond all human hearing; but, for each individual, the highest and lowest audible notes differ. Were there ears to hear, there are harmonies and articulate sounds above and below the range of man. The creatures of Mars, with the slightest anatomical differences in their organs, might hear, and yet be deaf to what we hear—speak, and yet be dumb to us. On either side the visible spectrum into which light is broken by a prism there stretch active rays, invisible to us. Eyes in structure very little different to ours might see, and yet be blind to what we see. So is it with all the senses; and, even granted that the unimaginable creatures of Mars had sense-organs directly comparable with ours, there might be no common measure of what they and we hear and see, taste, smell, and touch. Moreover it is an extreme supposition that similar organs and senses should have appeared. Even among the animals of this earth, we guess at the existence of senses not possessed by ourselves. Our conscious relations to the environment are only a small part of the extent to which the environment affects us, and it would be easy to suggest possible senses different to ours. With creatures whose evolution had proceeded on different lines, resulting in shapes, structures and relations to environment impossible to imagine, it is sufficiently plain that appreciation of the environment might or must be in a fashion inscrutable to us. No phase of anthropomorphism is more naive than the supposition of men on Mars. The place of such a conception in the world of thought is with the anthropomorphic cosmogonies and religions invented by the childish conceit of primitive man.

VI. *Evolution and Ethics*

> The history of civilisation is really the history of ... hesitations
> and alterations, the manifestations and reflections in this mind
> and that, of a very complex, imperfect, elusive idea, the Social
> idea ... struggling to exist and realise itself in a world of egotisms,
> animalisms, and brute matter.
>
> "The So-Called Science of Sociology"[1]

Like many of his contemporaries, Wells did not think
of science and ethics as separate and distinct from one
another. In his discursive writings he constantly relies on
science as the basis for defining the possibilities of *homo
sapiens*, both as an individual and socially, and thence he
infers judgments of value as to man's role and destiny.
Where he addresses himself explicitly to ethical matters,
the context of his speculations is specifically and fundamentally Darwinian. Abiding and recalcitrant ethical
questions such as the problem of pain and the relation
between moral and natural law arise for him out of his
understanding of the implications of evolution, which also
provides a model for the tentative solutions he offers. He
begins by considering theoretically the ethics of man's
biological condition and eventually arrives at a practical
scientific humanism, a program for humanly directed "artificial evolution."

Though he thought competition necessary to the survival of intelligence,[2] Wells was far from endorsing the Social

[1] H. G. Wells, "The So-Called Science of Sociology," *Independent Review*
6 (May 1905): 34; collected in *An Englishman Looks at the World* (London:
Cassell, 1914), pp. 203-204.

[2] See the passage from the *National Observer Time Machine* about "sanitary
science" (in "The Refinement of Humanity," chap. 3) and the Time Traveller's

Darwinist's view of a moral order entirely compatible with, because exactly analogous to, the natural scheme of conflict in a brute struggle for existence.[3] Indeed, one of his earliest essays on ethics, "Ancient Experiments in Co-

---

moralizing apropos the Eloi (p. 52 of the Heinemann edition): "What, unless biological science is a mass of errors, is the cause of human intelligence and vigour? Hardship and freedom: conditions under which the active, strong and subtle survive and the weaker go to the wall." The degree to which Wells agrees with these sentiments is perhaps determinable from *A Modern Utopia*, where he writes:

> The way of Nature . . . is to kill the weaker and the sillier, to crush them, to starve them, to overwhelm them, using the stronger and more cunning as her weapon. But man is the unnatural animal, the rebel child of Nature, and more and more does he turn himself against the harsh and fitful hand that reared him. He sees with a growing resentment the multitude of suffering ineffectual lives over which his species tramples in its ascent. In the Modern Utopia he will have set himself to change the ancient law. No longer will it be that failures must suffer and perish lest their breed increase, but the breed of failure must not increase, lest they suffer and perish, and the race with them.

Accordingly, "there must be a competition in life of some sort to determine who are to be pushed to the edge, and who are to prevail and multiply" (*AtlEd*, 9: 123, 124). These quotations from *A Modern Utopia*, it should be noted, clearly reflect Wells's shift (discussed below) from "natural" to "artificial" evolution as the hope for the future of the human race.

[3] Wells resisted the Social Darwinist-Spencerian dispensation probably less because of its inhumanity than its conservatism, its plea for "free enterprise" as a paradigm—rather than a brief phase—of man's evolutionary condition. In about March 1894 he wrote to his friend Arthur Morley Davies:

> I am very glad of the change in your views regarding our excellent Herbert Spencer—a noble and industrious thinker but lacking humour, the trick of looking at things with two eyes, the stereoscopic quality that makes a view real. The way you put it "individualism in ethics, socialism in economy" expresses I think my own position [in opposition to Spencer's] as well as yours. (University of Illinois Wells Archive, Urbana)

That is, Wells endorses the "opposite idea": the supplanting of laissez-faire economics by normative economics and of normative ethics by laissez-faire ethics (see also "The Rediscovery of the Unique"). Spencer, on the other hand, regarded ethical progress not as humanly initiated but as an adaptive response to external conditions (see, e.g., *An Autobiography*, 2 vols. [New York: D. Appleton, 1904], 2: 8), a belief which to Wells was a matter for satire: a reference to Spencer's *Data of Ethics* in "The Man of the Year Million" points to Spencer as the model for Professor Holzkopf of Weissnichtwo, the visionary prophet of the adaptive "perfection" of our remote descendants in that essay. Also, Wells was probably the one who ridiculed Benjamin Kidd (see Appendix, no. 58) because Kidd professed to discover a religious "instinct" of the poor and downtrodden to accept disease, poverty, and death for the greater good of the social organism.

Operation" (1892),[4] looks to nature for examples alternative to conflict. The law of strife, Wells suggests, may not
be the last word written by evolution. Like so many
cooperative and symbiotic entities in organic nature—"familiar cases of aid and self-abnegation"—men, too, it may
be, will someday coalesce into "unified aggregates," colonial organisms perhaps, in which the individuals have
"foregone the struggle"; yet, in their denial of self, each
may be effectually far more free than say, "a factory hand
in the body politic" today.

The idea of the withering away of the individuated ego
is carried a step further in "The Province of Pain" (1894).
Biologically, pain is necessary, even beneficent: it is our
"true guardian angel ... turning us back from death."[5]
Yet on the assumption of an evolutionary advance towards
quicker mental perceptions, the need for the protection
of pain becomes proportionately less "as science ousts
instinct." If it be true that "needless pain does not exist"
in the natural scheme of things, pain may well be only
a "phase" in the evolution of life from "the automatic
to the spiritual." The argument here, together with the
one put forward in "The Limits of Individual Plasticity,"
Wells reiterated in chapter 14 of *The Island of Doctor
Moreau*, where Moreau "explains" that he is not a "materialist" in regard to pain since he recognizes that finally,

[4] Formally rather than historically speaking, the term "Social Darwinism"
may designate any of the Darwinistic social analogies of the Victorian period,
from Marx's class struggle to Kropotkin's mutual aid (see Gertrude Himmelfarb,
"Varieties of Social Darwinism," *Victorian Minds* [New York: Knopf, 1968],
pp. 314-332). Organismic analogy was commonplace. In Spencer, for example,
intricate social-organic analogies supported a functionalist view of society (see
"The Social Organism," *Essays: Scientific, Political, and Speculative*, 2 vols.
[London: Williams, 1868], 1: 384-428). On the other hand, Wells's mode of
imagination in "Ancient Experiments" is heuristic and apocalyptic, primarily,
not sociological.

[5] Wells classified angels (see Appendix, no. 7) as the common white "plaster
cast" angel; the bright angel of art; and the "sombre and virile" angel of the
Old Testament. Here he refers to a variant of the latter type. In *The Wonderful
Visit* (1895), the angel shot down in mistake for a bird is the angel of art. Hitherto
ignorant of suffering, he falls into a world of pain where "the hairy sundew,
eater of careless insects, spreads its red-stained hungry hands to the God who
gives his creatures—one to feed another" (*AtlEd*, 1: 128).

in the evolutionary process, "pain gets needless."[6] The context in *Moreau* generates its own sardonic comment on this sentiment and on the hideous reality of pain as an evolutionary fact. Still, "The Province of Pain" is a vigorous speculative defense of an evolutionary possibility (just as "The Limits of Individual Plasticity" sets forth a possibility of medical science).

In the somewhat Wordsworthian essay, "The Sun God and the Holy Stars" (1894), Wells turns longingly from a world "too much with us" to the "natural" values of ancient peoples who were oriented towards the stars. The heavens always had a poetic intensity of meaning for Wells,[7] as indicated, for instance, in the all-enveloping sky of the "Gryllotalpa" canvas, where Christian and the Devil are reduced to "two of the littlest figures conceivable." In his valediction after the horrors of Moreau's island, Prendick commends himself to "the glittering hosts of heaven," where "whatever is more than animal within us must find its solace and its hope." So, too, in a world "refreshingly" lacking the rationalizations of science, the men of the old Nile knew the direct influence of the star-gods. Wells seems to see in the ancient consonance of stars, crops, and temples a model of that "interaction and correlation" of the whole of creation which he later said it was "imperative to believe" must transcend the "system of causes" revealed by science ("On Comparative Theology").

The next two essays here are more narrowly Darwinian. In "Bye-Products in Evolution" (1895), Wells attempted to reconcile hard-line biological utilitarianism with what might be called "Darwinian theodicy." The problem was how to account for those results of a painful evolutionary process which appear unnecessary to survival—man's aes-

[6] *AtlEd*, 2: 93; see also the introductory remarks in chapter 2.

[7] As a boy, Wells found and assembled an old telescope and was discovered by his mother "in the small hours . . . inspecting the craters of the moon" (*EA*, p. 106). Patrick Parrinder (*H. G. Wells* [Edinburgh: Oliver & Boyd, 1970], pp. 21, 28) comments on the symbolism of "the little stars" in a number of Wells's scientific romances and short stories.

thetic sense, say. Darwin had explained the inception of the aesthetic sense by analogy with, for example, insect-flower pollination and sexual selection among animals.[8] But Wells was concerned with the evolution of the higher aesthetic faculties, not their primitive forms. He was reacting to "Weismannism,"[9] which, by dealing the death-blow to the doctrine of the inheritance of acquired characteristics, left open no avenue of evolutionary innovation except through chance variations selected for "fitness" or extinction by the environment. Thus, when Wells tried to reconcile mechanistic selection with the existence of the human aesthetic sensibility, he could make sense of the latter only as an epiphenomenon (perhaps following Huxley's lead[10]): he speculated that although man's subtler mental appreciations are biologically useless in themselves, they may be necessary concomitants of biologically utile evolutionary structures. As "inevitably involved" "bye-products," the suffering entailed in their evolution would not be needless. Wells thereby arrived at what he evidently regarded as the hopeful view that the "spiritual" and the "nobler" attributes of man were evolved on the principle that "you cannot make a hay-cart that will refuse to carry roses."

"Bio-Optimism" (1895) marks the further retreat of Darwinian theodicy to its last line of defense, an iron Calvinism of struggle and the election of the "fittest." The tone of his discussion reflects Wells's professional scorn of the silly, pretentious "popularization" of biology which he was reviewing. What is otherwise notable, however, is the close resemblance between the substance of the first two essays mentioned above and the ideas that Wells now tears apart, as if in revulsion from his own earlier views. First ridiculing the artwork as "unmeaning distortions"

[8] *On the Origin of Species*, 6th ed. (New York: D. Appleton, 1896), 1: 249; 2: 282-284.

[9] On Wells and Weismannism, see chapters 1 and 4.

[10] Compare T. H. Huxley's "On the Hypothesis that Animals are Automata, and its History," in *Method and Results* (New York: D. Appleton, 1898).

of the "exquisite" forms of organic nature, then slashing "pulpit science" that preaches of symbiosis and "organically imperative . . . social virtues," Wells leads up to and drives home his message: "the names of the sculptor" of every evolving organic species "are Pain and Death." Such, he concludes, is "the Calvinism of science." Already he had spelled out the diabolism of the theme of the sculpting God in *The Island of Doctor Moreau*, the "theological grotesque" then awaiting a publisher.[11]

Though "Bio-Optimism" fails to dispose of the problem of evolutionary pain, Wells was not for long to repudiate his faith in moral progress, nor in the instrumentality of some type of evolutionism. The transition he was soon to make was to scientific humanism, adumbrated in "Human Evolution, An Artificial Process" (1896) and "Morals and Civilisation" (1897). The grounds of the shift lay in his continuing and further reaction to "Weismannism." Of necessity, he had bowed to the scientific acceptance of the germ-plasm theory, yet his initial response had been revealingly moralistic. He had disparaged "this metaphysical conception" that regardless of the father's "habits and vices and education," the children will "come into the world exactly as if his experiences had been the stuff that dreams are made of" ("The Biological Problem of To-Day"). Faced with the dilemma of harmonizing his need to believe in some kind of Lamarckian inheritance with the scientific disproof of Lamarck by Weismann, Wells suffered the pains of writing *Moreau* but then effected a characteristic "disentanglement"[12] from the impasse by the expedient of accepting Weismann's verdict while simultaneously denying that the "secular advancement of humanity" has depended upon biological evolution at all. That is, he ceased to speculate in biological terms of how man became man or will become any other entity, and turned instead to cultural evolution, which he labeled

[11] *AtlEd*, 2: ix; on the publishing of *Moreau*, see West, *op. cit.*, pp. 102-103, 113.
[12] Concerning "disentanglement," see chapter 1, note 22.

"The Acquired Factor."[13] He could then contend that man's progress has depended upon the ability to evolve the extrinsic, cumulative, transmissible mental environment of civilization. This ability came into existence with the first true men—by means of their susceptibility to social suggestion and their power of speech—and without it the paleolithic savage and modern man, Wells claims, would be interchangeable. In this view, the conservative factor in man is precisely his hereditary characteristics, especially his sexual and predatory drives; but there is reason to hope that "artificial" man can control these so that the progress from the Stone Age to the present may henceforth be accelerated and intelligently guided into the reality of "man ruling the future."[14]

The shift to scientific humanism meant, for Wells, dropping the issue of whether biology justifies us in believing man to be by "nature" a beast or a starry portent, and instead taking up—in his histories, utopias, forecasts, and social novels—the issue of man in society, in order to illuminate the workings of man's social and individual adaptive functions. Darwinism for Wells had always been a way of thinking rather than primarily a body of facts, and now he was able, with a sense of active implementation, to use the evolutionary model in areas other than biology. Freed from the "grotesque" theology of *Moreau*, the study of the man-making operation might become a hopeful affair and one that made a difference in one's

[13] This is the title under which appears Wells's review of C. Lloyd Morgan's *Habit and Instinct*, wherein Morgan, according to Wells, "shows ... that the body of man and the instinct of man ... are not at present undergoing evolution, that man is of all living things perhaps the most static" (see Appendix, no. 2).

[14] Ibid. In this regard, Huxley's Romanes Lecture (1893) presumably influenced Wells also:

The cosmic nature [says Huxley] born with us and, to a large extent, necessary for our maintenance, is the outcome of millions of years of severe training, and it would be folly to imagine that a few centuries will suffice to subdue its masterfulness to purely ethical ends. ... But ... I see no limit to the extent to which intelligence and will, guided by sound principles of investigation, and organized in common effort, may modify the conditions of existence. (*Evolution and Ethics* [New York: D. Appleton, 1897], p. 85)

actions—not just in one's beliefs—because man-making (Wells now felt) was a human enterprise rather than a natural process. He saw its conduct, moreover, as truly evolutionary, entailing "modification as well as addition" —whereby, for example, the morality of the civilized man was not a mere refinement of the barbaric morality but a slow, adaptive transformation of barbaric "virtue" into our present concept of "sin." Wells speaks of molding man by means of "an apparatus of moral suggestion," which he conceives of as made up of individual human beings— "prepotent persons, preachers, writers, innovators"—who bring the benefit of their unique energies into the human interplay of society. For civilization is not "material": it is "a fabric of ideas and habits" which "grows . . . through the agency of eccentric and innovating people" ("Human Evolution").[15] This formulation is analogous to Darwin's chance beneficial variations acted upon by the environment, but the environment in this case is mental, a wholly human fabrication, transmitted and modified by the mind. There is an element of Plato here. When Wells dreamt of "an informal, unselfish, unauthorised body of workers . . . shaping the minds and acts and destinies of men," he was thinking of Plato's Guardians.[16] But there may also be a kind of Platonism behind Wells's vision of an affinity between the spirit of man and the starry heavens, which led him to hope that "in Education lies the possible salvation of mankind from misery and sin" and their equivalents in the evolutionary process, "suffering and 'elimination.'"

[15] The emphasis on eccentricity and innovation correlates with Wells's concept of "the unique"; see chapter 2.

[16] Wells does not explicitly mention Plato in connection with "this body of workers," but they are evidently forerunners of the Samurai of *A Modern Utopia*, for whom Plato's Guardians were the models (*AtlEd*, 9: 230).

Wells vividly renders (in *EA*, pp. 106-107, 140, 147) the sense of power conveyed to him as a schoolboy on reading the *Republic*. The impact of Plato on him exhibits itself, *inter alia*, in the kinship between the Myth of the Cave and Wells's numerous parables about vision and the visionary, e.g., "The Country of the Blind" (1910), *The Wonderful Visit* (1895), and *The Invisible Man* (1897).

ANCIENT EXPERIMENTS IN CO-OPERATION

To guard against any disappointment, it will be well to confess at the outset that this brief paper is no inquiry into the graven records of the first historiographers, no startling discovery of "stores" in Babylon or strikes in ancient Nineveh. We have no tale to tell of an Owen of the Ganges, nor a picturesque presentment of William Morris, in a full-bottomed wig and a lotus-broidered robe, "organising labour"[1]—with fascinating side glances at the good old times of the sixth dynasty—in the shadow of a yet unfinished pyramid. Such comparatively recent attempts to reduce the too insistent individual for the good of society, if they occurred, are altogether too modern for our present scope. The first attempts at mitigating competition by union are of hugely remoter date than the first of human cities; and their success or failure is written, not on dead and decaying papyrus and stone, but vividly and with an animation, variety, and colour that a Carlyle or Froude[2] must envy, in the whole volume of living things.

For it is altogether false to find the nexus of life, and its changes, in competition alone. One gets an impression, from the current phraseology of our scientific teachers, that until the Christian Era the whole record of life from its beginning had been a frantic struggle of individuals to survive. A figure is conjured up of a growing crowd of units, battling at the too narrow portals of survival, with death sweeping off the hindermost. It is a horrible conception, as false as it is evil; and though a healthy man may include it in his beliefs and still live, by instinct, a wholesome citizen, it is there lying in wait against the

"Ancient Experiments"
Gentleman's Magazine 273 (Oct. 1892): 418-22. [Signed]
  [1] Robert Owen (1771-1858) and William Morris (1834-1896) were both socialists; Owen tried to put his "co-operative" ideas into practice by setting up an experimental commune in America.
  [2] Thomas Carlyle (1795-1881) and James Anthony Froude (1818-1894) both authored histories which attempt to bring the past imaginatively to life.

germinal time of depression, disaster, or trial, the seed of a savage pessimism. But an even cursory examination of the biologist's province will show that this element of individual competition is over-accentuated in current thought, and that not only human sentiment, but the great mother of humanity, Nature, has her sanction for self-sacrifice, and her own abundant recognition of the toiler and of the martyr.

The most familiar cases of aid and self-abnegation are to be found among gregarious and social animals. In the herbivora the herd will aid the individual; the majority of birds and land animals live and fight for their young, some will die for them. But these are far less striking instances than others less obvious to ordinary observation. The popular literature of natural history has made the ant and the bee so well-known to us, it would seem, that we leave them out of philosophical speculation. The mutual dependence of worker and soldier in the termite community, the certain harmony of disposition and desire between them, is surely forgotten when the "struggle for existence" is spoken of as one chaotic scramble. Here, growing indeed out of the very conditions of that struggle, is an instance of temperance and concession. In an anthill the rigour of competition has been softened, to the benefit and triumph of the species. But these cases of peaceful association are the merest beginnings of such unions, as a more careful analysis of zoological and botanical fact displays. It is in what are called colonial organisms that we find the next more pronounced phase of co-operative activity.

Beginning with such types as the coral polyps, we find individuals resembling one another in form and needs, but, because their food-supply is sufficient, living harmoniously together, linked as the Siamese twins were linked, by their bodies, and building up one common skeleton. In their relatives, the hydrozoa, we find another step along the line of organisation. Tree-like forms occur, made up of a branching system of polyps, with a common circulating system and a community of feeling; but here the individuals are not all alike. Some spread eager fingers through the water for food; some are concerned only in the budding off of colonising medusæ, which swim away to reproduce the kind in fresh localities. This division of labour is still greater in one subordinate group, the *Siphon[o]phora*. In such a form as *Physophora* there is a collection of diverse individuals, some of which cater for the colony, some of which are mere aggressive batteries of stinging cells; some act as protective coverings, some as egg-forming cases, and one—like a scientific essayist—crowns the colony and secretes gas to lighten it, as it floats through the waters of the ocean.[3] Here evidently there is something else than competition as a factor in the life of these various united zooids.

These numerous creatures, each equivalent to an ordinary animal, have foregone the struggle, and merged themselves into a higher unity. The same thing happens ordinarily in the sponges. The great group of the Polyzoa is made up of similar higher unities, and those near relations of the vertebrata, the Ascidians, include colonial forms, the colonies of which are so elaborated and specialised that they might at first be mistaken for a single creature.

But scientific analysis has not stopped here. It is not simply among individuals of the same kind that co-operative association occurs. During the last decade or so a great number of facts have been accumulated with regard to what scientists term *symbiosis*. Here two *dissimilar* organisms merge together for their common benefit. The typical case is that of the lichens. These familiar films and furs, the green and yellow blotches that soften and even glorify our old buildings and exposed rocky surfaces, and the rich

---

[3] Siphonophora are an order of free-swimming or floating hydrozoa (e.g., the jellyfish); physophora are a suborder of siphonophora which float by means of numerous bladderlike organs.

grey foliaceous forms that enrich the bare branches of our wintry woods, were once regarded as a group of lowly vegetables comparable to the mosses and liverworts. A microscopic examination of their substance reveals, however, a considerable departure from the structure of ordinary green vegetables. A network of felted fibres, such as we find in fungi, holds in its meshes a number of green threads and particles. These latter have exactly the same appearance as the green and bluish-green algæ of stagnant water. And experiment has manifested the truth of the suspicion this structure engendered, that the lichens are not simple vegetables at all, but co-operative unions of various fungi with green algæ; the fungus doing much the same work as the root of a higher plant, and the alga discharging the duty of a leaf. Later, many more instances of such united organisms have been adduced. Very probably the great majority of forest-trees obtain food, not by their roots directly, but through the intermediation of fungus filaments that interweave among their roots. The suspicion of symbiotic unions, indeed, now affects almost the whole Vegetable Kingdom, and many animals. Here again is an entirely different thing from destructive competition between individuals; instead, we perceive their harmonious agreement and the genesis of a higher unity.

Following the analytical process further, we discover still more sweeping objections to the idea of the competitive isolation of living things. The whole substance of a higher animal—and this term, of course, covers ourselves—is either made up of, or formed by, protoplasmic blebs[4] called cells; in bone, cartilage, connective tissue, and blood we find them, and again, with changes of shape and duty, in muscle and nerve. Now the commonest object of elementary microscopic work is the *amoeba*, one of a large class of creatures essentially identical in structure with one of these cells, a mere bleb of protoplasm living its life alone. Even to summarise the considerations in favour

[4] That is, bubbles.

of the theory of evolution would be quite outside the scope of this paper; it will suffice now to state that no zoologist or botanist of repute appears to have any doubt that the higher animals and the higher plants are alike descended from such forms, and are, in fact, *colonies* of imperfectly-separated amoeboid cells. Here, then, we realise that a thing essentially different from competition, the co-operative union of individuals to form higher unities, underlies the whole living creation as it appears to our unaided eyes. How complete that union is let our sense of individuality testify. The oldest fossils, the age of which the geologist indicates by such purely symbolical expressions as fifty and a hundred million of years, are remains of creatures consisting of many "cells," and before that time, therefore, their first ancient experiments in co-operation had been made and had succeeded.

A very curious, and to some minds a fascinating line of speculation, may be noted before we conclude. In the amoeba we have an isolated animal of one cell; in the great majority of animals we have a union of many cells; among the hydrozoa, ascidians, and polyzoa these unions again unite into unions of a higher order. In the gregarious assembly of cattle, in the social intercourse of rooks and wolves, and men also, we have the faint beginnings of such a further synthesis, into the herd, the pack, the flock, or the party. How far may we speculate in the future of further developments of the co-operative principle? Certain cities—Jerusalem, Florence, imperial and pontifical Rome—are no mere aggregates; they have a unity and distinctive character, an initiative and an emotion of their own. Again, we have ships that seem to have an individuality not entirely subjective. We perceive now in the Socialist a bold ambition for such a synthesis; we realise his drift. The village commune of the future will be an organism; it will rejoice and sorrow like a man. Men will be limbs—even nowadays in our public organisations men are but members. One ambition will sway the commune, a perfect fusion of interest there will be, and a perfect sympathy of feeling. Not only will there be "forty feeding like one," but forty writhing like one, because of toothache in its carpenter or rheumatics in its agriculturalists.

The recent work undertaken by physiologists to investigate the behaviour of the peculiar corpuscles in the body, the phagocytes, lends colour to this vision. These strange unities wander through the body, here engorging bacteria, and there crowding at an inflamed spot or absorbing an obsolete structure. They have an appearance of far more initiative and freedom than a factory hand in the body politic. It is as startling and grotesque as it is scientifically true, that man is an aggregate of amoeboid individuals in a higher unity, and that such higher unities as may be reasonably likened to man, the Polyzoa individuals and the Ascidians, have united again into yet higher individual unities, and that, therefore, there is no impossibility in science that in the future men should not coalesce into similar unified aggregates. There can be no doubt that such phenomena as the now almost forgotten Siamese twins and double-headed monstrosities are tentative experiments on the part of Nature towards a "colonial" grouping.

This is one of those numberless peculiar cases in which experience jars with reason. Mathematics abounds in such queer contrasts; at the very beginning of algebra we have to speculate about taking quantities away from deficiencies, as everybody knows; but the paradoxical aspect of biological science has not yet been so widely proclaimed. It is as much beyond dispute that the possibility of the utter extinction of humanity, or its extensive modification into even such strange forms as we have hinted at, human trees with individuals as their branches and so forth, is as imperatively admissible in science as it is repugnant to the imagination. Only a very ignorant and dull person would find in such conclusions the *reductio ad absurdum* of science, and only a very imaginative person could imagine he realised what those conclusions meant. But there are certainly enough facts accumulated by biologists to necessitate very considerable modification of our conceptions of individuality, and to have, if properly applied, an extensive influence on the tenor of current speculation.

THE PROVINCE OF PAIN

In spite of the activity of the Society for the Prevention of Cruelty to Animals in our midst, and of the zealous enemies of the British Institute of Preventive Medicine, there have been those who have doubted whether animals —or, at least, very many animals—feel pain at all. This doubt is impregnable, so far as absolute disproof goes. No scientific observer has, as yet, crept into the animal mind; no reminiscences of metempsychosis come to the aid of the humane. We can only reason that there is evidence of pain from analogy, a method of proof too apt to display a wayward fancy to be a sure guide. This alone, however, does not prevent us discussing the question—rather the reverse, for there is, at least, the charm of uncertainty about any inquiries how animals may feel pain. It is speculation almost at its purest.

Many people regard the presence of nerves as indicative of the possible presence of pain. If the surmise is correct, then every kind of animal, from the jellyfish up to man, suffers. Some will even go further, and make plants feel, and figure the whole living creation as groaning and travailing together. But the probabilities are that neither is life nor nervous structure inseparably tinted by the possibility of pain. Among the considerations that point to this conclusion is the fact that many of the nervous impressions of our own bodies have no relation either to pleasure or pain. Most of the impressions of sight are devoid of any decided flavour of the kind, and most sounds, and all those many nervous impressions that never awaken consciousness; those that maintain the tonic contraction of arteries, for instance, are, it goes without saying, painless. Then the little ganglia and nerve-threads that lie in the substance of the heart and keep it beating have nothing

"Province of Pain"
Science and Art 8 (Feb. 1894): 58-59. [Signed]

to do with pain. The nerves retain their irritability, too, in many cases, after death; and a frog's hind leg may be set moving after being cut off from the body. Here, again, is nerve, but no one will believe there can be pain in an amputated limb. From considerations such as these, one is forced to conclude that the quality of pain becomes affixed to an impression, not in the nerves that conduct, but in the brain that receives it.

Again, we may have pain without receiving nervous impressions—or, at least, we may have pain not simply and immediately arising from nervous impressions. The emotions of fear, jealousy, and even anger, for instance, have all their painful hue. Pain independent of sensation is possible, but so is sensation without pain. Pain without thought is possible, but so is thought without pain. Pain, then, though a prominent feature of our mental scheme, is not a necessary companion either to any living thing or nervous thread, on the one hand, or to any mental existence, on the other.

The end of pain, so far as we can see its end, is protection. There seems to be little or no absolutely needless or unreasonable pain in the world, though disconsolate individuals might easily be found who see no good in gout or toothache. But these, indeed, may be blessings in a still impenetrable disguise. The man in the story, at any rate, whose wish was granted, and who was released from pain, burnt first one hand and then had the other arm mortify, and was happily saved from dying of starvation through indifference by getting himself scalded to death. Pain, rightly seen, is, in fact, a true guardian angel, watching over the field of our activities, and, with harsh tenderness, turning us back from death. In our own bodies it is certainly only located where it is needed.

The whole surface of man's body has painful possibilities, and nerve-ends are everywhere on the watch against injury, but deeper the sense is not so easily awakened. In proof of this it is a common trick among medical students to thrust a pin into the thigh. There these nerve-ends are thinly scattered over the skin, and these once passed the muscle is penetrated with scarcely a pang. Again, as most people have read, the brain has often been cut in operations after injury to the head without causing pain. Internal pains are always less acute, and less definitely seated than external ones. Many grave internal disorders and injuries may manifest themselves merely as a general feverishness and restlessness, or even go on for long quite unsuspected. The province of pain, then, in man, so far as detailed government is concerned, is merely the surface of his body, with 'spheres of influence,' rather than proper possessions in the interior, and the centre seat of pain is in the mind. Many an operation which to describe gives an unpleasant thrill to the imagination—slicing away the brain, for instance, or washing away the brain with a jet of water—is, as a matter of fact, absolutely painless.

The relation of physical pain to the imagination and the emotions is worthy of consideration. There seems to be a direct relation between emotional and physical sensibility, the one varying inversely, to borrow a convenient technicality, as the other. Professor Lombroso[1] recently raised all the militant feminine by asserting that women felt physical pain less acutely than men. He hardly deserved the severely sarcastic retorts that appeared in the ladies' papers. His critics, from want of practice or other causes, failed to observe the compliment he was paying them. But a man must have been singularly unobservant if he has failed to notice that, while women are more sensitive to fear and to such imaginary terrors as reside in the cockroach and the toad, they can, when physical pain has secured its grasp upon them, display a silent fortitude quite impossible to ordinary men. Their pains are more intense mentally, but less so physically. This

[1] Cesare Lombroso (1836-1909), Italian criminologist, author of *La donna delinquente* [*Criminality in Woman*] (1893) and other studies. His article, "Physical Insensibility of Woman," appeared in the *Fortnightly Review* 51 (March 1892): 354-357.

is quite in accordance with the view that needless pain does not exist; where the quickness of imagination guards against danger there is evidently a lessened need for the actual physical smart.

Emotional states are anæsthetic. A furious man feels neither fear nor bodily pain, and there is even the clearest antagonism of pain and calm mental occupation. Do not let your mind dwell upon it is the advice of common sense. The *Ingoldsby Legends*[2] were the outcome of the struggle of one sturdy spirit against bodily pain. This is not the only way in which men can avoid the goad. In the use of anæsthetics we have men anticipating and meeting the warning. So far as pnysical pain goes, civilised people not only probably do not need it so much, but probably do not feel it so much, or, at any rate, so often as savages. Moreover, the civilised man evidently feels the spur of passion far less acutely than his less advanced brother. In view of the wise economy of nature, it is not immaterial to ask whether this does not open a probability of man's eventual release from pain. May he not so grow morally and intellectually as to get at last beyond the need of corporal chastisement, and foresight take the place of pain, as science ousts instinct? First, he may avoid pain, and then the alarm-bell may rust away from disuse. On the other hand, there is a quantitative relation between feeling and acting. Sit still, inhibit every movement, your sensations are at a maximum. So you behave when you would hear low music, and lose nothing. Struggle violently, the great wave of nervous energy flowing out neutralises the inward flow of feeling. A man when his 'blood is up,' when he is pouring out energy at every point, will fail to notice the infliction of a wound, which, if he were at rest, would be intensely painful. The struggles and outcries of animals being wounded have their merciful use—they shunt off so much energy that would register as pain. So the acts of

[2] Richard Harris Barham (1788-1845), who published a series of tales in comic verse and prose under the pseudonym Thomas Ingoldsby, was an invalid for most of his life.

sobbing and weeping are the proper channels of escape from a pressure that would otherwise be intolerable. Probably a great proportion of the impressions that would register as pain in man are immediately transmitted into impulses of movement in animals, and therefore cause no pain. With the development of the intelligence in animals there is, however, a diminution of the promptness with which an animal reacts to stimuli. The higher animals, like man, look before they act; with the distinction of approaching man in being less automatic and more intelligent, it seems credible that they also approach him in feeling pain. Probably, since their emotions are less subtle and their memories less distinct, the actual immediate smart of pain may be keener while it lasts than in man. Man being more intelligent, needs less severity, we may infer, from the hands of his great teacher, Nature, just as the woman needs less than the man.

Hence we may very well suppose that we have, as it were, a series among living things with respect to pain. In such an animal as the dog we may conceive that there is a fairly well-developed moral and intellectual rule, and a keen sense of pain. Going downwards, the mental factor diminishes, the smart of the pain becomes greater and greater in amount, but less and less enduring, until at last the mental disappears and the impression that would be pain is a momentary shock, translated into action before it is felt. On the other hand, as we ascend from the dog to the more complex human, we find physical pain becoming increasingly subordinate to the moral and intellectual. In the place of pains there come mental aversions that are scarcely painful, and an intellectual order replaces the war of physical motives. The lower animals, we may reasonably hold, do not feel pain because they have no intelligence to utilise the warning; the coming man will not feel pain, because the warning will not be needed.

Such considerations as these point to the conclusion that the province of pain is after all a limited and transitory one; a phase through which life must pass on its evolution from the automatic to the spiritual; and, so far as we can tell, among all the hosts of space, pain is found only on the surface of this little planet.

THE SUN GOD AND THE HOLY STARS

We who live in cities, with our innumerable variety of artificial lights, and with the great black house masses blotting out the sight of heaven, are assuredly forgetting the stars. It seems incredible to us that so large a part of the ancient Pantheon was but a version, in part poetical, in part sincere, of the common aspects of the sky. And we are all bitten with the vice of Herbert Spencer, and try to express our meaning as exactly and concisely as possible. The dawn to us is a dismal, chilly season of the day, best known to the yawning housemaid. But the men of the old Nile Valley had a clearer skyline, and were less busy with production and distribution. Moreover, they were inspiringly ignorant of elementary science. They saw the circumpolar constellations circle silently throughout the night, ruling over the darkness under cover of which the jackal ravaged the herd and the hippopotamus trampled the grain. So it seemed that up there was undying Set, the spirit of darkness, the dog-headed Anubis, Taurt, the ugly hippopotamus goddess, and the lords of all the terrors of the night. And the beam of the rising sun was the spear of Horus rising with healing in his wings to end the night when no man can work, and bring back the glory of the day.

Now Professor Norman Lockyer has thrown a curious light upon the nature of this festival by his consideration of the orientation of the great temple at Karnak. And his researches show, in a very brilliant manner, the advantage of a specialist in one department of science occasionally invading another. In the present case he is struck, as no archæological specialist would be, by the curious resemblance of the typical Egyptian temple to an astro-

"Sun God"
A review of Norman Lockyer's *The Dawn of Astronomy; PMG* 58 (Feb. 24, 1894): 3 [Ed. Attrib.]

nomical instrument. It is very long in proportion to its breadth, and, just as the astronomer's telescope has diaphragms at intervals to cut off any but the parallel beams of light from the sky, so diffused daylight and any reflections along the temple wall are prevented by rows of seated figures, pillars, and numerous doorways. Only the direct shaft of light from the morning sun at the season when it touched the horizon opposite the temple gateway could penetrate the deep shadow of the temple. On that day the expectant crowd standing in the mysterious darkness, and facing the holy of holies, their backs to the sunrise, saw for a moment the sanctuary brilliantly illuminated. Probably a figure of the god was placed to catch the transitory glory; and so Rā was manifested to his worshippers. One thing that has prevented this fundamental object of the building being recognized is the fact that at present the sun never shines into it at all; it points about a degree too far north even to receive the light of the sun at its most northward limit. And here the astronomer comes in again and shows us that, through a slow change in the angle between the ecliptic and the earth's equator, some seven thousand years ago, the solstice was not 23 deg. 27 min. north, as it is now, but 24 deg. 22 min. Since this change is calculable it follows that we can tell when the great temple of Amen Rā did receive the sunlight at the longest day in the year, and this date, if the description of the annual festival just given is correct, fixes the building of the temple. This occurred, says Professor Lockyer, 3,700 B.C.

We give this typical example to show the import this matter of orientation assumes in Professor Lockyer's hands. His inquiries have extended to a great number of temples, and the series of inferences he draws are very remarkable and far-reaching. The midsummer dawn temples occur throughout Egypt, but in the north we also find temples oriented due east and west to the spring equinox. Now this, though a not very significant epoch to the

Egyptian, was the celestial sign of the swelling of the Euphrates and Tigris to the Babylonian. So that Professor Lockyer's suggestion that these equinoctial temples mark the temporary predominance of an Asiatic culture is a very taking one. Finally, a great number of temples were oriented not to the sun but to various stars, Sirius among them, that once heralded his rising. But while the position of the sun shifts but a degree in seven thousand years, the stars have a regular progressive motion relative to the celestial equator that has long since carried them far away from their shrines; and again and again Professor Lockyer shows a temple has been rebuilt, and its axis twisted, to follow its inconstant stellar divinity.

The book is written with a minimum of technicality, and is luminous and attractive in style, and well illustrated. Professor Lockyer has a happy knack of pointing us to interesting side issues. In a maze of angles and temple plans he presently beguiles one to see a vivid picture of the priests of one star cult struggling with another; and, with a glance at Christian architecture, shows how, long after stars had ceased to be holy, the practice of orientation survived in temple building. In England still, the east window of a church properly built faces the sunrise at the festival of its patron saint; and St. Peter's at Rome, like the temple of Jerusalem, looks due eastward for the vernal sun. Thus the sun god and the holy stars survived as symbols after they had perished as divinities, and the sun that brings the harvest became at last the sun of righteousness that brings redemption to the world. But already in the ninth century the eastward orientation of Christian churches had been denounced as fire worship, and nowadays we build our temples on credit, and orient them to the gaslit street wherein the Great Democracy circulates for ever. And in the glare of our night illuminations the silent and eternal stars are forgotten.

BYE-PRODUCTS IN EVOLUTION

The evolutionary bye-product is a thing that still awaits appreciation even by some who profess science. It may even be that the phrase needs explaining here. Yet there are those who believe that all the best things in life are evolutionary bye-products. A concrete instance may serve to make the thing clear to any reader to whom the phrase is new.

A man, we will suppose, looks out of a window in the ground-floor of a house and sees a pillar-box opposite. In his hand he holds a letter of vital importance, and which he must post forthwith. Clearly he has to go through the front door, and over to the pillar-box and there post the thing. But the door of the house is locked and the key is upstairs, and he cannot take the letter until he has gone upstairs and obtained the key. Now to an observer who did not appreciate the locked door, his journey upstairs would be absolutely unmeaning. Suppose, too, that the key is covered with wet paint and enclosed in a sealed envelope. Then we find, as an outcome of the necessity to cross the road to the pillar-box, not only that the road is crossed, but that the man makes a journey upstairs, gets a certain amount of paint on his fingers, and breaks the seal of an envelope. The journey upstairs, the discoloured fingers, the broken seal, are as much bye-products in the process of crossing the road, as slag and various gases are bye-products of the reduction of iron. Or to put the thing in an abstract form, an end A can only be attained by a process that simultaneously produces B, C, and D, results not needed and yet inevitably involved.

The reader will perceive at once how this will apply to organisms. Let us say that a species under the pressure of changing conditions must either modify some organ in

"Bye-Products"
SR 79 (Feb. 2, 1895): 155-156. [*GW, GR*]

the direction A or perish. But that modification, we will presume, involves a disturbance in the whole physiological balance, more of this product and less of that, and so in parts of the body quite remote from the organ involved in the change A, other consequent changes are set up, and the directly unserviceable and yet absolutely necessary modifications B, C, and D ensue. For example, a species is under stress through the need of a certain pigmentary modification. The elaboration of the new pigment, or an increased elaboration of an old pigment, involves certain chemical bye-products which cannot be allowed to remain in the blood, and yet are products which the excretory apparatus of the animal is ill adapted to remove. It may be they are deposited about the body at points where they are least injurious, or even where they acquire a slight utility. For instance, for all we know to the contrary, the change of this or that animal from grey to drab may involve the appearance or disappearance of fleshy excrescences or horny outgrowths, and the development of hoof or horn, the profoundest changes in colour or kidney. Yet people who understand a little of the theory of evolution but not very much of it, will attempt to explain every feature of the structure of a living thing, down to its minutest curves, as the reaction of that organism to its necessities, and to an enormous majority of educated people, the instance of a perfectly useless organ would be considered an adequate objection to natural selection. But obviously, until we can be assured of every phase in the processes of physiological chemistry, such an objection is altogether beside the mark. It may be, that a large number of inexplicable colorations, inexplicable wattles, horns, manes, skeletal bars, and the like, will ultimately prove such evolutionary bye-products.

In the case of man particularly is such a speculation suggestive. His appreciation of musical harmony, his sense of visual beauty, are things that invariably puzzle the logical student of evolution, whose attention has been confined to immediate utility. But with regard to the subtle mechanism of mind, we are even more in the dark than when we deal with the chemical equilibrium. It may be true that we cannot show that the capacity for pleasurable emotion at the event A is inseparable from pleasurable emotion at the event B, but to prove the negative is equally impossible. You cannot make a hay-cart that will refuse to carry roses. Every new need may necessitate, not merely its satisfaction, but some collateral enrichment of life; and hunger, thirst, and lust, working upon our plastic specific substance, have truly engendered all the nobler attributes of the human soul. Our mother Want may have made the spiritual not because she sought it, but because it was inseparable from the maternal security she sought. And so the world of art and the body of literature become explicable among the bye-products of the evolutionary worker. Heaven forbid that we should say that actually the thing is so. All we would point out is that so common a difficulty may be at least plausibly explained.

BIO-OPTIMISM

It is not often that a reviewer is called upon to write art criticism in the columns of *Nature*. But the circumstances of the "Evergreen" are peculiar; it is published with a certain scientific sanction as the expression of a coming scientific Renascence of Art, and it is impossible to avoid glancing at its æsthetic merits. It is a semi-annual periodical emanating from the biological school of St. Andrews University. Mr. J. Arthur Thomson assists with the proem and the concluding article ("The Scots Renascence"), and other significant work in the volume is from the pen of Prof. Patrick Geddes. It may be assumed that a large section of the public will accept this volume as being representative of the younger generation of biological workers, and as indicating the æsthetic tendencies of a scientific training. What injustice may be done thereby a glance at the initial Almanac will show. In this page of "Scots Renascence" design the beautiful markings on the carapace of a crab and the exquisite convolutions of a ram's horn are alike replaced by unmeaning and clumsy spirals, the delicate outlines of a butterfly body by a gross shape like a soda-water bottle; its wings are indicated by three sausage-shaped excrescences on either side, and the vegetable forms in the decorative border are deprived of all variety and sinuosity in favour of a system of cast-iron semicircular curves. Now, as a matter of fact, provided there is no excess of diagram, his training should render the genuine biologist more acutely sensitive to these ugly and unmeaning distortions than the average educated man. Neither does a biological training blind the eye to the quite fortuitous arrangement of the black masses in Mr. Duncan's studies in the art of Mr. Beardsley,[1] to the

"Bio-Optimism"
A review of *The Evergreen: A Northern Seasonal* by Patrick Geddes et al.; *Nature* 52 (August 29, 1895): 410-11. [Signed]

[1] The English artist Aubrey Beardsley (1872-1898), famous for his black-and-white illustrations.

clumsy line of Mr. Mackie's reminiscences of Mr. Walter Crane,[2] or to the amateurish quality of Mr. Burn-Murdoch. And when Mr. Riccardo Stephens honours Herrick on his intention rather than his execution, and Mr. Laubach, rejoicing "with tabret and string" at the advent of spring, bleats

"Now hillock and highway
  Are budding and glad,
Thro' dingle and byway
  Go lassie and lad,"

it must not be supposed that the frequenters of the biological laboratory, outside the circle immediately about Prof. Patrick Geddes, are more profoundly stirred than they are when Mr. Kipling, full of knowledge and power, sings of the wind and the sea and the heart of the natural man.

But enough has been said of the artistic merits of this volume. Regarded as anything more than the first efforts of amateurs in art and literature—and it makes that claim—it is bad from cover to cover; and even the covers are bad. No mitigated condemnation will meet the circumstances of the case. Imagine the New English Art Club propounding a Scientific Renascence in its leisure moments! Of greater concern to the readers of *Nature* than the fact that a successful professor may be an indifferent art editor, is the attempt on the part of two biologists—real responsible biologists—writing for the unscientific public, to represent Biology as having turned upon its own philosophical implications. Mr. Thomson, for instance, tells his readers that "the conception of the Struggle for Existence as Nature's sole method of progress," "was to be sure a libel projected upon nature, but it had enough truth in it to be mischievous for a while." So zoologists honour their greatest! "Science," he says, has perceived "how false

---

[2] Walter Crane (1845-1915), English artist and illustrator.

to natural fact the theory was." "It has shown how primordial, how organically imperative the social virtues are; how love, not egoism, is the motive which the final history of every species justifies." And so on to some beautiful socialistic sentiment and anticipations of "the dominance of a common civic ideal, which to naturalists is known as a Symbiosis." And Prof. Geddes writes tumultuously in the same vein—a kind of pulpit science—many hopeful things of "Renascence," and the "Elixir of Life."

Now there is absolutely no justification for these sweeping assertions, this frantic hopefulness, this attempt to belittle the giants of the Natural Selection period of biological history. There is nothing in Symbiosis or in any other group of phenomena to warrant the statement that the representation of all life as a Struggle for Existence is a libel on Nature. Because some species have abandoned fighting in open order, each family for itself, as some of the larger carnivora do, for a fight in masses after the fashion of the ants, because the fungus fighting its brother fungus has armed itself with an auxiliary alga, because man instead of killing his cattle at sight preserves them against his convenience, and fights with advertisements and legal process instead of with flint instruments, is life therefore any the less a battle-field? Has anything arisen to show that the seed of the unfit need not perish, that a species may wheel into line with new conditions without the generous assistance of Death, that where the life and breeding of every individual in a species is about equally secure, a degenerative process must not inevitably supervene? As a matter of fact Natural Selection grips us more grimly than it ever did, because the doubts thrown upon the inheritance of acquired characteristics have deprived us of our trust in education as a means of redemption for decadent families. In our hearts we all wish that the case was not so, we all hate Death and his handiwork; but the business of science is not to keep up the courage of men, but to tell the truth. And biological science in the study still faces this dilemma, that the individual in a non-combatant species, if such a thing as a non-combatant species ever exist, a species, that is to say, perfectly adapted to static conditions, is, by virtue of its perfect reactions, a mechanism, and that in a species not in a state of equilibrium, a species undergoing modification, a certain painful stress must weigh upon all its imperfectly adapted individuals, and death be busy among the most imperfect. And where your animal is social, the stress is still upon the group of imperfect individuals constituting the imperfect herd or anthill, or what not—they merely suffer by wholesale instead of by retail. In brief, a static species is mechanical, an evolving species suffering—no line of escape from that *impasse* has as yet presented itself. The names of the sculptor who carves out the new forms of life are, and so far as human science goes at present they must ever be, Pain and Death. And the phenomena of degeneration rob one of any confidence that the new forms will be in any case or in a majority of cases "higher" (by any standard except present adaptation to circumstances) than the old.

Messrs. Geddes and Thomson have advanced nothing to weaken these convictions, and their attitude is altogether amazingly unscientific. Mr. Thomson talks of the Gospel of the Resurrection and "that charming girl Proserpina," and Baldur the Beautiful and Dornröschen, and hammers away at the great god Pan, inviting all and sundry to "light the Beltane Fires,"[3]—apparently with the dry truths of science—"and keep the Floralia," while Prof. Geddes relies chiefly on Proserpine and the Alchemy of Life for his literary effects. Intercalated among these writings are amateurish short stories about spring, "descriptive articles" of the High School Essay type, poetry and illustrations such as we have already dealt with. In this manner is the banner of the "Scots Renascence," and

[3] Wells would later light the Beltane Fires himself (*In the Days of the Comet* [1906], *AtlEd*, 10: 300ff.).

"Bio-optimism" unfurled by these industrious investigators in biology. It will not appeal to science students, but to that large and important class of the community which trims its convictions to its amiable sentiments, it may appear as a very desirable mitigation of the rigour of, what Mr. Buchanan[4] has very aptly called, the Calvinism of science.

[4] Untraced; possibly Robert William Buchanan (1841-1901), the poet, novelist, and playwright.

HUMAN EVOLUTION, AN ARTIFICIAL PROCESS

There is an idea abroad that the average man is improving by virtue of the same impetus that raised him above the apes, an idea that finds its expression in such works, for instance, as Mr. Kidd's *Social Evolution*.[1] If I read that very suggestive author aright, he believes that "Natural Selection" is "steadily evolving" the intrinsic moral qualities of man (p. 286). It is, however, possible that Natural Selection is not the agent at work here. For Natural Selection is selection by Death. It may help to clarify an important question, to point out what is certainly not very clearly understood at present, that the evolutionary process now operating in the social body is one essentially different from that which has differentiated species in the past and raised man to his ascendency among the animals. It is a process new in this world's history. Assuming the truth of the Theory of Natural Selection, and having regard to Professor Weismann's destructive criticisms of the evidence for the inheritance of acquired characters, there are satisfactory grounds for believing that man (allowing for racial blendings) is still mentally, morally, and physically, what he was during the later Palæolithic period, that we are, and that the race is likely to remain, for (humanly speaking) a vast period of time, at the level of the Stone age. The only considerable evolution that has occurred since then, so far as man is concerned, has been, it is here asserted, a different sort of evolution altogether, an evolution of suggestions and ideas. In this paper it is proposed to sketch an establishment of this view, and to indicate its bearing upon certain current conceptions.

The fact which so far has been insufficiently considered

"Human Evolution"

Fortnightly Review, n.s. 60 (Oct. 1896): 590-95. [Signed]

[1] An anonymous review of Benjamin Kidd's *Social Evolution* in the *PMG* is probably Wells's. See the Appendix, no. 58.

in this relation is the slowness with which the human animal breeds.[2] The consequences of that fact are very far reaching. In this country at the present time the average person becomes a parent for the first time about the age of one or two-and-twenty—at any rate, it will be sufficient for the purposes of this discussion to assume that is the case. An unrestrained human animal could not, as a rule, bear offspring before the age of fifteen or sixteen. Compare with this the state of the case in such an animal as the rabbit. A female rabbit is capable of bearing offspring within six months of its birth, and usually does so. That is to say, a century is spanned by, at the utmost, five generations of man, while a lineage of rabbits might conceivably have attained to the two hundredth generation in the same space of time. We may state the case of the rabbits in other words. Let us begin at the beginning; the matriarchal rabbit of our family was born, she escaped, by virtue of her special fitness for survival, the dangers incidental to leporine youth[†] and in the space of six months began to submit a number of samples to the selection of her circumstances. The fittest of these survived and repeated the process within the twelve-month. So the business proceeded. In the hundred years the family had therefore been picked over two hundred times by the hand of Natural Selection. Two hundred times had there been a rejection of unsuitable variations and a premium upon adaptive novelties. In the case of the human being this had occurred only five times. By virtue of its rapid breeding alone, then, it is evident that a rabbit must be, to express the thing in a numerical image, at least forty times more

[†]We are taking an average case from which, of course, good luck is eliminated. [Wells]

[2] See "The Rate of Change in Species." Between writing that and "Human Evolution" Wells may have seen an article by G. J. Romanes, abstracted in *Nature* (51 [Feb. 14, 1895]: 381) in part as follows: "Length of life is not the only factor which determines flexibility of type. There are at least three other such factors: (1) the period at which puberty sets in, (2) the number of times the individual breeds during its life-time, and (3) the number of young which it bears at each time of breeding."

amenable to the process of Natural Selection than a type of human being without the slightest sexual restraint, and at least fifty times more than the civilised human being.

But the lateness of maturity is not the only factor in this discussion. A doe rabbit has five or six litters yearly, averaging perhaps six in a litter; and the total average production by a doe of material upon which Natural Selection is to work may be (to guess at it) sixty or more. It is unusual for a woman to bear a fifth of this number of young. Here, then, is another consideration that carries the possible plasticity of the rabbit under changing conditions almost out of comparison with that of the human animal.

There is still a third difference, at least as between the rabbit and the civilised man of to-day. The normal death of a rabbit is a violent death; famine and pestilence as ever, beasts and birds of prey perhaps less than formerly, and man, ever more vigorously with snare, and poison, and gun, are busy upon the species, destroying *inter alia* all that do not conform to a certain standard of efficiency. The average rabbit, one is led to infer from the Theory of Natural Selection, must be altering in accordance with the changing standards that its changing circumstances impose. But the civilised human animal is under the harrow of death less than any animal perhaps that ever lived. The average duration of human life in a civilised community, for instance, is well above the season of maturity, while that of the fox or rabbit must be (happily) well below it. The weeding process is with us, then, incomparably less rigorous than it is with the rabbits.

Taking all these points together, and assuming four generations of men to the century—a generous allowance—and ten thousand years as the period of time that has elapsed since man entered upon the age of polished stone, it can scarcely be an exaggeration to say that he has had time only to undergo as much specific modification as the rabbit could get through in a century. Indeed, I believe it an exaggeration to say that he can possibly have undergone as much modification as the rabbit (under rapidly changing circumstances) would experience in fifty years. There are, I believe, statistics and resources in mathematical science, sufficient to determine this fact precisely, but for the present argument the recognition of this monstrous disproportion of specific plasticity is sufficient.

The fecund rabbit has been taken because it throws the factors of human stagnation (so far as Natural Selection goes) into effective contrast. In a lesser, though still considerable degree, the truth holds between man and all the higher animals. He breeds later and more sparingly than any other creature. Compared with that of the swarming microscopic organisms of the pond, or with the bacteria, the ratio of his specific inertia approaches infinity. Now there is reason (in the fluctuations of zymotic diseases) to believe that species of bacteria *have* altered in their nature within the present century. Their structure is, however, out of all comparison simpler than the human, and, apart from that, the known variations of animals, even the variations of fecund animals sedulously bred, are by no means striking. In view of which facts, *it appears to me impossible to believe that man has undergone anything but an infinitesimal alteration in his intrinsic nature since the age of unpolished stone.*

Even if we suppose that he has undergone such an alteration, it cannot be proceeding in the present civilised state. The most striking feature of our civilisation is its careful preservation of all the human lives that are born to it—the halt, the blind, the deaf and dumb, the ferocious, the atavistic; the wheat and tares not only grow together, but are impartially sheltered from destruction. These grow to maturity and pair under such complex and artificial circumstances that even a determinate Sexual Selection can scarcely be operating. Holding the generally-accepted views of variation, we must suppose as many human beings are born below the average in any particular as above it,

and that, therefore, until our civilisation changes fundamentally, the intrinsic average man will remain the same.

This completes the opening proposition of the argument,
the à priori case for the permanence of man's inherent
nature; but before proceeding, it may be well to glance
at another line of thought, which, followed out, would lead
to practically the same conclusion, that the average man
of our society is now intrinsically what he was in Palæolithic times. Regard his psychology, and particularly his
disposition to rages and controversy, his love of hunting
and violent exercise, and his powerful sexual desires. At
present normally a man's worldly interests, his welfare,
and that of his family, necessitate a constant conflict to
keep these dispositions under. A decent citizen is always
controlling and disciplining the impulses of anger, forcing
himself to monotonous work, and resisting the seductions
of the sporting instinct and a wayward imagination. I
believe it is a fact that most men find monogamy at least
so far "unnatural" as to be a restraint. Yet to any one
believing in the Theory of Natural Selection it is incredible
that a moral disposition, any more than an anatomical
one, can have come into being when it was—as are these
desires and dispositions just mentioned in civilised man—
directly prejudicial to the interests of the species in which
it was developed. And, on the other hand, it marches with
all our knowledge to suppose that in a state of complete
savagery the rapid physical concentration, the intense
self-forgetfulness of the anger-burst, the urgency of sexual
passion in the healthy male, the love of killing which has
been for ages such a puzzle in his own nature to man,
would have subserved with exactitude the interests of the
species. Here, again, is at least a plausible case for the
belief that the natural man is still what he was in the
stage of unpolished flint instruments—a stage which certainly lasted one hundred thousand years, and very probably many hundreds of thousands of years, which covered
many thousands of generations, which rose probably with

extreme slowness from the simian level, and in which he might conceivably have become very completely adapted to the necessities of his life.

Coming now to the second proposition of this argument, we must admit that it is indisputable that civilised man is in some manner different from the Stone Age savage. But that difference, it is submitted, is in no degree inherited. That, however, is a thing impossible to prove in its entirety, and it is stated here merely as an opinion arising out of the considerations just advanced. The cases of Wolf-Boys that have arisen show with sufficient clearness, at any rate, that the greater part of the difference is not inherited. If the child of a civilised man, by some conjuring with time, could be transferred, at the moment of its birth, to the arms of some Palæolithic mother, it is conceivable that it would grow up a savage in no way superior, by any standards, to the true-born Palæolithic savage. The main difference is extrinsic, it is a difference in the scope and nature of the circle of thought, and it arose, one may conceive, as a result of the development of *speech*. Slowly during the vast age of unpolished stone, this new and wonderful instrument of intellectual enlargement and moral suggestion, replaced inarticulate sounds and gestures. Out of speech, by no process of natural selection, but as a necessary consequence, arose tradition. With true articulate speech came the possibilities of more complex co-operations and instructions than had hitherto been possible, more complex industries than hunting and the chipping of flints, and, at last, after a few thousand years, came writing, and therewith a tremendous acceleration in the expansion of that body of knowledge and ideals which is the reality of the civilised state. It is a pure hypothesis, but it seems plausible to suggest, that only with writing could the directly personal governments coalesce to form an ampler type of State. All this was, from the point of view of the evolutionist, to whom a thousand years are but a day, a rapid and inevitable development of speech, just as the flooding of a vast country in the space of a few hours would be the rapid and inevitable consequence of the gradual sapping of a dam that fended off the sea. In his reference to this background of the wider state, and in its effect upon his growth, in moral suggestions and in knowledge, lies, I believe, the essential difference between Civilised and Palæolithic man.

This completes the statement of the view I would advance. The last paragraph differs from the development of the previous proposition, in being merely a sketchy explanation of the slightest texture inserted to suggest, rather than to establish, an idea. Should some of the details of the last paragraph even undergo inversion, the idea it completes will, I conceive, remain. That in civilised man we have (1) an inherited factor, the natural man, who is the product of natural selection, the culminating ape, and a type of animal more obstinately unchangeable than any other living creature; and (2) an acquired factor, the artificial man, the highly plastic creature of tradition, suggestion, and reasoned thought. In the artificial man we have all that makes the comforts and securities of civilisation a possibility. That factor and civilisation have developed, and will develop together. And in this view, what we call Morality becomes the padding of suggested emotional habits necessary to keep the round Palæolithic savage in the square hole of the civilised state. And Sin is the conflict of the two factors—as I have tried to convey in my *Island of Dr. Moreau.*

If this new view is acceptable it provides a novel definition of Education, which obviously should be the careful and systematic manufacture of the artificial factor in man.

The artificial factor in man is made and modified by two chief influences. The greatest of these is *suggestion*, and particularly the suggestion of example. With this tradition is inseparably interwoven. The second is his reasoned conclusions from additions to his individual knowledge, either through instruction or experience. The artificial factor in a man, therefore, may evidently be deliberately affected by a sufficiently intelligent exterior agent in a number of ways: by example deliberately set; by the fictitious example of the stage and novel; by sound or unsound presentations of facts, or sound or fallacious arguments derived from facts, even, it may be, by emotionally propounded precepts. The artificial factor of mankind —and that is the one reality of civilisation—grows, therefore, through the agency of eccentric and innovating people, playwrights, novelists, preachers, poets, journalists, and political reasoners and speakers, the modern equivalents of the prophets who struggled against the priests— against the social order that is of the barbaric stage. And though from the wider view our most capricious acts are predestinate, yet, at any rate, these developmental influences are exercised as deliberately, are as much a matter of design and choice, as any human act can be. In other words, in a rude and undisciplined way indeed, in an amorphous chaotic way we might say, humanity is even now consciously steering itself against the currents and winds of the universe in which it finds itself. In the future, it is at least conceivable, that men with a trained reason and a sounder science, both of matter and psychology, may conduct this operation far more intelligently, unanimously, and effectively, and work towards, and at last attain and preserve, a social organization so cunningly balanced against exterior necessities on the one hand, and the artificial factor in the individual on the other, that the life of every human being, and, indeed, through man, of every sentient creature on earth, may be generally happy. To me, at least, that is no dream, but a possibility to be lost or won by men, as they may have or may not have the greatness of heart to consciously shape their moral conceptions and their lives to such an end.

This view, in fact, reconciles a scientific faith in evolution with optimism. The attainment of an unstable and transitory perfection only through innumerable generations of suffering and "elimination" is not necessarily the destiny of humanity. If what is here advanced is true, in Education lies the possible salvation of mankind from misery and sin. We may hope to come out of the valley of Death, become emancipated from the Calanistic deity of Natural Selection,[3] before the end of the pilgrimage. We need not clamour for the Systematic Massacre of the Unfit, nor fear that degeneration is the inevitable consequence of security.

(In this paper the phrase "natural man" has been used as though all men were inherently alike. But it must be borne in mind that there are racial differences which, save for interbreeding and segregation of resultant types, have probably remained constant for many thousand years, and which must necessarily persist for many ages. The Aryan natural man is certainly not the Negro natural man; the Kelt, it may be, differs constitutionally from the Teuton, even as he claims. But the artificial man differs far more profoundly between nation and nation. The marked and, it is to be feared, growing divergence of the English type from the American, must be, for instance, a divergence purely of the artificial factor. Had we sufficient intelligence and unanimity to fight the forces of disruption, they could be fought and overcome.)

[3] Wells possibly coined "Calanistic" from Calanus, a philosopher of the fourth century B.C. who immolated himself when he became seriously ill; similarly the "Calanistic deity of Natural Selection" eliminates the "unfit." The word may also be a misprint for "Calvinistic."

MORALS AND CIVILISATION

In the *Fortnightly Review* for October, there was published a short paper entitled, "The Artificial Factor in Man," in which the view was advanced that the inherent possibilities of the modern human child at birth could differ in no material respect from those of the ancestral child at the end of the age of Unpolished Stone. And the difference between civilised man of to-day and the later Palæolithic savage, his ancestor, was presented as an artificial factor developed in him after birth by example and precept, by the complicated influences of the civilised body into which he was born a member. The conflict between his innate Palæolithic disposition and this artificial factor imposed thereon, was suggested as a new phrasing for the moral conflict, and the discordance was pointed to as expressing an evolutionary view of Sin. This article received a certain amount of notice in various quarters, and nowhere was it adequately gainsaid. And almost simultaneously from two directions came independent parallel utterances. At the Church Congress[1] practically the same view was expressed in a more orthodox phrasing, while Professor Lloyd Morgan, in his book "Habit and Instinct,"[2] arrived at the same conclusion in an inductive enquiry, which placed the proposition on a foundation altogether more solid than the *à priori* considerations advanced in my article.

This conception of a civilised man as composed of these two factors, will be found, if it is accepted and its consequences followed up, a remarkably far-reaching one. And, in this paper, it is proposed to restate certain fundamental principles of morality, in these new terms, and to make a suggestion that arises out of this restatement.

"Morals and Civilisation"
Fortnightly Review, n.s. 61 (Feb. 1897): 263-68. [Signed]

[1] See the Archdeacon of Manchester's address to the Shrewsbury Church Congress of 1896, "The Bearing of the Theory of Evolution on Christian Doctrine," *Times*, Oct. 8, 1896, p. 9, cols. 1-3.

[2] See note 13 and text, chapter 6; also the Appendix, nos. 2 and 53.

In the former paper it was suggested that morality is the padding of suggested emotions and habits, by which the round Palæolithic man is fitted into the square hole of the civilised state. In accordance with which view we must needs regard social organization and individual morality as determining one another. Indeed, if the reader will consider the matter, the whole form of the social organization, the shape of our civilisation, is nothing more nor less than the algebraic sum of the artificial factors of its constituent individuals—a fabric of ideas and habits. Civilisation is not material. If, in a night, this artificial, this impalpable mental factor of every human being in the world could be destroyed, the day thereafter would dawn, indeed, upon our cities, our railways, our mighty weapons of warfare, and on our factories and machinery, but it would dawn no more upon a civilised world. And one has instead a grotesque picture of the suddenly barbaric people wandering out into the streets, in their night-gear, their evening dress, or what not, as chance may have left them at the coming of the change, esurient and pugnacious, turning their attention to such recondite weapons as a modern city affords—all for the loss of a few ideas and a subtle trick of thinking.

Now, it is scarcely necessary to say that, in accordance with this view, there is no morality in the absolute. It is relative to the state, the civilisation, the corporate existence to which the man beast has become adapted on the one hand, and to the inherent possibilities of the man on the other. And the data of morality must vary with the state, the social environment rather, in which the man exists; the alternative judgments of right and wrong in action, that is, must vary. Civilised man, speaking roughly, seems to have progressed through a series of stages from the merely bestial state in which unqualified instinct sufficed, to his present condition; of which stages, gregarious animalism, tribal savagery, the militant barbarism and the militant civilised state may be taken as typical. Beyond the militant civilised state, many people anticipate a non-militant cosmopolitan civilisation in the future, a condition which such things as the rules of war and the perfect security of non-combatants away from the immediate seat of war foreshadow. A practical local anticipation of such a non-militant civilisation has occurred transitorily at least twice in the world's history in certain phases of the Roman and Chinese empires.

The three typical stages: tribal savagery, barbarism, and militant civilisation, have developed out of each other in a regular order, through the growth and development of the common body of ideas. It does not follow, however, that the individual morality of the barbaric man is simply the morality of the tribal savage enlarged, and that of the civilised man simply a further extention of the barbaric phase. We have also to consider a process of modification as well as addition, whereby, it may be, what was eminent virtue in the tribal savage may ultimately become sin in the civilised man.

The proposition may perhaps be best illustrated by our glancing at the development of sexual morality, a topic too rarely discussed in an unemotional way. In the mere solitary beast—solitary after the feline fashion—there is practically no sexual morality, but only a group of more or less complex and interacting instincts, the net object of which—to state the matter without prejudice in a convenient theological dialect—is to direct the energies of the individual towards an abundant propagation of vigorous offspring. Now the instincts that would effectually secure this object while man was in a quite solitary animal phase, must needs become modified directly he has begun to aggregate into herds or communities. The mere aggregation, the facilities for intercourse, and the consequent danger of wasting energy needed in the hunting and warfare of the community, the injury to offspring wrought by promiscuity, the innate aggressiveness of the males, and the passion of jealousy alike demanded that a certain rudimentary idea of continence (of which the taboos so hateful to Mr. Grant Allen[3] are one mode of expression) should arise before even the tribal community could exist —even indeed before a flock could exist. Habit, the trick of imitation, had to come to the help of instinct. In other words, so soon as we step from solitary animal to tribal savage, to tribal beast even, the propagation and survival of the individual type becomes complicated by the conditions of survival of the tribe. The abundant propagation of vigorous offspring is still, however, the sole end in view;—that is, indeed, the ultimate condition of all successful and aggressive tribal existence. The ideal sexual virtue of this tribal phase would seem to be found in a sober polygamy; and among the ancient Hebrews and the modern Zulus, the culminating triumphs of tribal savagery, we find this condition. The tribal barbarism succeeded the tribal savagery, and its population problem did not greatly differ from that of the preceding condition. The entire sexual code of the tribal barbarism of the Hebrews, at about the stage of aggregation into an ampler state, remains completely on record. With the sanction of polygamy removed, it is the basis of the sexual morality of the vigorous, militant, civilised states of the Europe of to-day. And the essential feature of it is the elaborate prohibition of any waste of energy along the sexual line of escape. "Increase and multiply and replenish the earth," is the spirit of it all.

The replacement of polygamy by monogamy marks, however, a new phase in human development, the imposition of a new restriction, the ideal observance of which is still too much for common men. Monogamy is, and has been, the professed morality of our country, for instance, for many centuries, but one may doubt its virtual triumph until quite recent times. It marks a phase when a violent death has become sufficiently remote and the community so complex, that the importance of the moral and even

---

[3] See Wells's review of Allen's *The Evolution of the Idea of God* in "On Comparative Theology," chapter 2 above.

the intellectual training of offspring had come to weigh against the importance of their number and physical efficiency. Whatever its sources, the organic corollaries of the monogamic idea were feminine self-respect and a better education (using the word in its widest sense) of the children. The emancipation of woman indeed has no meaning for anyone but the individual woman, apart from the children's welfare. And the monogamic family, with an entire prohibition of wasted energy, is no doubt the moral ideal, so far as sex is concerned, of the modern militant civilised state. States and nations that fall away from that ideal will inevitably go down before States that maintain it in its integrity. France, for instance, wanes, for the simple reason that the circle of ideas of the common French household severs marriage and offspring.

Our state is militant and aggressive, and Mr. Kipling is its poet. But, there have been in the history of the world, and there may come again, phases when civilisation is static, when there is no pressure of antagonism from without to demand an answering internal pressure of population, and correlated with the establishment of such a state, conceptions of sexual morality necessarily alter. This has obtained in certain periods of Roman history, in Persia, and in China. For such speaks Omar Khayyám.[4] In all such periods, there has been a distinct development of conceptions tending to keep the total population at an unvarying number from generation to generation. These make for the most part in the direction of relaxing the reprobation attaching to the waste of energy, and, further, the spirit of infanticide raises its head. The moral condition of the individual in what we generalise and call the "Oriental" world, is the more or less perfect expression of a general static condition. We find the monogamic respect for woman as wife and mother has passed; we find the honoured courtesan and a recognition of infanticide;

---

[4] A *carpe diem* philosophy pervades Omar's *Rubáiyát* and is apparent in lines like: *Ah, make the most of what we yet may spend, / Before we too into the Dust descend* (trans. Edward Fitzgerald, XXIV, ll. 93-94).

culture tends to an æsthetic impotence, and religion dimly apprehending a vanished conflict, becomes perverted to the whims of the Durtals[5] of the time, renounces the world and takes refuge in monasticism. We need not go east of Suez to find this moral state, for it grows up together with the cosmopolitan idea in all great cities. And, had it not been for the development of war material and commodities consequent upon scientific discovery, and the possibility of expansion opened by the geographical explorer, our own civilisation might very possibly be even now passing into the static condition. Already, in the days of Malthus, the static sexual morality had found an imperfect but suggestive formulation.[6] And before the geographical discoveries of Tudor times, the static condition seemed imminent throughout Europe.

Hitherto, this has been the final phase of all civilisations, the establishment of a broad area of physical security, then a moral dry rot spreading outward from the cities, the loss of energy through sexual vice, and then, since no civilisation has so far been universal, pressure from without and collapse. But, in the case of a universal civilisation, the dry rot would involve no collapse, at least until disintegration occurred.

This has been the history of sexual morality under civilisation so far. But it is not an organic law. Each civilisation is unique and has its own unique possibilities. A civilisation is merely an aggregation of ideas, and prepotent persons, preachers, writers, innovators, may, more or less, con-

[5] That is, exponents of religiosity: Durtal is the hero of a trilogy by J. K. Huysmans who converts from spiritual doubt to "monasticism"; in the words of an anonymous reviewer of *En Route* (the second volume of the trilogy), Durtal, after his conversion, returns "to Paris . . . as selfish, egotistical, useless, parasitic, and diseased as when he set out" ("Whither?" *SR* 82 [August 8, 1896]: 139). (This view of Durtal is not Huysmans's; but Wells—whether he knew the novel directly or only from notices of it—undoubtedly shared the *SR* reviewer's opinion.)

[6] Thomas Robert Malthus (1766-1834), the English economist, contended in his *Essay on the Principle of Population* (1798) that as the wealth of a nation is a ratio of riches to population, the only way of avoiding increasing poverty is by limiting population. The principal means for insuring this static condition, Malthus argued, was through "moral restraint."

sciously mould that aggregate. It is no inevitable force which changes militant into static civilisations. As much as anything it is the demoralisation due to security,—a disorganization of the forces of moral suggestion. And, hitherto, moral ideas of vital import have been presented to men as correlated with religious conceptions, with which error, or the suspicion of error, of a more or less obvious description was interwoven. Sexual morality has been shattered by the downfall of the creeds. Nowadays, for instance, we are told that this practice is to be reprobated and that commended, because it is God's will. Men may doubt God, men may doubt his interpreter, and so, unhappily, vice takes refuge under the conscience clause. The conventional conception of marriage is still a ceremonial. But the very basis of a sound morality in such a state as ours is surely not a sacrament, but the monogamic family. Morality is made for man, and not man for morality, and the essential fact of monogamic marriage is not the marriage service and a joint honeymoon, as the modern Young Lady has been very foolishly taught, but the birth and education of children. People shrink from rationalising these questions, grow shame-faced and angry. But upon the consistent presentation of sexual morality as existing entirely for the sake of offspring and of the general stock of energy, the continuation of the present progress of our civilisation most assuredly depends. At present this matter is neither treated with consistency nor lucidity in our literature, or in our other vehicles of moral suggestion.

And along another line, too, the existing conceptions of morality are vague and unsystematic, and that is along the line of property. When all personal property was portable, "Thou shalt not steal," snatch and bolt, reiterated until it became a habit of mind, was possibly a sufficient moral education in this respect, sufficient to render possible the wholesome corporate existence of man. But the mere fact of the irresponsible useless millionaire wandering wastefully at large, points clearly to a defect in our existing structure of moral conceptions. And indeed, the Hebrew prophets, with their repeated denunciation of such as grind the faces of the poor, admit the early failure of their barbaric code so far as property was affected by it. To many people nowadays, however, people chiefly of the propertied classes, the "Rights of Property," the principle of "findings, keepings," without analysis of ownership, is more sacred than any sacrament. And this growth of irresponsible property, together with the abortion of the monogamic family and the enfeebled reprobation of sterile and sterilizing indulgences, is one of the common features of all civilisations passing from the militant to the static state of civilisation.

Now, if what is here laid down is valid, it follows that the future of our civilisation depends upon the possibility of constructing a rational code of morality to meet the complex requirements of modern life, and of efficiently organizing the forces of moral suggestion to render it operative.

We have been discussing moral ideas simply from the point of view of function, of their part in the operations and destiny of the civilised body, and without any reference to the mental processes by which they have arisen. Their development is inseparably interwoven, on the one hand with the development of theological ideas, and on the other with political institutions. To trace that development in detail, the reader must go to those who have a more intimate knowledge of anthropology than I have. The idea which pervades this paper, although it has not been distinctly formulated so far, the idea that a moral theory should be deduced from an ideal social state, has, however, played its part. Christianity, for instance, arose when the militant civilisation of Rome, surviving its rivals and its circumadjacent barbarism, became for a time a non-militant state of physical security. And the Founder of Christianity would certainly seem to have derived the chief lines of his teaching from an ultra-civilised conception of universal human brotherhood. Christianity has been the nominal religion of militant barbarism and militant civilisation, but everywhere Articles XXXVII. and XXXVIII. must needs come in as a codicil to the testament of the Prince of Peace. "It is lawful for Christian men, at the commandment of the Magistrate, to wear weapons and serve in the wars," is a very courageous gloss on Christ's "Thou shalt not kill"; and "The Riches and Goods of Christians are *not* common," Article XXXVIII. further explains—whatever you may have happened to understand from Him.

Moreover, in Socialism, we have a very complete theory of social organization, necessarily involving a scheme of private morals.

And the question for which this paper has been written, with which it may end, is this. Are we not, at the present time, on a level of intellectual and moral attainment sufficiently high to permit of the formulation of a moral code, without irrelevant reference, upon which educated people can agree? The *apparatus of moral suggestion*, the people who write, preach, and teach that is, needs only too evidently the discipline of a common ideal. One sees the favourite writer, alert for the coming of the boom; the eminent preacher, facing bishopric-ward, with one eye on the Government and the other on the reporters; the distinguished teacher before the camera; the dexterous politician, unconscious as to the sources, but precise as to the direction, of that wind of popular feeling that shall presently bear him to power. But a definite stress of effort to determine the development of the public ideals is wanting. And yet one may dream of an informal, unselfish, unauthorised body of workers, a real and conscious apparatus of education and moral suggestion, held together by a common faith and a common sentiment, and shaping the minds and acts and destinies of men.

Appendix. A Selective Bibliography [with Abstracts] of H. G. Wells's Science Journalism, 1887-1901

This survey is a selective record of H. G. Wells's science journalism, from his earliest surviving efforts up to 1901 (with exception made for "The Scepticism of the Instrument," included as an appendix to *A Modern Utopia* [1905] but also essentially related to these early writings, especially "The Rediscovery of the Unique" [see chap. 1], and thus an important nexus between Wells's interest in science and his later sociological concerns). Without claiming to be exhaustive, the listing comprises 60 articles derived from a comprehensive sifting of periodical contributions attributed to Wells by *GW* or *GR*, augmented by 35 previously unnoticed pieces, most of which we assign to Wells on the basis of evidence found in the Wells Archive at the University of Illinois. We have included all the essays and reviews that we deem relevant to Wells's science fiction, as well as two uncollected short stories of a somewhat essayistic nature (nos. 86, 93). Our arrangement of the material is alphabetical, by title, and we have provided an abstract of any item not reprinted in this anthology.

Of the 35 previously unlisted articles, 1 is a transcript of a lecture by Wells, 5 are signed, 13 are identifiable from Amy Catherine Wells's cue-titles on a document in the Wells Archive (these are quoted in our attribution brackets that follow the bibliographic information), and 16 (of which 6 allude to, or are alluded to in, essays or reviews known to be by Wells) are included on grounds of style and content (in which case there is a bracketed asterisk after the entry). For this bibliography, we are supplementing our table of abbreviations with the following:

ET *The Educational Times*
FR *The Fortnightly Review*

GM   *The Gentleman's Magazine*
SSJ   *The Science Schools Journal*

1. ABOUT TELEGRAPHS. *PMG* 60 (Jan. 5, 1895): 4. [*ACW*: "Telegraphs"]
Wells praises A. L. Ternant's *The Telegraph* (trans. R. Routledge) for its wide-ranging historical exposition of the development of various telegraph systems, ancient and modern.

2. ACQUIRED FACTOR, THE. *Academy* 51 (Jan. 9, 1897): 37. [Signed]
Wells approves the constructive Weismannism of C. Lloyd Morgan's *Habit and Instinct* (so like his own position in no. 38). Morgan infers from analysis of the proportionate shares of instinct and habit (i.e., education) in higher animals, including man, that the human body and instincts are no longer evolving. The mental environment alone evolves. Despite his brute ancestry, man can shape his world through science, art, and education, and so "cease to be driven, a dry leaf before the wind."

3. A.D. 1900. *PMG* 59 (Oct. 12, 1894): 3 [*GW*]
In 1900 the giving of a dinner party or the hanging of a picture may be forbidden by court order if either is deemed unwholesome by Mrs. Hallelujah, Mr. Peahen, or other guardians of public morality.

4. ADVENT OF THE FLYING MAN, THE. *PMG* 57 (Dec. 8, 1893): 1-2. [*GW*; but *GW* inadvertently masks the identity of this unreprinted essay by confusing it with "The Flying Man"; the latter, a short story collected in *The Stolen Bacillus*, appeared in the *PMG* 60 (Jan. 4, 1895): 1-2]
Wells portrays the flying man, present and future. The nineteenth and twentieth centuries witness his fiascoes and hardier triumphs. By A.D. 21,000 (Wells adopts the quasi-visionary tones of no. 52) batlike human swarms darken the evening air, homing to suburban "rookeries" from the dome of St. Paul's. The flying man holds the future: "Even now the imaginative person may hear the beating of his wings."

5. ANCIENT EXPERIMENTS IN CO-OPERATION. *GM* 273 (Oct. 1892): 418-422. [Signed]

6. ANGELS AND ANIMALCULAE. *PMG* 59 (Oct. 9, 1894):

4. [*ACW*: "Angels & Animalculae"]
Wells cheerfully labels J. W. Thomas's *Spiritual Law in the Natural World* "what one may perhaps call the New Theology, theology 'up-to-date,'" scientifically smartened up.

7. ANGELS, PLAIN AND COLOURED. *PMG* 57 (Dec. 6, 1893): 3. [*GW*]
Wells catalogues angels: the common white angel of "the oleograph, the Christmas card, the illustrated good book, and the plaster cast"; the art angel of "fiery red and celestial blue," "of brightness rather than sentiment"; and the biblical angel of the Hebrew and of Milton, "a vast winged strength, sombre and virile."

8. ANOTHER BASIS FOR LIFE. *SR* 78 (Dec. 22, 1894): 676-677. [*GW, GR*]

9. BELATED BOTANIST, A. *PMG* 59 (Nov. 13, 1894): 4. [*ACW*: "Belated Botanist"]
E. Sandford, author of *A Manual of the Exotic Ferns and Selaginella,* is "an extreme expression of the specialist type." Knowing all about the cultivation of ferns, he has not a suspicion of the findings of botany in the last 40 years—facts of fertilization, reproduction, and classification, known to "almost any high-school girl."

10. BIOLOGICAL PROBLEM OF TO-DAY, THE. *SR* 78 (Dec. 29, 1894): 703-704. [*GW, GR*]

11. BIO-OPTIMISM. *Nature* 52 (Aug. 29, 1895): 410-411. [Signed]

12. BYE-PRODUCTS IN EVOLUTION. *SR* 79 (Feb. 2, 1895): 155-156. [*GW, GR*]

13. CENTRE OF TERRESTRIAL LIFE, THE. *SR* 79 (Feb. 16, 1895): 215. [*GW, GR*]
On the basis of the geological theory that continental land masses have persisted fundamentally unchanged in scope in geological time, Wells reasons that terrestrial life must have begun in the higher northern latitudes and "in the struggle for existence between the older and the newer type [i.e., species], generally the newer prevailed and drove the older southwards."

14. COLOURS OF ANIMALS, THE. *PMG* 60 (Jan. 25, 1895): 3. [*ACW:* "Mimicry of Animals"]

Whereas the man in the street supposes that "everything is trying its very best to resemble something else," the truth is that "many of such resemblances are still unaccountable and apparently quite accidental." Wells cites as his main source F. E. Beddard's *Animal Colouration.*

15. COMPARATIVE THEOLOGY, ON. *SR* 85 (Feb. 12, 1898): 211-213. [Signed]

16. CONCERNING OUR PEDIGREE. *GM* 274 (June 1893): 575-580. [Signed]
Wells muses, with satirical overtones, on the evolutionary ancestry of man, which he follows from the anthropoid apes *backwards* in time.

17. CONCERNING SKELETONS. *SR* 81 (June 27, 1896): 646-647. [*GW, GR*]

18. CONCERNING THE NOSE. *The Ludgate,* n.s. 1 (April 1896): 678-681. [Signed]
Light-hearted speculation, with satiric undertones, on the future evolution of the inexplicable human nose. "The nose of to-day . . . is in . . . a transitory and developing stage. One may conceive 'advanced' noses, inspired with an evolutionary striving towards something higher, remoter, better—we know not what. We seem to need ideals here."

19. "CYCLIC" DELUSION, THE. *SR* 78 (Nov. 10, 1894): 505-506. [*GW, GR*]

20. DARWINIAN THEORY, THE. *PMG* 60 (Jan. 1, 1895): 4. [*ACW:* "Darwinian Lectures"]
For the general reader, A. Milnes Marshall's *Lectures on the Darwinian Theory* is "the clearest modern exposition"; and, says Wells, "when such dark speculations as those of Weismannism" are used by the "small fry of science" to belittle Darwin, Marshall's is "a needful tribute to the memory of the greatest biologist" of all time.

21. DEATH. *SR* 79 (Mar. 23, 1895): 376-377. [*GW, GR*]

22. DECADENT SCIENCE. *PMG* 58 (April 5, 1894): 4. [Allusions in nos. 65, 81] [*]
Wells demolishes Henry Pratt's *Principia Nova Astronomica* and its "brand-new" solar system, "a very nice affair, with a Central Sun, and a Polar Sun, and an Equatorial Sun, over and above the visible sun of your vulgar astronomers."

23. DISCOVERIES IN VARIATION. *SR* 79 (March 9, 1895): 312. [*GW, GR*]
    A discussion of new biometric studies of variation in species, wherein Wells observes: "Variation occurs in every direction [i.e., all possibilities are tried], with complete symmetry; it does not occur in a definite direction as if it were following some inherent tendency of the animal to develop in a particular fashion. These minute variations offer a fair field for natural selection to reject or select."

24. DISEASES OF TREES, THE. *SR* 79 (Jan. 19, 1895): 102-103. [*GW, GR*]
    A review of R. Hartig's *The Diseases of Trees*, together with a brief discussion of plant pathology.

25. DREAM BUREAU, THE. *PMG* 57 (Oct. 25, 1893): 3. [*]
    With increasing knowledge of dream-physiology, the time approaches for investigators "to bring the control of dreaming as a fine art into the realm of possibilities." We may imagine the dream-addict someday ordering up a night's supply, of any sort he pleases.

26. DURATION OF LIFE, THE. *SR* 79 (Feb. 23, 1895): 248. [*GW, GR*]

27. ELECTRICITY. *PMG* 59 (Dec. 22, 1894): 4. [*]
    Wells reviews J. A. Fleming's *Electric Lamps and Electric Lighting* and R. Mullineux Walmsley's *The Electric Current*. The one is a "readable volume" for nontechnical people, the other a second-hand handbook of batteries, circuitry and "professorial disregard" of "the real substance of electrical engineering" today, the dynamo.

28. EXCURSION TO THE SUN, AN. *PMG* 58 (Jan. 6, 1894): 4. [*]
    Wells admires the plain style and "inhumanity and serene vastness" of the subject of Sir Robert Ball's *The Story of the Sun*. The idea of electromagnetic tides brushing by "our little eddy of planets," unsettling our compasses, making solar storms, then passing on to "the illimitable beyond," is "so powerful and beautiful as to well-nigh justify that hackneyed phrase, 'the poetry of science.'"

29. EXTINCTION, ON. *Chambers's Journal* 10 (Sept. 30, 1893): 623-624. [*GW*]

30. EXTINCTION OF MAN, THE. *PMG* 59 (Sept. 25, 1894):

3. [Reprinted, with a slight addition, in *CPM*]
Man is dominant today, but the fossil record never shows "a really dominant species succeeded by its own descendants." Man may be displaced by crustaceans, cephalopods, ants, or even plague bacilli—to name but four possibilities "out of a host of others."

31. FALLACIES OF HEREDITY. *SR* 78 (Dec. 8, 1894): 617-618. [*GW, GR*]
This essay raises, but leaves unanswered, the problem of what causes genetic "idiosyncrasy"—i.e., differences among offspring of the same parents, even between twins—which Wells finds one of the fascinating enigmas of heredity.

32. FLAT EARTH AGAIN, THE. *PMG* 58 (April 2, 1894): 3. [*ACW*: "The Flat Earth Again"]

33. FLINT IMPLEMENTS, OLD AND NEW. *PMG* 58 (April 3, 1894): 4. [*]
Wells recommends Worthington G. Smith's *Man, the Primeval Savage* to the general reader for its accounts both of ancient bones and implements and of modern forgeries of same.

34. FOUNDATION STONE OF CIVILIZATION, THE. *PMG* 58 (May 22, 1894): 3. [*GW*]
A cyclist with a tire ripped up by flints listens perforce to an old man's dissertation showing that flints attended the demise of savagery and were, in fact, "the only thing that could engender civilization."

35. GEOLOGY IN RELATION TO GEOGRAPHY. *ET* 47 (July 1, 1894): 287-288. [Signed]
Using England as an example, Wells points out that "all the chief facts in the geography of a country may be obtained in a quasi-inductive fashion from its geological structure." Thus "a few elementary geological considerations ... bind together what are otherwise disconnected facts in a singularly powerful manner." (The argument here anticipates Wells's position in no. 82; see also no. 87).

36. GOOD INTENTIONS OF NATURE EXPLAINED, THE. *PMG* 58 (Feb. 9, 1894): 4. [*]
Wells regrets Edith Carrington's *Workers Without Wage*, a children's nature book which holds up to "vile" man the "lowly goodness" of the "affectionate" spider and the "pa-

tient" snail. Hiding nature's cruelty from children is bad practice.

37. HUMAN EVOLUTION. *Natural Science* 10 (April 1897): 242-244. [Signed]
This open letter of Wells's defends the position he had taken in no. 38. "My interest in these theories [about the nature of man]," he writes, "lies chiefly in their application. ... After Darwin it has become inevitable that moral conceptions should be systematically restated in terms of our new conception of the material destiny of man."

38. HUMAN EVOLUTION, AN ARTIFICIAL PROCESS. *FR* n.s. 60 (Oct. 1896): 590-595. [Signed]

39. HUXLEY. *Royal College of Science Magazine* 13 (April 1901): 209-211. [Signed]
Wells recalls his student days under T. H. Huxley. "I believed then he was the greatest man I was ever likely to meet, and I believe that all the more firmly today."

40. INFLUENCE OF ISLANDS ON VARIATION, THE. *SR* 80 (August 17, 1895): 204-205. [*GW, GR*]
"Isolation on islands has played a larger part in the evolution of the animals and plants than is usually attributed to it," since this isolation—which according to modern geological findings is intermittent—gives rise in its periodicity to "an immense number of new species." Among these natural selection takes place when the island resumes its connection with the mainland.

41. INSECTS AND FLOWERS. *SR* 79 (April 6, 1895): 440-441. [*GW, GR*]
A discussion of examples of pollination by various insects.

42. INTELLIGENCE ON MARS. *SR* 81 (April 4, 1896): 345-346. [*GW, GR*]

43. IN THE NEW FOREST. *SR* 79 (April 27, 1895): 544-545. [*GW, GR*]
Wells mentions some animals to be met with in the forest and raises some questions about their behavior.

44. J.F.N. *Academy* 56 (May 6, 1899): 502-504. [Signed]
Wells pays tribute to the philosopher J. F. Nisbet and his "quest—that perpetual quest!—of the unassailable truths of being." "It has a touch of the heroic," says Wells, that Nisbet, "feeling, as he certainly did, a strong attraction towards

certain aspects of devotion, ... would defile himself with no helpful self-deceptions ... but remained, as he was meant to remain, outside, amid his riddles." (Compare the conclusion of no. 15, where Wells defines his own own, similar position in regard to the "imperative to believe").

45. LIFE IN THE ABYSS. *PMG* 58 (Feb. 9, 1894): 4. [*]

46. LIFE OF PLANTS, THE. *SR* 82 (August 8, 1896): 131-132. [*GW, GR*]
The differences between animals and plants are not so great as most people imagine. All plants have at least local motion, with the "lower forms of plant life" moving "as actively as animal protoplasm." Also, the process by which plants absorb and assimilate nourishment is not as mechanical as it is usually supposed to be.

47. LIMITS OF INDIVIDUAL PLASTICITY, THE. *SR* 79 (Jan. 19, 1895): 89-90. [*GW, GR*]

48. LIVING THINGS THAT MAY BE, THE. *PMG* 58 (June 12, 1894): 4. [Allusion to no. 32][*]
A review of J. E. Gore's *The Worlds of Space*. Finding Gore unimaginative when it comes to extraterrestrial life, Wells suggests such possibilities as a silicon base for life outside planet earth (see no. 8).

49. LUMINOUS PLANTS. *PMG* 59 (August 25, 1894): 4. [*ACW*: "Pr. v. Kerner"]
In the interests of "the general reader," Wells approves Anton Kerner von Marilaun's *The Natural History of Plants* (trans. F. W. Oliver). In particular the section on luminous lichens and seaweeds inspires Wells to regard the deepest growths (which overhang "the perpetual night of the plant world" and glow red in utilizing their chlorophyll) as emblems of apocalypse—"so to speak, the sunset of marine vegetation."

50. MAKING OF MOUNTAIN CHAINS, THE. *Knowledge* 16 (Nov. 1, 1893): 204-206. [Signed]
An account of various contemporary hypotheses—which Wells illustrates with homely examples—about how mountains are formed, concluding with his own synthesis of these ideas.

51. MAMMON. *SSJ*, no. 2 (Jan. 1887), pp. 53-54. [*GW*; signed "Walter Glockenhammer"]

Thoughts on two paintings by G. F. Watts, *Mammon* and *Visit to Æsculapius*: together these canvases "signify ... that this nation is, as it were, two dissevered parts ... ease, elegance, and pleasure are floated to-day on an ocean of toil and ignorance and want."

52. MAN OF THE YEAR MILLION, THE. *PMG* 57 (Nov. 6, 1893): 3. [Reprinted in *CPM* as "Of a Book Unwritten"; a lost version, "The Past and Future of the Human Race," went back to 1885 (see Geoffrey West, *H. G. Wells: A Sketch for a Portrait* [London: Gerald Howe, 1930], p. 111) or perhaps 1887 (*EA*, p. 549)]

    As man evolves, says Professor Holzkopf of Weissnichtwo, the "purely 'animal' about him is being, and must be, beyond all question, suppressed in his ultimate development." He forecasts the hypertrophy of the organs of intellect—head, eyes, hands—and the atrophy of the "animal organs"—nose, external ears, digestive tract. Our descendants, immersed in nutritive baths deep underground, will survive until the sun itself burns out.

53. MIND IN ANIMALS, THE. *SR* 78 (Dec. 22, 1894): 683-684. [*GW, GR*]

    In this review of C. Lloyd Morgan's *An Introduction to Comparative Psychology*, Wells intimates that he has a higher opinion of animal intelligence than Morgan. "It may be that Professor Lloyd Morgan's dog, experimenting on Professor Lloyd Morgan with a dead rat or a bone, would arrive at a very low estimate indeed of the powers of the human mind."

54. MODEST SCIENCE, THE. *PMG* 58 (Feb. 19, 1894): 4. [Allusion in no. 79] [*]

    To the general reader, says Wells, H. N. Dickson's *Meteorology* is "exceptionally entertaining," combining "the most modern conclusions" with accurate folk-knowledge of the still unpredictable ways of the weather.

55. MORALS AND CIVILISATION. *FR* n.s. 61 (Feb. 1897): 263-268. [Signed]

56. MORE BACON. *PMG* 58 (June 22, 1894): 4. [Allusion in no. 65][*]

    Wells expounds the "scientific method" of Orville W. Owen's *Sir Francis Bacon's Cipher Story*. Owen pasted up pages of all "Bacon's" works—*The Faerie Queene, The Anatomy of Melancholy*, Shakespeare's plays, and the rest—and rolled them back and forth on a thousand feet of canvas until every line mated with a physically distant one to produce a secret history of Elizabethan profligacy. Two earlier Bacon articles—"Mysteries of the Modern Press," *PMG* 58 (April 23, 1894): 3; and "A Remarkable Literary Discovery," *PMG* 58 (May 3, 1894): 3—may also be Wells's.

57. MOUNTAINS OUT OF MOLECULES. *PMG* 59 (Nov. 29, 1894): 4. [Allusion in no. 81][*]
Wells debunks both the thesis that "heat is a current of ether running in and out of molecules" and the overblown style of its presentation in Frederick Hovenden's *What is Heat? A Peep into Nature's Most Hidden Secrets.*

58. NEW OPTIMISM, THE. *PMG* 58 (May 21, 1894): 4. [Wells mentions Kidd in no. 38][*]
In reviewing Benjamin Kidd's *Social Evolution*, Wells not only doubts Kidd's belief that nations survive in the struggle for existence by subordinating intellectual development to "virtue, altruism, and the habit of self-sacrifice," he questions the name "optimism" for a creed which gives the future to the Anglo-Saxons because they are "so stupid, so pious, so sentimental."

59. NEWLY DISCOVERED ELEMENT, THE. *SR* 79 (Feb. 9, 1895): 183-184. [*GW, GR*]
A popularized account of Lord Rayleigh's discovery of argon. "All their lives [people] had, without knowing it, been breathing argon."

60. OBSERVATORY, FROM AN. *SR* 78 (Dec. 1, 1894): 594-595. [Reprinted in *CPM*]
If our moon were brighter, we might never suspect the existence of the stars. "We can imagine men just like ourselves [but] without such an outlook": in that case, what an enlargement of vision it would be if that bright moon faltered in its luminosity—perhaps perturbed by the passing of a dark star—and the heavens were unveiled. There is a fear of the night "that comes with knowledge, when we see in its true proportion this little life of ours."

61. ORIGIN OF THE SENSES, THE. *SR* 81 (May 9, 1896): 471-472. [*GW, GR*]

Wells talks about the evolution of three organs of sense: the nose, from primitive chemotropic, and the eye, from primitive phototropic mechanisms, and the ear, as "an organ for translating vibrations into touches."

62. PAINS OF AN IMAGINATION, THE. *PMG* 59 (Sept. 20, 1894): 3. [*GW*]
    The author used to be cursed with a restless florid imagination that led him about as if tied by a string. But he cured himself of it. He proposed that it earn him a living by writing a book, and it has never troubled him since.

63. PECULIARITIES OF PSYCHICAL RESEARCH. *Nature* 51 (Dec. 6, 1894): 121-122. [Signed]
    Wells in this review of Frank Podmore's *Apparitions and Thought Transference* attacks "psychical research" into occult phenomena as unscientific because its results are unverifiable by repeated experiment.

64. "POLYPHLOISBALLSANSKITTLOGRAPH," THE. *PMG* 58 (May 8, 1894): 3. [See no. 22][*]
    Wells spoofs apparatuses of unknown function exhibited by unintelligible foreigners at Royal Society soirees.

65. POPULARISING SCIENCE. *Nature* 50 (July 26, 1894): 300-301. [Signed]
    Wells begins by pointing out the need for popularizing science, then criticizes how scientists usually go about it (in language that is too technical and jargonized or absurdly and condescendingly simplistic). "Intelligent common people come to scientific books . . . for problems to exercise their minds upon . . . there is a keen pleasure in seeing a previously unexpected géneralisation skilfully developed."

66. POSITION OF PSYCHOLOGY, THE. *SR* 78 (Dec. 29, 1894): 715. [*GW, GR*]
    Wells uses George Trumbull Ladd's *Psychology, Descriptive and Explanatory* to launch an attack on the state of contemporary psychology, which he regards as being weighed down by a priori, hence unscientific, assumptions.

67. POSSIBLE INDIVIDUALITY OF ATOMS, THE. *SR* 82 (Sept. 5, 1896): 256-257. [*GW, GR*]

68. PROTEAN GAS, THE. *SR* 79 (May 4, 1895): 576-577. [*GW, GR*]
    A quizzical discussion of the controversy surrounding the

discovery of argon.

69. PROVINCE OF PAIN, THE. *Science and Art* 8 (Feb. 1894): 58-59. [Signed]

70. PURE AND NATURAL MAN, THE. *PMG* 57 (Oct. 16, 1893): 3. [*GW*]

Wells's hero, a rigid logician, recognizing that "the essence of all civilized ills" is man's "entirely artificial life," retires from society, goes nudist, and abstains altogether from the use of soap, an alkali.

71. PYGMY PHILOSOPHY. *PMG* 60 (April 11, 1895): 4. [*ACW*: "Pigmies"; *GR* links this cue-title to *SR* (July 13, 1895), but *ACW* enters it under "Sat Review" and "PMG" in title-groups published no later than April, and only "PMG" is crossed off (indicating publication); also, the *SR* (but not the *PMG*) review is uncommonly colorless for Wells]

Wells rejects the efforts of J. L. A. de Quatrefages, in *The Pygmies* (trans. Frederick Starr), "to establish the high moral standards of these primitive people, and to imply the primordial elevation of humanity."

72. RATE OF CHANGE IN SPECIES, THE. *SR* 78 (Dec. 15, 1894): 655-656. [*GW, GR*]

73. REDISCOVERY OF THE UNIQUE, THE. *FR* n.s. 50 (July 1891): 106-111. [Signed]

74. REMINISCENCES OF A PLANET. *PMG* 58 (Jan. 15, 1894): 4. [Allusion in no. 65][*]

Wells commends an "able and popular exposition of modern geology," Thomas Bonney's *The Story of Our Planet*. The earth's age and life-span are the main topics of this review.

75. ROYAL COLLEGE OF SCIENCE, AT THE. *ET* 46 (Sept. 1, 1893): 393-395. [About 1893 or 1894, *ET* "paid Low £50 a year as editor and another £50 a year for contributors. He and I found it convenient that I should be the contributors—all of them": *EA*, p. 291] [*]

Things have changed little, Wells writes, since his student days at South Kensington; and he hopes that through brief "glimpses of the hall, the lift and staircase, a laboratory full of students, methodical teaching, and errant rebels sitting over rare books in the 'Dyce and Forster,' or cultivating art in the picture galleries," he can give the reader a student's view of that institution.

76. RUDIS INDIGESTAQUE MOLES. *PMG* 60 (March 13, 1895): 4. [*ACW*: "Rudis Indigestaque Moles"]
Wells reviews Sir Archibald Geikie's *Memoir of Sir A. C. Ramsay*, in which one eminent geologist shuffles the life of another into a detritus "shaken up together and thrown down before the reader."

77. SCEPTICISM OF THE INSTRUMENT, THE. *Mind*, n.s. 13 (July 1904): 379-393. [Signed; given first as a paper to the Oxford Philosophical Society, Nov. 8, 1903; reprinted, altered, and abridged by about 15 percent in *A Modern Utopia*]
This essay develops ideas first bruited in nos. 67 and 73. Wells mistrusts the uniformity of formal logic because: (1) it classifies "uniques as identically similar objects" under some term that automatically accumulates a specious significance thereby; (2) "it can only deal freely with negative terms by treating them as though they were positive"; and (3) it projects onto one plane at a time, and thus places in mutual opposition, ideas which in fact are stratified at various levels of meaning, and thus are really complementary. In Wells's universe of "uniques," "ethical, social and religious teaching [come] into the province of poetry." Since philosophy, too, is self-expression, this essay contains much autobiographical material.

78. SCIENCE, IN SCHOOL AND AFTER SCHOOL. *Nature* 50 (Sept. 27, 1894): 525-526. [Signed]
Mainly in school: a critique of the predominant pedagogical approach to science, which inculcates fact but not the method of discovery (compare nos. 80, 82, 87).

79. SCIENCE LIBRARY, SOUTH KENSINGTON, THE. *PMG* 58 (May 3, 1894): 2. [*GW*]
Wells slashes the cataloguing system of the Science Library of the Royal College of Science, which classifies the lives of entomologists under "Insects" and the subject "Meteorology" before 1891 under "Physics" and after 1891 under "Astronomy" (among other examples).

80. SCIENCE TEACHING—AN IDEAL AND SOME REALITIES. *ET* 48 (Jan. 1, 1895): 23-29. [Identified in *ET* as a transcript of Wells's lecture before the Royal College of Preceptors, Dec. 12, 1894]
Wells contrasts the "idealistic standpoint" towards the

curriculum with "things as they are." Ideally, education should be primarily and fundamentally scientific: there should be an overall sequence of studies, emphasizing the interrelatedness of various disciplines. Structurally also, within any given area of study, "generalizations" should be arrived at "inductively" on the basis of "object-lessons and physical measurements" which enable the student to "see certain visible facts as connected with certain other visible facts." In practice, on the other hand, school curricula are unorganized and chaotic. Rather than providing "an ample background of inductive study"—the prerequisite for "exact thinking" and consequently for exactness of expression— schools instead offer a bewildering array of courses in which facts—purveyed as dogma—are presented in isolation from one another and without regard for any experiential or experimental basis. (This lecture is the fullest expression of notions Wells brings up in nos. 78, 82, and 87).

81. SCIENTIFIC RESEARCH AS A PARLOUR GAME. *SR* 79 (April 20, 1895): 516. [*GW, GR*]

A review of I. W. Heysinger's *The Source and Mode of Solar Energy Throughout the Universe*, in which Wells, pointing out Heysinger's ignorance in equating solar energy with electricity, attacks this kind of dilettantism generally.

82. SEQUENCE OF STUDIES, THE. *Nature* 51 (Dec. 27, 1894): 195-196. [Signed]

Wells here reviews three scientific textbooks and criticizes them all for the absence "of that progressive reasoning process which is the very essence of genuine scientific study" —that is, the process of establishing evidence for why something is so.

83. SINS OF THE SECONDARY SCHOOLMASTER, THE. *PMG* 59 (Dec. 15, 1894): 1-2. [*ACW*: "Sins of the Schoolmaster"; this, the last of three parts, deals with science teaching; two earlier parts appeared on Nov. 28, pp. 1-2, and Dec. 8, pp. 1-2]

Generally ignorant of the present state of science, schoolmasters must needs teach it anyway. They do so mechanically, without sequential progression and without realizing that "not knowledge, but a critical and inquiring mental habit, is the aim of science teaching" (see no. 80).

84. STRANGENESS OF ARGON, THE. *PMG* 60 (March 15, 1895): 3. [*ACW*: "Argonn"]

Many are the curious properties of argon, not least the lateness of its recognition. "Surely there are still wonders left in the world, and the healthy discoverer may keep a good heart yet, though Africa be explored." (See also nos. 59 and 68).

85. SUN GOD AND THE HOLY STARS, THE. *PMG* 58 (Feb. 24, 1894): 3. [*]

86. TALK WITH GRYLLOTALPA, A. *SSJ*, no. 3 (Feb. 1887), pp. 87-88. [*GW*; signed "Septimus Browne"]

87. TEACHING OF GEOGRAPHY, THE. *ET* 46 (Oct. 1, 1893): 435-436. [Signed]

Ranged in ascending order of complexity, the pedagogical approaches to geography proceed from "Where is A?" through "What kind of a place is A?" to "Why is A what it is?" They proceed, that is, towards a "descriptive"—"inductive" or scientific—view of the subject. Ideally, with a proper sequence of studies (see nos. 80 and 82), the study of geography can become "something altogether wider, a great and orderly body of knowledge centering about man in his relations to space." (See also no. 35).

88. THROUGH A MICROSCOPE. *PMG* 59 (Dec. 31, 1894): 3. [Reprinted, slightly modified, in *CPM*]

"All the time these creatures are living their vigorous, fussy little lives in this drop of water they are being watched by a creature of whose presence they do not dream." "Even so, it may be, the [observer] himself is being curiously observed."

89. TRANSIT OF MERCURY, THE. *SR* 78 (Nov. 24, 1894): 555. [*GW, GR*]

There are many things about the planet Mercury worth noting as it crosses the sun's disc—its erratic behavior, for example.

90. VERY FINE ART OF MICROTOMY, THE. *PMG* 58 (Jan. 24, 1894): 3. [*GW*]

Wells describes the preparation of a variety of substances for observation under the microscope and whimsically envisions a time when the slides prepared in his day will become collector's items.

91. VISIBILITY OF CHANGE IN THE MOON, THE. *Knowledge* 18 (Oct. 1895): 230-231. [Signed]

92. VISIBILITY OF COLOUR, THE. *PMG* 60 (March 7, 1895): 4. [*ACW*: "Colour Vision"; *GR* links this cue-title to *SR* (Sept. 14, 1895), but *ACW* enters it under *PMG* only and in a group all published by mid-April; again, the *SR* (but not the *PMG*) review is uncommonly bland for Wells]
Wells welcomes W. de W. Abney's *Colour Vision*, a "fairly exhaustive account of the sensations of colour from the scientific side" and a work particularly stimulating to "the artist and art critic among those who find pleasure in untechnical scientific books addressed to the general reader."

93. VISION OF THE PAST, A. *SSJ*, no. 7 (June 1887), pp. 206-209. [*GW*; signed "Sosthenes Smith"]

94. YARDS SACRED AND PROFANE. *PMG* 60 (March 4, 1895): 4. [*ACW*: "Measures"]
With a perfunctory nod to reform, Wells turns with relish from the rationalized standards of measurement urged in Wordsworth Donisthorpe's *A System of Measures* to Donisthorpe's account of such "natural" standards as the hand's-length or the ox's "furrow-long" ("growing" says Wells, "visibly out of the soil"). (Compare no. 85).

95. ZOOLOGICAL RETROGRESSION. *GM* 271 (Sept. 1891): 246-253. [Signed]

Index of H. G. Wells's Writings

Index of Names

Sophocles, 169
Spencer, Herbert, 9, 23, 77n, 108n, 127, 180n, 181n, 200
Sprigg, Christopher St. John, 7n
Stephens, Riccardo, 207

Tennyson, Alfred, Lord, 14, 108n
Ternant, A. L., 230
Thomas, J. W., 231
Thomson, Sir John Arthur, 206
Thomson, Sir Joseph John, 119n, 120-121
Toulmin, Stephen, 4n
Tylor, Sir Edward Burnet, 43

Varigny, Henry Crosnier de, 129
Vorzimmer, Peter J., 10n

Wallace, Alfred Russel, 10n, 15, 29, 34, 133
Walmsley, Robert Mullineux, 233
Watts, George Frederick, 237
Weeks, Robert P., 7n
Weismann, August, 9-10, 77n, 107, 124-127, 132, 133, 136n, 138, 183-184, 211, 230, 232
West, Geoffrey (pseud. of Geoffrey Harry Wells), 5n, 15n, 48n, 184n, 237
Wilsing, Johannes, 111
Wilson, Edmund Beecher, 127
Wolff, Kaspar Friedrich, 123-124, 127n
Wordsworth, William, 23, 182